Caffeine Ni

In The Know

Dougie Brimson

Fiction aimed at the heart
and the head…

Published by Caffeine Nights Publishing 2020

CONDITIONS OF SALE

Published in Great Britain by
Caffeine Nights Publishing
4 Eton Close
Walderslade
Chatham
Kent
ME5 9AT
caffeinenights com
caffeinenightsbooks.com
Also available as an eBook and audiobook

British Library Cataloguing in Publication Data.
A CIP catalogue record for this book is available from the British Library

ISBN: 978-1-913200-08-4

Everything else by
Default, Luck and Accident

Also by Dougie Brimson

Follow Billy Evans story in

The Crew
Top Dog

Published by Caffeine Nights

Also:
Wings of a Sparrow

For Tina.

Who puts up with me.

Acknowledgments

Huge thanks to Marina Darling for her help, input and fabulous editing, and to my fellow Hornet Neil Stevenson for being both my beta reader and consistently more miserable than I am.

Also, thanks to my screenwriting partner, Gary Lawrence, to Karl (and Sue) Wiggins for his notes and to Dee Atkins for being my number one fan (and not like Annie Wilkes at all).

Finally, a massive thank you to everyone who's read The Crew and Top Dog and urged me to write this third instalment. I hope it's worth the wait.

PART ONE

Chapter One
Thursday 2nd August 2018

01.40

Graham Hawkins lay in his bed staring at the ceiling. Not simply because he couldn't sleep but because every fibre of his being was screaming at him, telling him that something was wrong. Very wrong. Whether instinct or sixth sense, Hawk's awareness of trouble was as real as his ability to see, smell and touch. Having been honed over decades in pubs, railways stations and on terraces across Europe, it had never let him down.

His anxiety was heightened by the fact that he had no idea what might have triggered it. He couldn't imagine it being the dreaded six o'clock knock, not after all this time. The Saturday Scene had been consigned to his past years ago. These days he was firmly established as just another of the many old faces that inhabited the bars around The London Stadium when West Ham were at home. More respected than most for sure, even held in awe by some as one of the legendary faces of *The Cockney Suicide Squad,* but no longer a player in the game that was hooliganism. No, those great halcyon days were long gone. Not that the Old Bill had ever let a little thing like time get in their way. There were still plenty in uniform who harboured both long memories and deep-rooted grudges but why would they come after him now?

Inevitably, as they always seemed to when thoughts turned to football, his mind led him not to away days, great days or even manic terrace days, but to his friend Billy Evans. In particular the devastation he went through following his beloved wife's brutal and tragic murder. Even now, over twelve years later, recalling it angered Hawk. There had never been a sniff of justice thanks to the police and their sham of an investigation nor an ounce of compassion from the press who had seemingly delighted in crawling all over his friend with fantasy tales of Irish paramilitaries and crippled footballers. Cunts the lot of them.

Yet through all the shit that had been thrown at him, Billy had somehow managed to hold it all together. Hawk had lost count of the times he'd been astounded by his mate's resilience in the face of what must have been soul shattering grief but he knew Billy better than anyone and as a consequence, knew only too well that there had been equally as many times when emotionally, the man who was his brother in all but blood had been clinging on for dear life. Not that anyone else would ever have known.

Only once in all the intervening years had the two of them ever actually talked properly about it but even then, despite the pain, the tears and the alcohol, Billy still hadn't fully explained how the woman he continued to refer to as his soul mate had ended up underneath an articulated lorry on the A12 and Hawk certainly hadn't pressed. If even in the very depths of despair his best mate hadn't felt able to share something with him, he had a reason. That was good enough.

Thankfully, having brought his two boys to the point where they were now fine young men, Billy had recently begun to show flashes of his old self. The cheeky grin and the banter that had not only helped him build his various businesses into hugely profitable enterprises but which had aided his rise from foot soldier to leader of *The CSS* back in the 90's, had become the norm rather than the exception. But to those in the know it was clear that the shadow of despair still haunted Billy. He was on the mend for sure, but there was a way to go yet before the ticking time bomb of depression would be banished forever.

Hawk glanced across at the empty space where Julie would normally have been snoring gently. He'd never had a problem with her being on nights at the hospital but every so often, he missed her being beside him that feeling of closeness. This was one of those times. Still, at least he still had his wife in his life which was more than poor Billy had.

He sighed again as his senses fired another warning shot across his bows. There was definitely something...

'Fuck this,' he muttered out loud as he slid from under the duvet. If it was Old Bill coming knocking, he was at least going to have a final smoke before they carted him off.

It took barely a minute for Hawk to pull on some joggers, slide on a pair of well-worn Adidas Gazelles and make his way through the darkness down to the back door. But even as he pulled a cigarette from the packet he'd left on the kitchen windowsill something caught his eye.

He stared at it for a second and then frowned as realisation hit. 'Shit'.

Barely ten miles away, Billy Evans was also wide awake although in this case it was far from unusual. His relationship with sleep was a fleeting one and had been for many years.

In truth, that was how he liked it. For in the dead of night, when life had slowed to a stop and he was totally alone, that was his time. The time when he didn't have to put on a front for anyone else but could instead reflect, regret and try to find some kind of peace with the demons that haunted his dreams. And haunt them they did. A constant reminder that he and he alone was responsible for the fact that his two sons had grown up without a mother and that he had endured over a decade of life devoid of any real emotion except guilt. Not just for what had happened, but for what had not.

All it would have taken was for him to tell the truth. Explain how he had incurred the wrath of a group of Irish Paramilitaries by crippling a young footballer and how they had brutally murdered the love of his life in revenge. Yet instead, even though the police had eventually unwrapped the whole sorry saga, Billy had stayed quiet and refused to confirm or deny anything. Not because he'd been concerned about incriminating himself, but because he'd been genuinely afraid that the Irishmen would come for him and his boys. As a result, the police had been left with nowhere to go. The consequence being that the investigation had quickly stalled and was now long since forgotten. The Irishmen, wherever they were, had escaped any kind of punishment.

Yet whilst Billy had never doubted that he had done the right thing, the safest thing, the fact that his beloved wife, his soul mate, had never received the justice she deserved had been a source of constant shame. And whilst he loved his sons as much as any father ever could, their presence provided him with a permanent memorial not only to his failings as a human, but of his eternally broken heart.

That however, was the price karma had handed him and even though at various times Billy had tried to block it out with both pills and alcohol or even neutralise it with therapy, he had eventually come to the conclusion that the only way to come to terms with his grief was to embrace it. If a life of sadness and sleepless nights was his penance, then so be it.

With a sigh, he reached for the remote, turned on the TV and began channel surfing. Searching for anything that might occupy his thoughts and pass the hours until sunrise.

Hawk stuffed his phone back into his pocket and glared through the window at the side of his garage. 'Bastard Old Bill,' he muttered to himself. 'Fucking useless.'

Even as he spoke, another flash of light shot from the slightly open side door of the garage and not for the first time, Hawk imagined whoever was inside doing God knows what to his beloved Harley Davidson. 'Bollocks to this,' he growled.

For a brief second, he thought about grabbing a knife from the draw but just as quickly, dismissed the idea. He'd never used a blade in his life and he certainly wasn't going to start now. But what else was there to hand? He could hardly confront a burglar with a ladle or a pasta scoop. No, if he was going into battle there was only one thing going with him. He darted for the cupboard under the stairs and within seconds was back in the kitchen with an old and familiar friend swinging in his hands. Now he was on it. His mind racing as it ran through every possible scenario. Not out of fear, there was no fear, but to prepare himself to react to whatever might unfold in the coming minutes.

Preparation, that was the key to violence. It was a lesson learnt in hundreds of pubs and motorway services, on thousands of railway platforms and of course, on the terraces.

If you were ready for when it kicked off, you had more than half a chance of coming out on top.

The thought suddenly struck Hawk that maybe he should just wait for the police. After all, he had no idea who or what was in his garage. They could be wired pill-heads, professional bike thieves or just chancers looking to make a few quid. However, as quickly as it had arrived the thought was set aside. Hawk had spent most of his life hating and fighting the filth and he'd be bollocksed if he was going to sit back and rely on them for anything now. If someone was on his property trying to have it away with something that was his, he was going to front them up and make them pay. The old bill could pick up the pieces.

And then it came, embracing him like an old friend, the buzz. The once all too familiar cocktail of adrenaline, arrogance and power that accompanied the anticipation of combat. Fuck, how Hawk had missed that feeling. No wonder so many clung on to it for so long.

He took a final deep breath, clasped the baseball bat in both hands and gave it a gentle swing.

It was time.

Billy had all but given up trying to find anything to capture even a fraction of his attention when an episode of something called *American Chopper* appeared on his screen.

Despite a lifetime in the motor trade, the inner workings of the internal combustion engine had always remained a total mystery to Billy and his interest in motorcycles was, at best, negligible. However, the same could not be said of Hawk who in recent years, had developed a passion for Harley Davidson's and now spent most of his spare time either riding here, there and everywhere or tinkering with his bikes in his garage.

Although Billy took the piss mercilessly, the truth was that he was envious. His life lacked many things but chief amongst them was anything that provided the kind of escapism that Hawk had found and now enjoyed so much in his motorbikes. Billy wanted that, craved it even. With his boys having now left home and with lives of their own, that need was becoming more pressing than ever.

But what? That was the question. He'd tried everything from golf to gambling but nothing had ever held his interest beyond more than a few weeks. Even meeting up with the lads at games had lost much of its appeal although even he could admit that he'd recently started to feel more comfortable being amongst it again. Yet if anything, those few hours and their constant reminders of the past somehow made the rest of the time even more difficult to deal with.

The one thing Billy was certain of was that despite the emptiness and sadness he felt, he would never become embroiled with another woman. Not because of his guilt, but because he knew that any woman who came into his life would always be a poor second to the memory of his wife. That wouldn't be fair on her or for that matter, on him.

He was still pondering this when the noise of the ever feuding Teutul's drew his attention back from his thoughts and after lowering the volume to a suitable level, Billy dropped the remote onto the bed, settled back into his pillows and waited for sleep to find him.

Graham Hawkins eased open the back door and slid through it into the darkness before making his way silently along the short path and taking station about five feet from the open garage door. For a moment or two he was unsure if there were anyone still inside and that maybe they'd already done the off. But just as he was about to move forward for a closer look, a barely audible metallic clink followed by strands of hushed conversation gave them away.

With a wry smile, Hawk adjusted his stance to place himself to one side of the door, his bat swinging loosely in his clenched hands. If a ball had come at him, he'd have been ready.

'OK you cunts,' he called, his voice dripping with threat. 'Out!'

The garage fell silent. Hawk stood poised, his eyes fixed on the blackness of the open door as he waited for a sound or a movement. He slowly swung the bat, practicing the trajectory, rehearsing the movement. Chest height, not the head. More chance of hitting something.

'I ain't fucking about! Out!'

More silence. Then the senses pinged again. They were coming.

It took an instant for the veteran of a thousand battles to register the details of this new enemy. Two of them, not men, not kids, teenagers. Dressed from head to foot in black, their black faces coated in fear as they fought desperately to gain momentum and get past whatever was waiting for them outside the confines of the garage. Most importantly, even in the faint light, Hawk could see that their hands, whilst gloved, were empty. Result.

He swung the bat with all the strength and deliberation he could muster at the leading youth who instinctively threw up his arm in a vain attempt to protect himself. The resultant crack echoed through the dark like a gunshot yet even as an agonised scream began to pour from the youth, Hawk had the bat back on his shoulder, his eyes and brain busily working out the most efficient and effective use of the second strike.

However, before he could unleash another blow the youths had bundled past him and were off, sprinting through the open garden gate and out into the street.

Without a moment's hesitation, Hawk took off after them. Instinct telling him to focus on the one he'd injured. Another valuable lesson hard learned. Nothing slows someone like pain and even with lungs polluted by a lifetime of Marlboro consumption, he had little difficulty in catching his foe. Grabbing his collar and wrenching him backwards.

'Got you you little fucker,' gasped Hawk as he dragged the youth to a halt.

'You broke my arm you bastard!' he wailed.

'Shut up for fucks sake,' growled Hawk in response. 'You'll wake my neighbours'.

He quickly glanced around for the other youth but there was no sign of him or anyone else and so he returned his attention to his captive. In spite of the obvious agony he'd already inflicted, it was all Hawk could do to stop himself from lashing out and delivering more pain. Instead, devoid of either sympathy or regret, he shoved the youth across the road and slammed him against a brick wall. The action causing yet another blast of agonised screaming as the teenager desperately clutched his limb to his chest in an effort to keep it still.

'Sit down there and shut the fuck up.'

The youth glared angrily at his captor then pulled a phone from his pocket. However, before he could dial Hawk had snatched it off him.

'Give me that you little shit!' he barked.

'I need an ambulance. I was calling 999.'

'The old bill will be here in a minute; they'll sort you out. Until then I told you to shut the fuck up.'

'It's fucking killing me!'

'Good. Remember that next time you think about breaking into some poor bastard's house, you arsehole.'

'Let 'im go you wanker!'

Hawk span around to find the second youth standing barley ten feet from him. Almost instantly, he saw the knife in his right hand. Six inches long, the steel glistening in the orange glow of the street lighting. A quick glance around revealed no sign of anyone else let alone the police and in spite of the pained screams that had come from the injured teenager, no lights were showing in any of the houses nearby although that didn't mean that there weren't people lurking behind the nets watching the drama unfolding outside.

'Are you fucking serious?' laughed Hawk who, even as he was talking and without taking his eyes from the knife being pointed at him, moved to one side to bring the injured youth back into his line of sight. If one had a blade, chances are they both did and standing there in little more than a pair of jogging bottoms and some old trainers, Hawk had suddenly realised that he was both isolated and extremely vulnerable. Although he was at least comforted by the feel of the baseball bat clasped firmly in his right hand.

'Danny! Come on! Let's go!' the armed youth called. This time more urgent, desperate even.

Hawk glanced at the injured youth as he struggled to his feet. Although part of him still wanted to rip them both apart, decades of street-fighting experience were telling him that he was in a situation which had the potential to go very bad very quickly and that the best and safest tactic was to defuse it by handing his enemy an escape route. Better that than risk a kicking, or worse. Besides, he'd done more than enough to be able to hold his head up and walking away unscathed was infinitely preferable to doing something stupid simply to satisfy some misplaced sense of ego.

'Go on, piss off before the filth turn up,' Hawk barked as he took another step backwards to put additional space between himself and the injured youth. 'I ever catch so much as sniff of you again, you're fucking history. Got it?'

The injured youth glared at him, his eyes burning with rage and pain.

'You're a fucking dead man! You got me!'

'Do yourself a favour son,' said Hawk calmly. 'Leave while you got a chance 'cos if you don't, you're gonna end up in the nick or hospital. Your call.'

The injured youth continued to glare for a second but slowly, an almost imperceptible smile crept onto his face. The slight curling of the lips and the darting eyes enough to tell Hawk that someone was behind him. Now he really was in trouble.

The first blow came crashing into him with such force that it blasted every ounce of breath from his lungs and sent the baseball bat spinning from his hands. The second came even as he was struggling to retain his balance and keep on his feet. Yet somehow Hawk managed to grab hold of his attacker and not only drag himself upright but land a punch of his own. The blow affording him a split second's respite which he used to full advantage by swinging the youth around and slamming him into the wall with every ounce of strength he could muster.

However, just as Hawk was about to follow up with another punch, he felt an arm tighten around his throat and another blow hit him in the back. Instinctively, he threw his head back as hard as he could. The resultant crunch and subsequent yelp all the evidence he needed that whoever it was now had a broken nose for their trouble.

Another blow pummelled his kidneys and this time, it came with such force that Hawk couldn't help but slide to his knees. The first kick hitting him even before he could yell out in pain.

'You cunt!' came the scream. 'That's for my fucking arm!'

The second kick came as Hawk was curling himself into a ball. His mind racing between thoughts of self-preservation and what he was going to do to extract some semblance of revenge at some point in the future. However, as quickly as it had begun, the attack was over. The thudding of boot on flesh replaced by the patter of three sets of trainers receding quickly into the darkness.

Hawk gave them a few seconds and then, once he was sure they'd gone for good, unrolled himself and lay on his back. His eyes focussed on the streetlamp burning above him as he tried to work out which part of him hurt most. Head, ribs, shoulder, back or pride, he was spoiled for choice.

It had been a while since he'd taken a kicking, a bloody long while. Stoke away, 2005, over fourteen years. 'Jesus,' he wondered, 'was it really that long ago?' He couldn't remember it feeling like this though. In fact, from memory, not only had he got to his feet almost immediately, but he'd led the line against the *Naughty 40* when it had kicked off again shortly afterwards. Back then, repairs to dented pride and reputation were swift and sweet, revenge even sweeter. Now, Hawk felt like he could barely move, and he'd taken probably no more than ten blows.

'Christ', he groaned out loud. 'I'm too old for this bollocks'.

'Mr. Hawkins?'

Hawk turned his head to see two policemen approaching. Their torches panning the road as they approached.

With a sigh, he dragged himself into a sitting position. 'I called you bloody lot ages ago.'

'What happened?' asked one of the officers. 'We received a report of a break in.'

'Yeah, my garage,' replied Hawk. 'Two of the bastards. I…' He stopped talking as the second policeman suddenly frowned and shone his torch onto the road behind where Hawk was sitting. 'What is it?'

For the first time, Hawk realised that he was sitting in something damp. It took barely a second to register that it was his own blood.

Billy had finally drifted into something approaching sleep when the sound of his mobile rattling on the bedside table snapped him back to consciousness.

Even as he reached for it, he knew something was wrong. The sight of 'Julie' on the screen highlighting one of his darkest fears in bright green reality. 'This ain't good,' he muttered to himself as he pressed the answer button.

'Julie, what's wrong?'

He listened for a second as a strange voice spoke to him. The words making no sense as he struggled to understand how or why someone else was talking to him when his brain was telling him it should have been his best mates' wife. Then, suddenly, everything caught up. By the time the voice had finished talking, Billy was already half-dressed.

Chapter Two
Thursday 2nd August 2018

03.15

Less than 25 minutes after the phone call, Billy burst into the Accident and Emergency department at Queens Hospital, Romford. As usual, even in the early hours of mid-week, the place was littered with dregs. Almost all having arrived there as a result of their own inability to adhere to even the basics of self-control or the simplest rules of common decency.

Billy loathed them, all of them. He loathed their self-destructive lifestyles, loathed what they represented and loathed their selfishness and stupidity.

For that reason, on the rare occasions he had to visit such places and be amongst them, he tried, as best he could, to blank them. Totally. It was safer all round.

On this occasion however, it required no effort on his part for he had far more pressing things on his mind. Without even pausing to look around, he headed directly toward the reception desk where a middle-aged woman was staring at her computer.

'Excuse me,' he said, as calmly as he could. 'My mate was brought in…'

'One moment please sir,' she replied without looking up. 'I'll be with you in a second.'

Billy took a deep breath to settle himself. In any normal circumstance, he would have taken the time to take in his surroundings but not now. His heart was already racing thanks to a heady mixture of adrenaline and fear and the last thing he needed was anger adding to it. Instead, he fixed his gaze on the woman. Willing her to finish whatever it was that was taking up her time. His precious time.

'I'm sorry,' she said with without even a flicker of a smile. 'What's your friend's name?'

'Hawkins. Graham Hawkins. His wife called me, she's one of the duty sisters. Julie Hawkins.' Billy watched her face closely as he spoke.

'Could I have your name sir?'

'Billy. Billy Evans.'

'If you take a seat, I'll let her know you're here'.

Billy remained at the desk until she had vanished from sight. His concern heightened by the fact that the woman had broken eye contact a millisecond after he'd mentioned Julie's name and hadn't re-engaged it again. A classic tell. Whatever was going on with Hawk, it was bad.

He took another deep breath and finally turned away from the reception desk. A move which, for the first time, brought his surroundings into proper view. It was a familiar and painful landscape. Not because of the grey and anonymous shapes that littered the seating area, but because of the memories it reawakened. Broken bones, sick children, his father's accident, aunt's, uncle's, mates, neighbours… they'd all dragged him here at some time or another. Above all, he was reminded of Samantha and all the times they'd sat there waiting to be seen. Him at his most impatient, her at her calm, caring and loving best.

'Billy!'

Billy snapped from his daydream and turned to find Julie approaching him. He'd seen her many times in uniform, both at work and at home, and had always been struck by the assured confidence which poured from her. But all of that was gone, replaced by what he could only describe as terror. He certainly couldn't recall ever seeing tears in her eyes before.

He held out his arms and she sank into them.

'Thank God you're here,' she said. The relief in her voice almost tangible. 'I didn't know who else…'

'Hey, you don't have to thank me. First things first, are you OK?'

'I don't know,' she replied flatly. 'I came back off my break and he was just being brought in.'

Billy gave her a final squeeze and then released his hold. 'What happened?'

'Apparently, some kids broke into the garage and he chased them. They…' She stumbled as she spoke. The tears choking her. 'The police are waiting to take a statement.'

Billy baulked at mention of the police. 'The old bill are here?'

Julie looked at him and her eyes filled again. 'He's in a bad way.'

Billy felt his chest tighten as his heart started to race. He was suddenly acutely aware of the fact that they were surrounded by people, all of whom were staring at them and taking in the drama that was unfolding in front of them like some kind of sick soap opera. He took hold of her hand.

'Not here,' he said quietly. 'Is there somewhere a bit less public?'

Julie forced a half smile and led him toward the double doors leading into the department proper. However, even as they approached them a nurse appeared, her eyes settling instantly on Julie. When she spoke, Billy immediately recognised her voice as the one that had spoken to him earlier but of greater concern was the look on her face.

'What's wrong?' he asked before Julie could speak. The nurse looked at him, puzzled. 'I'm Billy, we spoke earlier.'

'Oh, I'm Claire,' she responded with a brief smile before turning to Julie. 'Mister Carter wants a word.'

'OK,' replied Julie. The anxious tone in her voice clear. 'Could you take Billy to my office?'

'Can't I see him?' he asked a little too urgently.

The two women exchanged the briefest of glances. 'Not at the moment,' said Claire softly.

'Why not? What's going on?' Billy asked. His eyes flashing between the two women. 'How bad is he?'

Claire flashed Billy a look and then turned to her colleague. 'Julie, Mr. Carter's waiting. Don't worry, I'll look after things here,' Julie nodded a silent reply and with a final half smile, she turned away and headed through the double doors. Billy watched her go, his spirits sinking further with every step she took from him. Something was wrong, very wrong.

'Who's Mister Carter?'

'He's a surgeon,' said Claire calmly as she gestured toward the doors.

The word made Billy's blood run cold. 'A surgeon? What does he need a surgeon for?'

'Come on, I'll rustle you up a tea or something. You look like you need it.'

'Look, I don't need tea,' said Billy. Struggling to retain his cool. 'I need to know how my mate is.'

Claire looked at him and smiled the disarming smile of someone who'd been through this experience a million times. 'OK, but let's get you into sisters office first. It's more private.'

Billy followed her through the double doors and was immediately struck by the total contrast to the waiting area. Whereas that had been reasonably calm, the working side of the department, even at this early hour, was a hive of both noise and activity. Yet even as he gazed upon the staff scurrying around, his eyes were drawn to the sight of four policemen loitering outside a cubicle at the far end of the room. Their look and presence totally at odds with the environment but as good as a neon sign in showing him where Hawk was. The very sight of them made his blood run cold.

'Billy!' He turned to find Claire staring at him. Her expression fixed and firm. 'Don't worry. It's all quite routine.' She smiled again. Another disarming smile.

Reluctantly, he turned away from where his friend lay and followed her to a small office at the opposite end of the room. The journey taking him past a number of cubicles full of people busy enduring their own kind of personal, possibly life changing trauma. However, Billy resisted the natural temptation to glance in their direction. He had enough to handle at the moment and the very last thing he either needed or wanted was anything else clinging to his emotions. Instead, he remained firmly focused on the direction of travel and his destination at the far end of the room. Only when he reached it did Billy relax.

'What's the story?' he asked even as Claire pulled the door closed.

Claire turned and looked at the man standing in front of her. 'So, this is Billy Evans,' she thought. Her mind flashing briefly back to some of the many times his name had been mentioned by Julie during late night conversations when shifts were slow and time needed filling. The widower, the father, the successful businessman, the criminal, the violent former football hooligan and according to Julie, the killer. Could this guy standing in front of her really be all those things?

She glanced him up and down again. There was certainly something about him that intrigued her.

'Well?'

Claire took a deep breath and refocussed. She'd been a nurse long enough to know that when friends and family asked how serious something was, not all of them actually wanted to know. The man in front of her however, was a different kettle of fish. He not only wanted to know, he needed to know.

'He has a fractured skull and a broken rib,' she said abruptly. 'He also has four stab wounds. Three in the back, one on his left side.'

'Jesus!' gasped Billy. 'How bad is it?'

'It's extremely serious. I'm sorry, but they're doing everything they can.'

'What the fuck does that mean?' Billy asked desperately. 'He's not… I mean he's gonna be OK right?'

'As I said, they're doing everything they can,' she replied calmly. 'The injury to his skull is a problem as he keeps lapsing in and out of consciousness.'

'Is that why the surgeon's here?'

'No,' she responded after a pause. 'The stab wounds have caused some internal damage. We don't know how much yet as we don't know how deep the wounds are.'

'But you've got an idea?'

Claire paused for thought but before she could speak again, the door opened, and Julie entered. Her face coated in fear. Billy took her in his arms for a second and held her.

'You should see him before he goes to theatre,' she said tearfully as she pulled away. 'He'll like that,'

'I'll take him,' said Claire. 'You stay here for a minute and gather your thoughts OK?' Julie nodded in response. 'I'll be back in a second.'

Claire gestured to the door and with a last glance at Julie, they left the room and headed toward the cubicle where Hawk lay.

'He's got a tube in his throat,' whispered Claire as they walked. 'So, he won't be able to talk. Just remember, the machines are there to keep him comfortable. There's nothing to be frightened of'

Billy nodded but kept his eyes fixed firmly on the approaching curtains. Her words, like everything else in the room, were a blur and his heart was beating so hard that he would have sworn everyone else within a few yards were hearing it.

'They'll be along for him in a couple of minutes, OK?' she hissed. Billy nodded his reply and with a final smile, Claire pulled open the curtains and led him inside.

The scene which met him was, thanks to a million films and fly-on-the-wall TV shows, oddly familiar. A body lay on a bed connected by all kinds of tubes and cables to machines which were busily beeping and flashing in response to whatever was being pushed to or from them. The only thing out of place was that the body wasn't some anonymous individual, it was his friend Hawk. But whereas he had feared the very worst, as soon as their eyes met Billy found himself enveloped by a feeling of calm relief as his fears evaporated. His mate was alive and in the best hands he could be in and that was all Billy had needed to know. His job now was to simply be himself.

Hawk held up his fist and Billy bumped it. 'I knew that bloody bike would be trouble,' he said the second Claire pulled the curtains closed behind her. 'You better not have left me it in your bloody will either. Poxy thing will be on eBay that night.' Hawks eyes smiled up at him and Billy took hold of his hand. 'You know you're going under the knife, right?' Hawk nodded gently. 'Well I'm telling you now, you see any bright lights, you tell 'em to piss off OK?'

Hawk smiled again and tried to speak. Billy squeezed his hand again. 'Don't even think about it. Whatever it is can wait.'

Hawk slowly shock his head and frowned. The inference clear. He released his hand from Billy's and held up three fingers.

'Look, you've got to relax,' pleaded Billy. 'You can tell me all this shit tomorrow.'

Hawk frowned and began to get agitated. Billy put his hand on his shoulder to calm him down. 'OK, OK,' he whispered. 'D'you want me to get the Old Bill in? They're just outside?' Hawk gently shook his head and once again, held up his three fingers. 'Three of them?' asked Billy in a hushed voice. Hawk nodded then pointed to his face and tapped his cheek. 'White lads.' Hawk shook his head and tapped his face again. 'Black?' asked Billy. Hawk winked then held up one finger. He then moved that to his nose and Billy couldn't help but notice an involuntary wince. 'One of them smelled of something?' Hawk shook his head and then thought for a second before clicking his fingers. Billy frowned. 'You clicked his nose? What does that mean? Oh, you broke his nose?'

Hawk took a deep and obviously painful breath before giving Billy a thumbs up. He then held up two fingers before pointing to his arm and clicking his fingers again. 'You broke the second one's arm?' Hawk nodded again. 'And what about the third one?' Hawk gently shook his head but then after a second or so, he slowly pointed to his side. Billy frowned. 'It was the third one who stabbed you?' Hawk gave an almost imperceptible nod and closed his eyes in obvious pain. Billy took his hand and squeezed it. 'OK I got it. Now you just relax OK? You can fill in the blanks tomorrow.'

The curtains suddenly opened behind him and Billy looked up to see not just Julie and Claire, but a whole group of people dressed in theatre scrubs. It was obviously time. He took hold of Hawks hand, bent down and whispered, 'love you bruv. Don't you forget it,' before standing aside and letting the medics go to work.

'Come on, let's get you that cuppa,' said Claire gently.

'No,' said Billy without turning away. 'I want to...'

'It's OK Billy,' said Julie calmly. 'I'll go with him. Claire will bring you up once he's in theatre.'

Billy half smiled in response then reached out and took her hand. 'You're the boss,' he said quietly and then, after a brief embrace, she turned and followed Hawk as he was wheeled away through another set of doors and out of sight. Billy stood for a second and stared after them. It had been a long time since he'd felt so helpless or so empty. Or so choked.

'Mister Evans?'

Billy turned to find one of the policemen staring at him. The other three close behind. The enemy. The fact that they'd referred to him by name did not go unnoticed and put Billy immediately on his guard. 'What?' was the only word he felt able to utter.

'Did he manage to say anything about what happened?'

Billy lowered his eyelids and took a breath. His loathing of both the police and the law was as good as a part of his DNA and on top of that, he'd never grassed anyone to the Old Bill. Not even in the very gravest of times. 'Are you shitting me?' he hissed. 'The fucking doors are still swinging!'

'Yes sir, I'm well aware of that,' replied the policeman in a tone that suggested he was no stranger to either abuse or aggression. 'But we didn't get a chance to speak to him so anything you might be able to tell us could help us catch whoever stabbed him.'

Billy eyeballed the policeman and felt his hackles rising as the emotional turmoil he'd somehow managed to keep suppressed throughout the previous few hours began to simmer.

'Billy?'

He turned to Claire, still standing beside him. Her voice soft and soothing. Oil on extremely troubled waters.

'Did he say anything? If he did, you've got to tell them.'

Billy stared at her. In any normal circumstance he'd have told this bloody woman to mind her own business, or worse. But this wasn't a normal circumstance. It wasn't about football or dodgy motors or even his own past, it was about Hawk and the fact that thanks to some scumbags, he was currently on his way to an operating theatre. As such, Billy knew he had little choice but to overcome his natural instincts and comply. 'He said there were three of them. Black lads.'

'Anything else?' asked the policeman eagerly. 'Even the smallest detail.'

'He said he broke the first one's nose and the second one's arm. It was the third who stabbed him.'

'He broke his arm. How?'

'He's resourceful,' replied Billy irritably.

Before the policeman could say anything else, another of the officers stepped forward. Billy was instantly struck by how much older he was than the other three, but it was also immediately apparent that he had a calm assurance the others didn't possess.

'Maybe we should go somewhere more private,' he said quietly. 'Is there a room we could use?'

'I'll take you to one of the family rooms,' said Claire. 'If you'll follow me.'

Billy stepped aside to let her pass but not before he noticed a rapid exchange of glances passing between the four policemen. He'd had enough dealings with Old Bill over the years to know that what went unspoken was usually far more important than any actual words but whilst it was obvious that something was going on, he had no idea what it might be. His suspicions were heightened when two of the policemen walked off in the opposite direction. 'Where are they going?' he asked.

'Let's go somewhere more private,' said the older policeman calmly. 'After you.'

Billy stood resolute for a second before turning to follow Claire through the double doors and along the corridor where only a few minutes previously, Hawk and Julie had travelled. However, for some reason he couldn't fathom, with each step he took his unease grew until by the time Claire opened the door to the small family's room, he was ready to blow. 'I'll get you some tea,' she said before vanishing from sight.

Even before the door had closed behind her, Billy rounded on the two policemen.   'OK, What's the bloody story?'

'Please, sit down Mister Evans,' said the older policemen who had obviously taken charge of the whole process.

'I don't want to sit,' replied Billy angrily. 'I want some bloody answers.'

'I understand how you're feeling but we are actually trying to help. Now, please, sit down.'

Reluctantly, Billy sat. A move that was mirrored by the two policemen. The younger of whom took out a notepad and began writing.

'Right, first things first. This is PC Bryant, I'm PC Moore. Rob, if you like. Is it OK if I call you Billy?'

Billy frowned. 'How d'you know my name anyway?'

'I'm West Ham,' said Moore with a half-smile. 'My dad's West Ham, his dad was West Ham. Why else d'you think I'm called Robert Moore? Junior here might not know all about you and *The CCS*, but I do. I know about you from way back.'

'Gotcha,' scoffed Billy dismissively. 'This must be a right touch for you then. Karma in action.'

'Look, whatever you might think of us, we're on your side here OK?' replied Moore. 'But if we're gonna to get these shits, we need your help. Understood?'

Billy considered the question carefully. As ingrained as his distrust of the police was, he knew Moore was right and that for Hawk and Julie's sake, he had no choice but to set aside his personal feelings and adopt a neutral stance. However, his gut instinct was telling him that something was going on that he didn't know about and if he was going to discover what it was, he had to retain control of the exchange. 'What have you got?' he asked.

Moore threw a glance at his colleague who shrugged his shoulders. 'We received a report of a burglary from Mr. Hawkins at about 02.00. Officers attended shortly afterwards but there was nobody at the house. It was about 15 minutes before they found him by which time…'

The door burst open and Claire entered carrying a tray of tea which she carefully placed on the table. 'Sorry, but I've got to get back. I'll let Julie know where you are Billy so don't worry. She'll probably come here anyway.'

'It's OK,' said Moore. 'We won't be long, I promise.' He waited until Claire left and then turned back to Billy. 'By the time they found him he'd lost a lot of blood, but he was able to give us a brief description of three black youths aged between 16 and 20. That was about it.'

'He didn't say nothing about a ruck then?' asked Billy who, even as he was speaking was thinking about who he might be able to pass the information on to.

'No, he only said he'd gone after them and been jumped. So, you see,' continued the policeman, 'anything you can tell us which adds to that is useful.'

'I've told you everything he told me,' said Billy. 'As it was it was like a shit game of charades.'

'Don't worry. That's a real help.'

'What happens now?'

'We find them. Simple as that.'

'You better, before we do.' The words flew out of Billy instinctively. Even he didn't know where they had come from but the resultant change in the atmosphere inside the small room was tangible.

'Look,' said Moore softly. 'I know how you're feeling, honestly, I do. But leave this to us OK?'

Before Billy could answer, Bryant's radio burst into life and he stood and moved swiftly from the room. Moore watched him go before standing and turning to face Billy who remained sitting on the sofa. His eyes fixed firmly on the policeman standing over him.

'I mean it. The last thing we need right now is anything getting in our way. Understood?'

The two men eyeballed each other for a second before Moore turned away and walked out of the room leaving Billy alone with his anger.

Outside in the corridor, Moore and Bryant strode briskly back toward the main unit.

'I take it he was once some kind of face at West Ham?' asked Bryant.

'He wasn't *a* face, he was *the* face,' replied Moore. 'And a lot more besides.'

'What's that mean?'

Moore laughed to himself as his memory reeled off a list of crimes Billy had been linked with over the years. Not simply football related violence but extortion, car ringing, murder and even the death of a copper. That was just the stuff they had on record; God only knows what else he was guilty of. 'Put it this way,' he said. 'There are a lot of retired coppers who'll tell you that their biggest regret was not being able to put him away. Or Hawkins for that matter.'

'Maybe there is such a thing as karma then,' scoffed Bryant.

Moore grabbed Bryant by the shoulder and pulled him to a halt. 'Listen, I know you're a probationer, so I'll cut you some slack,' he said quietly. 'But don't underestimate what we've got here. These two were once in the top ten hooligan targets, not just for the Met, I mean nationally. More importantly, they're fucking legends at West Ham and when word gets out that Hawkins has been stabbed, we could have the entire bloody *CSS* crawling all over East London trying to find who did it. Pound to a pinch of shit he's on the blower as we're standing here.'

Bryant smiled. 'Come on skipper. All this *Cockney Suicide Squad* stuff. Ain't it all a bit *Green Street*?'

Moore shook his head and headed off toward the A&E department. 'I despair, really I do.'

Billy had fallen back into his seat and was staring at the ceiling as he tried desperately to get a handle on the emotional turmoil that had engulfed him. He couldn't even work out if he was angry or terrified because everything was dwarfed by a sense of complete and utter helplessness.

For a fleeting second, he wished that he had belief. At least then he'd have the power of prayer to call on and maybe that would give him the strength to cling onto the hope that was ebbing from him. But religion had never been a part of his life and the only thing he had ever truly believed in was himself. Although even that had been tested in the wake of Sam's death.

But what if he was missing something? What if her murder had been punishment for all the wrongs he'd done up to that point and now he was being confronted by another dose of karma? Or was it all merely a test? Part of some grand plan to tempt or even drag him back into the spiritual fold.

Yet how could he ever put his faith in something that had done so much damage not to him, he had never cared about himself in that sense, but to his boys? And what about Julie? She'd dedicated her life to helping others and here she was, facing the loss of the love of her life in the worst kind of circumstances. And for what? A fucking motorbike!

However, before he could ponder it any further, Billy felt himself being overcome with a feeling he couldn't quite understand. It was as if the blood was being drained from the bottom up leaving his joints numb and incapable of movement. As the feeling crept upwards through his body, the thought struck him that he was having if not a heart attack, a stroke. Another kick in the bollocks from the almighty for daring to question either his existence or his tactics. 'Is this it?' he wondered. 'Am I fucked as well?'

Yet even as the words rattled around his head, the blood began to surge back through his veins. It was almost as if it had been sucked out, warmed up and was now being pumped back in bringing with it a strength he hadn't felt in years.

Within a matter of moments, the feeling had returned to his body but this time the anxiety and anguish that had gripped him only moments before had gone. In its place a long dormant but all too familiar sense of confidence and determination.

'What the fuck was that all about?' he said out loud as he pushed himself to his feet. As much to prove to himself that he could still actually function as for any other reason.

'Are you OK?' Billy turned to find Claire standing in the doorway staring at him with a bemused expression on her face.

'Yeah', he said. A little too abruptly. 'I'm… I think so.'

'You sure?' she asked. 'You were talking to someone.'

'Just myself,' he replied. 'I was getting stir crazy I think. Any news?'

Claire stared at Billy. She'd seen a lot of strange things happen in hospitals over the years and very little shocked her, but something had obviously happened to this man. He was different somehow, more assured, sharper. She wondered for a fleeting moment if he'd taken something but dismissed the thought almost immediately. He wasn't the type, that much was obvious, but his mind was clearly racing. 'He's in theatre.' she said. 'I just wondered if you wanted to sit with Julie.'

'Yeah, of course,' replied Billy calmly even as plans formed in his head. 'But could you give us a minute?'

'Sure, just come and find me when you're ready.'

The second Claire was gone, Billy pulled his phone from his pocket. It took a few moments to find what he was looking for and almost instantly he was tapping away. The second he'd hit send, he thrust the phone back into his pocket and turned toward the door only for a small poster to catch his eye. He smiled to himself as looked at the list of telephone numbers offering religious support and comfort in times of need. 'You might move in mysterious ways mate,' he thought to himself, 'But I bloody don't. Not any more.'

Even as he pulled the door open and headed toward the accident and emergency department, his phone pinged to signal the arrival of the first response. He took it out, glanced at it and then as further messages arrived, he switched it to silent and with a wry smile, thrust it back into his pocket before continuing his walk.

It had begun.

06.10

Billy stared into the empty plastic cup clasped gingerly in his hands as he fought desperately to remain calm. He had always hated waiting but this, this was unlike anything he'd ever had to endure. He'd sat there for almost two hours drinking endless cups of tea brought in by Claire and various other nurses but aside from that, there had been no news, no information, no nothing. Just desperate hope. It was purgatory.

For what seemed like the thousandth time, he glanced across at Julie who was busily losing herself in paperwork as she also waited for news from the operating theatre. 'How the fuck can she do that?' Billy wondered to himself whilst at the same time marvelling that she was able to. But that, he guessed, was what years of nursing taught you. The ability to run on autopilot in the face of adversity and deal with the emotional aftermath when you were away from the hospital. Was that, he wondered, why so many of the nurses he'd known over the years were party animals? If what he was going through was typical, Billy could hardly blame them.

He finally succumbed and crushed the cup between his fingers, the noise of crunching plastic finally dragging Julie's attention from her endless forms and earning him a disapproving glare. 'You should go get some fresh air,' she said. 'I'll come and find you if there's any news.'

Before Billy could answer, his phone pinged earning not merely another glare but a sigh heavy with exasperation. A sure sign that he was getting on her tits in a big way. 'Sorry,' he said. 'I must have knocked it off silent. I'll go out for a bit.'

As Julie returned to her escapism, Billy stood and quietly left the room only to find PC Bryant standing in the corridor staring at him.

'What's up?' he asked. 'Is it Hawk?"

'No,' replied Bryant. 'Nothing like that. Might I ask where you're going?'

'I need a slash and some fresh air. Why?'

'We'd prefer it if you remained in the office for now.'

'To be honest, I don't give a fuck what you want,' said Billy calmly. 'My back teeth are floating and if I don't have a piss soon...' He moved to walk past Bryant, but the policeman blocked his way.

'If you need a toilet, there's one along the corridor back there sir. I'll show you.'

Billy eyeballed the policeman who simply smiled in return before gesturing back up the corridor. Much as he was desperate to unload some of the frustration coursing through his veins, a more pressing need was to empty his bladder and so reluctantly, he turned around and headed off closely followed by Bryant.

Moments later, suitably relieved and with hands freshly washed Billy was about to leave the washroom when his phone pinged again. He pulled it out and even as he began to read, he felt his hackles rising. Barely a second later, he had burst out into the corridor where PC Bryant was waiting.

'What the fuck's going on?' he barked. 'My mates in the car park and he's saying that you lot won't let him in.'

'I can't comment on that,' replied Bryant. 'Other than to say that for operational reasons, A&E is currently on lockdown.'

'What does that mean?'

'What it says. Now, if you'd like to return to...'

'I'm not going anywhere other than outside,' growled Billy. 'I've been staring at the walls for hours. I need some air.'

'I'm sorry sir,' said Bryant nervously. 'I can't allow that.'

A smile spread across Billy's face. 'You're gonna stop me going outside? Seriously? On what grounds?'

'As I said sir, we have a situation in A&E. It's for your own safety.'

Billy almost burst out laughing but before he could reply, PC Moore appeared and walked toward him. 'What's going on?'

'Junior here is telling me I can't go outside,' Billy said calmly. 'And I'm telling him that he can't stop me.'

'Yes, he can,' replied Moore abruptly. 'Because those were his orders. However, we have a bit of a situation developing and I need your help to calm it down before it gets out of hand. Come with me, please.'

With a glance at Bryant, Moore turned and headed off in the direction of A&E. Billy, his mind racing, followed him as Bryant fell in behind him. However, before they reached A&E, Moore took a left turn and led them through the ambulance bay. As they stepped into the open air, he stopped and turned to Billy. 'Some of your er… colleagues are gathering outside and they're being a pain in the arse. I need you to tell them to go home.'

'And why would I do that?' asked Billy. Desperately struggling to contain the swell of pride and relief he was feeling. 'They're concerned citizens.'

'Because if you don't, I'm under orders to nick the lot of them for obstruction. Your choice.'

Billy stared at the policeman standing in front of him. He'd had enough dealings with the police over the years to know how far he could push his luck and he sensed that for some reason, Moore was close to breaking point. In the past, he'd have pushed a little more just to see the reaction but the last thing Julie needed was any more grief and he certainly didn't want to be sitting in the back of a van when Hawk came out of surgery.

'OK,' he said calmly. 'I'll speak to them. But I don't need either of you on my shoulder OK? Give me five minutes.'

'Thank you,' replied Moore in a voice which sounded almost relieved. 'Come back here when you're finished.'

Billy strode across the car park, his eyes taking in every detail of his surroundings as he walked. Parked by the entrance to A&E were three police cars and two police Transit vans which Billy presumed were empty. Standing in the road were four policemen, one of whom he recognised as one of the spotters who trawled the bars around the London Stadium on match days and beyond them stood six familiar and trusted faces. Older maybe, but each possessing the same aura of self-assurance and bond of comradeship that only military combat and a lifetime on the terraces seemed capable of instilling in people. From their demeanour, Billy could see that like him, they were clearly pissed off.

'About fucking time,' said Stretch as Billy approached. 'Bastard Old Bill slung us out soon as we asked for you. What's the score?'

Without a further word, Billy embraced the men in turn.

'How's Hawk Billy?' asked PJ.

'Give us a smoke for fuck's sake.' gasped Billy, continuing to speak even as he placed the cigarette in his mouth and lit up. 'He's still in surgery. Two hours so far. Fuck me...' he whispered as he allowed the smoke to drift from his mouth. 'That tastes good.'

'What happened?' pressed Stretch.

'About one o'clock this morning he caught three scrotes in his garage trying to nick his bike. He gave two of 'em a hiding but the third one stuck him in the back.'

'Cunts.'

'Who were they?'

'Dunno. Black lads. Hawk reckons he gave one a broken nose, the other has a broken arm.'

'They won't be hard to find then,' said PJ.

'I hope not,' replied Billy. 'Cos, I want 'em found.'

'Word's already out,' said Stretch.

Billy smiled. 'Good. Whatever it takes OK? I'll put a grand up as a sweetener for whoever puts them on offer.'

'Then what?' asked Geoff calmly as he glanced in the direction of the four policemen. 'You know Old Bill will be all over us like a bloody rash.'

'Leave that to me. Just get 'em found and call me when you have news OK. I best get back and you lot best do the off or they're gonna lift you. I'll call you soon as I have any news.'

Billy went to turn away but then stopped in his tracks. 'Any idea what's going on in there? They told me it's on lockdown or something.'

'Dunno,' said Geoff. The meat wagons were here when we turned up.'

Billy shrugged his shoulders and with a wave of his hand, headed back toward the hospital.

As he entered the ambulance bay, Billy was surprised to find neither Moore or Bryant waiting for him and so out of curiosity, rather than head back toward Julie's office he headed toward A&E which was, as he expected, chaos. However, what struck him was the number of policemen dotted around. Most notably two who seemed to be standing guard over one of the bays at the far end. A sure sign that someone had been nicked…or was about to be.

'I told you to meet me at the ambulance bay!'

Billy turned to find Moore staring at him. His face a curious mix and anger and panic. 'You weren't there,' he replied irritably. 'What am I supposed to do? Hang around until you turn up?'

Moore moved to one side and held out his arm. 'Come on. You shouldn't be here.'

With a shrug, Billy allowed himself to be led back through the double doors and along the corridor toward Julie's office but as they passed the ambulance bay, Moore took hold of his arm and pulled Billy to a halt.

'Look, I'm sorry but there's no easy way to tell you this,' said the policeman. 'Your mate, he died in theatre about fifteen minutes ago.'

Chapter Four
Thursday 2nd August 2018

08.30

Few of the paramedics delivering a steady stream of anguish to the A&E department of Queens Hospital noticed the man sitting quiet and alone on a wall by the entrance. Those that did barely gave him a passing glance.

They'd seen enough of the consequences of death to recognise that this man, whoever he was, had suffered some kind of loss and if he wanted to be alone, then that was his choice. They had pressing work to do, life to preserve.

What they didn't know, couldn't have known, was that far from grieving, this seemingly quiet man was busy formulating plans to give them more custom.

When Moore had told him about Hawk, his initial instinct had been to go to Julie to try and offer whatever support he could but she had already vanished into the bowels of the hospital to spend whatever time she needed to with Hawk's body. His second instinct was to think about himself and how he was ever going to come to terms with another loss, but he quickly pushed that to the back of his mind. Primarily because he knew deep down that he was never going to be able to and the fear that he was once again going to fall into the grip of the dreaded black dog had already begun to simmer.

So instead, Billy had simply walked out into the fresh air and sat on a wall to think about his next move. And that move was revenge.

'There you are, I've been looking for you.' Billy looked up to find Claire standing above him. Her face ashen and a trace of urgency in her voice which brought Billy to his feet.

'What's wrong? How's Julie?'

'She's fine, her parents have just arrived.'

'That's good,' said Billy. 'Poor cow must be going through the ringer.'

Claire took hold of his hand and began to pull him away from the ambulance bay toward the car park. 'I need to talk to you,' she hissed. 'But not here.'

Billy allowed himself to be led until they were out of earshot of anyone else at which point Claire stopped and turned to face him. She stared at him for a moment and then grabbed him. Pulling him as close as possible to her. So tight that he could feel every curve of her against him. He returned the embrace, albeit reluctantly. It had been a long time since he'd been held by a woman and he wasn't sure if he was ready for it. 'It's OK,' he began. 'I...'

'Listen,' she whispered, 'You didn't hear this from me but a few hours ago the police brought someone into A&E. I think it's one of the people who stabbed Graham.'

Billy felt his blood run cold. 'Why do you think that?' he replied calmly.

'Not just me, everyone thinks that. We're nurses, we're not stupid.'

'Have you seen him?'

'No. I've been with another patient. They wouldn't let me in anyway. The police are trying to get him out of here as quickly as they can.'

'Why?'

'Because of you. And to be honest the staff aren't exactly thrilled to be dealing with someone who may have killed the husband of…'

'OK,' interrupted Billy. 'I get it. Do you know his name?'

'Ashley Bennett. I got it off the board.'

Billy released his embrace and smiled at her. 'Thanks,' he continued. 'I appreciate that.'

'Well at least you know,' said Claire. 'Now I'm off home. It's been a long night and I'm back on duty in a few hours.'

Without another word, she turned and headed toward what Billy assumed was the staff car park. He watched her for a moment then started walking toward the entrance to A&E with only one thing on his mind. However, even as he approached, the doors slid open and a group of policemen walked out. In their midst, a black youth, his left arm cradled in a sling.

Seeing him, Billy instinctively broke into a sprint. He knew he had mere moments to do what he had to do and only one chance to do it. If he failed, they'd have him in the back of the waiting van and away.

'Stop right there!'

Billy ignored the shout and continued running. His eyes firmly fixed on his target even though he could sense PC Moore approaching him from his left.

'Stop him!' yelled Moore. 'Stop that man!' The shout instantly bringing all eyes to bare on the rapidly approaching Billy, including those of Ashley Bennett.

Billy slowed to a stop. His eyes oblivious to everything happening around him as he sucked in every single detail of the person standing less than thirty feet from him. To all intents and purposes, the killer of his friend.

It took a matter of seconds and then, as the police bundled him away, Billy continued to stare at the youth until he had been forced into the van and the doors closed. 'OK!' he barked as he shook the police hands off him. 'I'm cool.'

The police retreated and Billy turned to find Moore standing behind him. 'I told you to leave it to us!' he said calmly. 'And I also told you I'd nick you if you did anything.'

'What did I do?' asked Billy arrogantly. 'Did I smack him? Did I shout anything? No. I did fuck all and you know it.'

The two men eyeballed each other for a few moments. 'Just leave it to us OK?' said Moore. 'Nothing's going to be served by you going on some bloody crusade. Besides, shouldn't you be thinking about his wife?'

Billy continued to eyeball Moore for a moment and then smiled. 'You're right,' he said quietly. 'I best go and see how she is.'

Moore watched Billy head back toward the hospital, took a deep breath and glanced at his watch. Fourteen hours he'd been on duty and he was physically and mentally drained. It had been a horrific night.

He'd been a copper for over 25 years and during that time, on more occasions than he dared to remember, he'd found himself in the middle of situations which weren't just heartbreaking, they were devastating. Usually, he'd been able to deal with them with the thought that whatever he might be feeling, it was always much worse for someone else. Yes, he could empathise but be they victim or family, and it was always one or the other, the bad news element of the event wasn't his to cope with, it was theirs. His job was to remain professional and make the best out of what was all too often, a nightmarish situation. This time was different.

This time he didn't just feel distraught or frustrated at what had unfolded, he felt angry. Angry at the lack of faith he felt in the law he had sworn to uphold and angry at his own impotence when it came to being allowed to enforce it. But most of all, he was angry at the fact that he could no longer hide the fact that the law had lost. Beaten by an underclass who held little enough respect for themselves let alone the police. Christ, they barely even recognised right and wrong.

The night could have been so different. For even as Hawkins had been on his way to hospital, two of his colleagues had stumbled across a youth clearly in pain from what had turned out to be a broken arm. Despite his protests, they had brought him into A&E where, even as Billy Evans had been arriving at reception, two and two were already being put together. They had their man, at least one of them.

However, as soon as they had begun to question the youth about his movements, he had switched from being cagey to aggressive. Denying all knowledge of any stabbing and instead, claiming that he'd just been walking along when a man had come out and attacked him with a baseball bat for absolutely no reason. From the description he'd given, that man, clearly, had been Graham Hawkins. He'd even had the cheek to demand that his attacker be arrested and charged with assault.

This was nothing new to a seasoned copper like Rob Moore who had seen pretty much everything, but it was clear, that with no witnesses to counter the youths' claims, the testimony of Hawkins was going to prove crucial.

Then, news had come through that he had died on the operating table and Rob Moore had been forced to watch on whilst his wife had been told that most awful of news. And of course, they'd also been told that everything possible would be done to bring the killers to justice, but they were idle words. For like every copper there, Moore had known in his heart of hearts that barring a miracle, the chances of a major conviction were pretty much zero. The result being that the little bastard was going to walk away with at best, a slap on the wrists and there was nothing he or anyone else was going to be able to do about it. The very thought made him feel sick.

Well that was it for him. He was done. As soon as was practical he'd be putting his papers in and if he used the holiday owed to him, he'd probably only have to work a few more shifts before he became just another retired copper.

He already felt relieved.

Far from seeking out Julie, Billy had made his way through the hospital and back out into the car park where he had climbed into his car and headed home as quickly as he could.

Once through his front door and without even breaking stride, he had headed for his study and switched on his computer. Now, having logged on to his rarely used Facebook account and trawled around for barely five minutes, he was staring at Ashely Bennett. The youth's face cloaked in the kind of arrogant smirk which seemed to define the grubby crime fuelled culture that had spawned him and a thousand others.

'Gotcha you bastard.'

Chapter Five
Tuesday 2nd October 2018
14.45

Billy sat in his car, eyes closed, the radio on low. He needed a few moments of solitude and refection otherwise he'd crack, and he was determined that he wouldn't let that happen. Not today. Today was the day he'd been dreading.

Ironically, it had gone smoother than he had dared to hope. His eulogy, delivered to a packed crematorium, had gone without a hitch and had drawn both laughs and an approving smile from Julie that had filled him with pride. Even the noise of the curtains closing around the coffin hadn't shaken him although like many, he had masked the anguish of that moment by humming along to the music that had filled the room. Oddly, given the angst her husband's relationship with football had caused her over the years, 'I'm forever blowing bubbles' had been Julie's choice but it had been spot on.

Now it was over. Hawk was gone and here he sat, trying to compose himself ahead of the wake. It was an impossible task. For whilst his mate might have gone, Billy didn't have the one thing he desperately craved. He didn't have closure.

Having identified Ashley Bennett, Billy had immediately put the word out and demanded that he be found. However, he had also insisted that no one touch him, for Billy wanted that satisfaction himself. Once he'd had his pound of flesh, *The CSS* could have their fun.

It had taken barely hours before he'd had an address, but Bennett had been nowhere to be found. Instead, Billy had become embroiled in a confrontation with his family which had resulted in the police being called. Regretful only for the fact that he'd received a caution and a severe warning of the consequences for him were Bennett to come to any harm at any time.

Mindful of the impact that would have on Julie if nothing else, Billy had reluctantly taken a step back from his desire for revenge and had instead thrown himself into supporting the grieving widow whilst at the same time, helping to arrange the funeral. An onerous and painful task which Julie had happily abdicated full responsibility for sure in the knowledge that Billy wouldn't let her, and more importantly Hawk, down.

Then the crushing blow had come when the Crown Prosecution Service had decreed that the case wasn't even going to court. For with the other two youths involved having been identified and backing up Bennett's story about Hawk attacking them first, the lack of any evidence to counter their version of events left them with little confidence that they would be able to secure any kind of conviction. Far better to leave the case open and hope that the murder weapon or a witness would turn up in the future. At least then they'd have a chance.

Julie had naturally been distraught at their decision but whilst Billy had feigned anger, it had been purely for show. His faith in the law had long since evaporated and by that time his mindset had already been locked into revenge mode. The police and whatever they might have had planned for Ashely Bennett, were wholly irrelevant. The key questions for Billy were when and how? And they would be addressed as soon as today came to a close.

A tap on the window dragged him back to real time and he opened an eye to find Claire staring at him. She tapped her watch and gestured in the direction of the hotel where people clad in black suits were streaming through the front entrance.

Claire. The silver lining in this shit show.

Initially, he had fought desperately against the idea of forging any kind of relationship but as the weeks had passed and they had talked, Billy had eventually began to accept that whilst she clearly had feelings for him, he also had growing feelings for her. So much so that he had even broached the subject with his sons who had both voiced not merely approval, but relief. 'About bloody time' they'd both said. So,

41

he'd gone for it. Not in a big way, it was early days after all, and she was certainly no replacement for his beloved Sam, but it had been a start and for the first time in a long time, he had begun to feel comfortable in the company of a woman.

He looked up at her again and forced a half smile before pushing open the door and stepping out of his car.

'You OK?' she asked softly.

'Yeah, I just needed a minute to myself. You know.'

Claire smiled knowingly at him then held out her hand. 'Come on mister,' she said. 'People are waiting.'

Billy took her hand and then pulled her close. Their arms locking gently around each other as if it were the most natural thing in the world for either of them.

They held the embrace for a few moments and then, hand in hand, walked slowly toward the hotel.

Billy stood at the bar quietly nursing a bottle of Budweiser as he took in the packed room in front of him. He had been touched by the show of faces from other clubs who had been at the crematorium, but he'd been genuinely surprised at how many more characters from 'their' world had turned up at the hotel to pay their respects. Amongst the inevitable West Ham faces were numerous lads from other clubs some of whom had travelled significant distances. Some Billy knew well, others not at all but be they friend or former foe, he had welcomed them all personally and warmly. Now, with the speeches done, tears shed and the food and alcohol flowing, the gathering had begun to make the transition from solemn occasion to old-school reunion and with Julie now firmly ensconced in the bosom of her family and friends, Billy had finally begun to relax as he flitted between groups. A task helped by the fact that few people had felt the need to go too deeply into the reasons why they were there. It was shit; everyone knew that. There was no need to rehash it.

There was however, one subject which kept cropping up and that was the small matter of Ashley Bennett and the fact that he had seemingly evaded justice. Having taken the conscious decision not to discuss it at the funeral for fear it would tip him over the edge, Billy had shied away from getting too deeply involved in any such conversation and instead, had maintained a dignified silence on the matter. 'Now wasn't the time or the place,' had been his only response whenever the subject had been touched upon

Yet in truth, Billy hadn't worked out what he was going to do, at least not yet. He had chapter and verse on Bennett and his little crew as well as any army of lads willing to tear them and their world apart on his say so. Yet he also had the police looking over his shoulder and whilst he was happy that the inevitable spell inside would be a small price to pay for the justice he personally craved, he was also well aware that as a single parent, he had his boys to think about.

But equally, he was acutely aware of the responsibility that sat on his shoulders in terms of *The CSS*. The scene might have moved on a bit since the halcyon days when he and Hawk had called the tunes but they were still a force to be reckoned with and the current crop remained just as fiercely protective of their reputation as he had been back in his day. Billy knew he had time, respect and loyalty demanded it, but it wasn't finite, and he'd already started to hear a few rumblings of discontent, some from closer to home than he felt comfortable about. *The CSS* wanted their pound of flesh, and they wanted it soon.

'You alright fella?' Billy snapped from his daydream and turned to find Stretch standing beside him. The seemingly standard look of amusement on his face. 'You look miles away.'

'Just thinking about Hawk. He'd have enjoyed this.'

'He'll be up there kicking off about all these faces drinking at his expense,' Stretch replied with a wry smile. 'Tight fucker.'

Billy smiled at the thought. Tight was one word you could never have attached to Hawk. He'd never knowingly ducked a round in his life.

'Listen,' Stretch continued, his voice lower and more serious. 'There's a couple of geezers floating around. Something about 'em ain't right.'

'So why didn't you front 'em?'

'I didn't like to in case they were family or something.'

'They still here?'

Stretch nodded in the direction of the doors leading out into the hotel grounds where two men stood quietly taking in everything going on around them. Smartly dressed and well groomed, they certainly blended in but like Stretch, Billy felt instantly uneasy as he scrutinised them. For a second he considered the idea that they might be policemen but that particular and well-tuned alarm bell wasn't sounding which left only one other alternative. 'Fucking journalists' he muttered as the blood began to course through his veins and his temper began to tingle. 'Come on.'

He placed his bottle on the bar and closely followed by Stretch, began to work his way through the crowd toward them. However, even before he was barely halfway across the room the two men spotted him heading in their direction and slid out through the doors. A move which if anything, made Billy even more irritated and move even faster.

However, as he burst out into the garden expecting the men to have vanished, Billy was surprised to find them both standing waiting for him.

'Mr. Evans,' said the first one calmly. His accent a curious mixture of middle English punctuated with a twang of Yorkshire. 'It's nice to finally meet you.'

Billy studied the two men standing in front of him desperately searching for anything approaching recognition but none came. 'I take it we've not met which begs the question…'

'Not actually met,' interrupted the first man calmly. 'We do know all about you though. You have quite a reputation.'

'Impressive I'd say,' said the second. 'You could say that's why we're here.'

'Who are you then?' asked Stretch. 'Some kind of shit double act?'

'I think what my friend is trying to say,' said Billy without taking his eyes from the men standing in front of him. 'Is that if we've not met you didn't know Hawk and you're obviously not family so who the fuck are you and what are you doing here?'

The two men exchanged a look and then smiled. 'Well, we actually wanted to talk to you. Privately.'

'Then you call the office and set up an appointment with my secretary,' said Billy. 'You don't come to my mate's funeral and give it large. That's bad manners.'

'We don't really do formal appointments,' said the second man. 'We prefer the more, er... direct approach.'

'I don't care what you prefer,' replied Billy irritably. 'That's how it is. Now whoever you are, fuck off before I lose my rag and say something I won't regret.'

The first man nodded and then retrieved a card from his pocket which he handed to Billy. 'My numbers on the back. We'll be around until tomorrow evening if you'd like to talk.'

'That depends what you want to talk about,' replied Billy calmly.

'Let's just say I think it'll be to your advantage,' said the first with a wry smile. 'But we should let you get back. Nice to have met you Mr. Evans.' He thrust out his hand, but Billy ignored it and with that, the two men turned and walked away. Billy watched until they were out of sight and then shook his head.

'What the fuck was that all about?' he said out loud.

'Pair of nonces if you ask me,' replied Stretch. 'Come on, let's get a beer. I'm bloody parched.'

Stretch headed back into the hotel but Billy stood and pondered for a moment. Decades of dealing with moody characters both at football and in business had equipped him with the gift of being able to size people up almost instantly but these two had left him stumped. Having looked them in the eye, he wasn't even sure that they weren't coppers let alone journalists although if they were, they were unlike any he'd ever encountered before. Not only that, but he was still none the wiser about what they actually wanted with him which was most baffling of all.

With a sigh, he glanced at the card in his hand. One side was totally blank but on the other was a handwritten phone number and a single name; Ashley Bennett.

Billy drew his car to a halt and turned to look at Claire who was dozing quietly in the passenger seat. It was only half nine but having been on nights all week and then spending the morning with Julie and her family as they prepared for the funeral, she'd barely managed any sleep in the previous 24 hours so it was hardly surprising that the motion of the car, coupled with the numerous glasses of wine she'd consumed at the hotel, had taken its toll.

Unsure if he should wake her or not, Billy settled back in his seat and allowed his mind to wander back over the events of the day. It had actually been tougher than he'd expected not least because of the memories it had triggered of the last funeral he'd had to arrange, that of his beloved Sam. The irony that Hawk had been by his side throughout that horrific time had been uppermost in his thinking throughout the previous weeks and he'd been determined to repay that debt by doing his friend proud and he had. He was absolutely confident of that.

Yet with the funeral now over and those obligations dealt with, Billy knew that he was now going to be faced with a fresh series of problems. Not least the very real and terrifying idea that his life would have to return to what passed for normality. Everyday life and carrying on as if nothing had happened had been a source of constant struggle in the years after Sam's death and the nagging fear that the dreaded black dog would return to consume him once again had already started to take a grip. It wasn't helped by the fact that he was now missing the one person he'd been able to call on for emotional support and indeed, in that sense he was already feeling very much alone. He could hardly vent to his boys and he was still wary of unloading anything on Claire for fear of scaring her off which left him with little or nothing to lean on. In quieter and reflective moments, he'd even considered the idea of giving bereavement therapy a crack but had shied away from it. Not just because he was fearful of what secrets from his past he might let slip, but because he could never shake the notion that taking that path was akin to admitting not merely weakness, but defeat. Yet here he was, staring into an even darker abyss with barely a glimmer of either hope or escape. Maybe, he wondered, the time might have come to revisit that particular idea.

There was also the increasingly pressing issue of Ashley Bennett which had been brought into even sharper focus by the curious encounter at the wake. He still had no idea what that had been about but Billy had never been averse to playing mind games if they suited him so he could hardly complain if someone was trying to employ them on him. Yet whilst he had various courses of action open to him, Billy had already decided to make that particular call first thing. Whatever these chancers were after, he needed to know who they were and what their particular interest was in both him and Bennett.

He glanced across at Claire who having shifted in her seat, was now starting to snore gently. Billy smiled at the sight and sound of her, yet he knew that of all the problems he was going to have to confront in the near future, she was potentially going to be the most difficult for him to deal with.

Billy had still been in his teens when he and Samantha had met, and it had been pretty much love at first sight for both of them. The progression to marriage, home and children had been natural and smooth and even despite some of his more questionable activities, she had never seriously doubted him just as he had never doubted her.

Yet whilst Sam would forever be the love of his life, she was, thanks to him, gone. Her presence reduced to memory and photograph. The idea of replacing her was quite frankly terrifying yet however much Billy had fought it, Claire had reignited feelings that he had thought consigned to history. However, the emergence of emotions such as attraction had also generated huge swathes of guilt and despite the years since his beloved wife's death, Billy had allowed those to stifle all other feelings. That had been fine whilst he'd been involved with the planning of the funeral but now that had passed, he was left exposed and on the edge of unknown territory. Was he ready to take that leap of faith and confront everything that a relationship would bring?

The very idea raised more questions than answers yet whilst issues such as how his boys would react, what Sam's family would think and even the potential reawakening of his long dormant libido fought for his attention, it was the issue of his past which kept pushing its way to the front.

He had never had to explain nor justify himself before but were he and Claire to become an item it was inevitable that at some point, history would show its hand and whilst he was aware that she had been well briefed by Julie, the truth was that his past was heavy with secrets he hadn't even felt able to tell Hawk. Would he be able to keep those events quiet in the face of what he suspected would be intense scrutiny? And if he couldn't, if at some point he let slip the very worst of it, how would she react to the discovery that his litany of crimes included the murder of one man and involvement in the deaths of two more, one of whom had been a policemen?

Yet even as he pondered this, Billy began to realise that another fear had begun to make its presence felt and that was the fear that if he didn't step up, she would walk, and he'd be back to being alone. The more he thought about that, the more he began to understand just how much of an impact Claire had made on him since they'd first met on that fateful night. Billy had never sought nor needed approval from anybody for anything yet the fact that no one had thought it out of the ordinary when he had walked in holding hands with a woman had come as a huge relief.

Billy smiled to himself as he looked at her, still snoring gently. Maybe he was actually ready to step into that minefield after all. 'Hey,' he said softly. 'We're home.'

'Just throw something over me and leave me here,' she murmured without opening her eyes. 'I'm too comfortable to move.'

'I would, but I'd have to walk home and it's bloody cold.'

'Then stay,' she said. 'Why go back to an empty house?' The words hit Billy like a sledgehammer. So, this was it, either knowingly or unknowingly Claire had taken the decision out of his hands and it was now or never. Of all the things he'd ever done, of all the situations he'd ever been in where he'd had to front someone or something up, he'd rarely been as terrified as he was at that instant. Was this woman who he'd barely even kissed, about to change his life and fill a void which he'd kept empty for over a decade?

Billy turned to stare out into the darkness as he struggled to settle his heart which was thumping almost audibly. 'OK,' he said turning back to her. 'If you're sure.'

Claire opened an eye and looked at him. 'It's not me who needs to be sure mister,' she said. 'The question is, are you sure?'

Billy smiled and as he did so, he felt his previously crippling anxiety evaporate. 'I'm more than sure,' he said. 'I'm certain.'

Chapter Six
Wednesday 3rd October 2017

10.30

The red Mini pulled away from the kerb, Billy watching it until it had been consumed by the mid-morning traffic. Only once it was out of sight did he climb into his Range Rover and settled back into the leather clad opulence of the interior. 'Fuck.' he said out loud. 'Fuck, fuck, fuck!'

Last night had not gone well.

When he had taken the decision to stay, he had made it in good consciousness however it had become clear fairly quickly that he hadn't fully considered the potential implications of having to overcome 15 years of self-imposed celibacy. It hadn't been a total disaster, but it hadn't been far off and whilst Claire had been both understanding and patient with him, Billy had been left feeling both embarrassed and emotionally drained by the experience. Primarily because from the moment they had entered Claire's bedroom, his mind had kept turning to Samantha and whilst he'd somehow managed to keep that to himself, it had inevitably had a crushing effect.

Billy sat for a minute, staring into space until with a sigh and another curse, he gave up beating himself up and instead, pulled the business card from his pocket and dialled the number. It was answered within two rings.

'Good morning Mr Evans. Thanks for calling.'

'Well either you're good at guessing or you're using a dodgy phone,' said Billy with a calm which belied both his mood and his surprise. 'Either way, you wanted a meet, so let's meet.'

'Good. We're at the…'

'I don't care where you are,' said Billy abruptly. 'You want to meet me; I'll say where and when.'

'Fair enough,' replied the voice.

'There's a pub called *The Top Of The World* on the A12 just outside Brentwood. I'll meet you there in an hour.' Before they could answer, Billy killed the call and after waiting for a few seconds to see if they'd call back, flicked through his contacts until another name appeared. He clicked on it and waited for a few seconds until a female voice answered. 'Good morning, *The Top Of The World*. How may I help you?'

'Could I speak to Simon please. Tell him it's Billy. Billy Evans.'

Despite its rather odd location on a major road on the edge of a tough Essex town, *The Top Of The World* enjoyed a good reputation both with the locals and those who passed regularly.

Much of this was down to the landlord Simon who, as a former Royal Marine, not only refused to put up with any crap from his patrons but was fanatical about standards. As a consequence, the place was clean, safe and served excellent food which explained why, at 11.00 on a cold October morning, the car park was already half full.

Its location also served another purpose. For being easily accessible and relatively discreet, it was the perfect place for meetings be they business, social or even clandestine which was how Billy and Simon had become friends. It also explained why he was now parked up in a bay which gave him a clear view of both the entrance to the car park and the pub. Not just because he wanted to be there when they turned up but because he wanted Simon to run the rule over them first. As a judge of character, the landlord of *The Top Of The World* had few peers which was why he was so good at his job. If there was anything remotely dodgy about the men who wanted to meet him, Simon would sniff it out.

However, with half an hour to kill, Billy's mind inevitably began to wander back over the events of the previous night and in particular, the issue of Samantha. He hadn't planned on that although on reflection, since even after 15 years he could remember every single thing about her and still missed her desperately, it was pretty obvious that there would be an element of comparison the first time he effectively replaced her. Yet even he had to admit that he had actually enjoyed waking up beside someone for the first time in a decade and a half and it was clear that Claire had felt the same. She'd certainly shown no sign of being disappointed, quite the opposite. They'd been laughing and joking right through until the time had come for her to leave for work so was it really fair for him to feel guilty? After all, you can't cheat on a memory, not even when it's of the love of your life. Or can you?

It was a lot to process and not for the first time, Billy wished he had Hawk to talk to although he was fairly certain what his friend would have told him. 'Don't be a twat, go for it' would have been pretty close.

Billy was still imagining how that conversation would have unfolded further when his attention was grabbed by a black Mercedes pulling into the car park. He knew instinctively that it was the two men from the funeral and checked the clock on his dashboard to see that they'd arrived ten minutes early.

Without taking his eyes off the car, he picked up his phone and pressed redial. It was answered even as they stepped out of the car and headed toward the entrance. 'They're just coming in. Two men, dark suits.' The line went dead.

Billy cradled the phone in his hand ready to answer the instant the response came. He was tempted to take a look over the Mercedes but thought better of it and instead, kept his attention fixed on the entrance as he ran through the various scenarios that might unfold. There was every possibility that this was some kind of trap and if he was going to avoid walking into it, he had to banish all thoughts of Samantha and Claire and make sure that he was fully on his game.

After what seemed an age but was actually nearer to four minutes, Billy's phone rang, and he tapped the green button. 'What's the story?' he asked.

'They're vet's,' said Simon in a hushed tone.

'What d'you mean vet's?' asked Billy.

'Well not the sort who stick their arms up cow's arse's. What do you think I mean? They're ex-military.'

'You sure?'

'Yep. They're both wearing veterans' badges on their jackets, so I asked 'em. There's something else.'

'What?' Billy listened intently for a moment and then, when the line went dead, he slipped his phone into his pocket, reached forward and started the car. However, even as he was slipping the automatic gearbox into drive, he paused. His head was telling him to get out of there, but his gut was telling him something entirely different. The question was, what?

'Fuck it,' he muttered aloud, not for the first time that morning, and within a matter of moments, Billy Evans was striding purposefully across the car park toward the entrance of *The Top Of The World* ready to take on whatever fate had in store for him.

The two men both stood as Billy approached. 'Mr. Evans,' said the first holding out his hand. 'Welcome. What would you like to drink?'

Billy shook both their hands and sat down. 'Call me Billy,' he said. 'Let's just get down to business, shall we?'

'As you wish,' said the first man. 'First things first, I'm Paul, this is Tom. I'm sure your friend the barman told you the rest.'

'He did indeed,' replied Billy with a wry smile. 'You caught me.'

'Not really,' said Tom with a grin. 'It was just an educated guess. If we were in your shoes we'd be just as cautious.'

'But I hope that shows you,' continued Paul, 'that we've got nothing to hide from people we trust.'

'Trust!' said Billy with a hint sarcasm. 'That's a big word to throw at someone you barely know.'

Paul smiled. 'Oh, we know all about you Billy. In fact, we've been looking for someone like you for quite a while.'

'Someone like me. What does that mean?'

Tom held up his hand in apology. 'Wrong choice of words, sorry. What Paul meant was, we've been looking for someone with your abilities.'

Billy leant forward and rested on his elbows. 'OK, let's stop pissing about shall we? What do two ex-military coppers want with me? And what the fuck have you got to do with Ashley Bennett?'

Paul and Tom exchanged glances and then turned back to Billy. 'OK,' began Paul. 'We have a proposition we think will interest you.'

'What kind of proposition?'

'Before we talk about that, could you please erase everything you've recorded so far and then turn off your phone?'

Billy eyeballed the two men opposite for a moment then reluctantly pulled out his phone. Once he'd complied with their request, he placed it on the table and leant forward.'

'So? What's all this cloak and dagger bollocks about?'

Normally, as long as they didn't impact on anyone else, Simon was happy to leave people to whatever business they were up to inside his bar. However, there was something about this particular liaison which had piqued his curiosity and he had kept a wary eye on the booth in the corner where the three men had remained ensconced in deep conversation for over an hour.

Having spent 12 years in the Royal Marines and another 6 as a member of the Special Boat Service, he had developed numerous skills when it came to judging both people and situations and whilst the alarm bells weren't ringing, they were certainly jingling. Then again, that tended to be the case whenever Billy Evans was huddled over a table in his bar. Simon didn't know him well, but he knew enough to know that he was a character with a checkered past and a somewhat hazy attitude to the law. Not that he personally had cause to complain, far from it. The two cars he'd brought from Evans Motors over the last three years had both come courtesy of hefty discounts and Billy had certainly put more than enough money across his bar to make his patronage welcome. More importantly, he'd never caused an ounce of concern which made him pretty much the perfect customer. Truth be told, Simon actually quite liked him, even envied him a little.

The other two men, however, were a different kettle of fish. Simon had sussed them as ex-military the second they'd stepped into the bar, but he'd been surprised at how easily they'd offered up the information about being former military policemen. As a breed, RMP's tended to keep their background quiet when amongst other veterans primarily because of the piss taking that would inevitably ensue.

There was of course, always the chance that they had checked out the location Billy had chosen for their meeting and having discovered that they had a special forces veteran behind the bar, had put two and two together and surmised that any information learned ahead of that meeting would be immediately passed on. That, however, would have involved a degree of either intuition or intelligence that had been lacking in the majority of military policemen he'd met during his career.

It was all very curious and as Simon busied himself with the demands of his other customers he wished, not for the first time, that he'd installed hidden microphones in all the booths.

If he had, he would have quickly learned that his interest was well founded. For the discussion that he'd been observing from a distance was about to kick start a chain of events which would, within a matter of a few months, change the course of his nation's history. And Billy Evans would be slap, bang in the centre of it.

Chapter Seven
Friday 9th November 2018

23.45

Gary Williams took a final draw on his cigarette and flicked it into the middle of the road. He stopped to watch it until the rain had extinguished the final burning embers and lit another before continuing his late-night stroll through the damp streets of Brockley.

When Mandy's dad had died, it was inevitable that as an only child she would feel duty bound to adopt his dog and whilst he had been reluctant at first, primarily because he knew that the walking duties would fall firmly on his shoulders, Gary had tempered this with the knowledge that not only was the Jack Russell banging on in years, he came with almost a half a million pounds worth of house attached.

Yet fairly quickly, the little dog had done the one thing that Gary never thought any animal could ever do, it had gotten under his skin. Now, three years later, as the old dog struggled with a variety of age-related ailments, Gary had actually started to wonder how he was going to cope without his buddy once that fateful day arrived.

He took another drag on his cigarette and glanced around for his canine companion, but he was nowhere to be seen. 'Charlie', he called quietly, mindful of the late hour, 'come on you old bugger.'

The response was an almost instant yap from across the road. Then another, and another. Even before Gary could call out again, a porch light went on almost exactly where the barking was coming from. Instinctively, Gary hurried toward it. He was well aware that not everyone in this part of South-London was a fan of dogs crapping on their front step and the last thing he wanted, or needed, was any kind of row.

However, by the time the front door of the house had been opened by a large middle-aged Asian man wearing a dressing gown which was clearly too small for him, an argument was the last thing on Gary's mind. For just like Charlie, his attention had become entirely focused on the lifeless body propped against the wall outside number 46 Cartwright Avenue.

A little over 220 miles north, Claire finished reapplying her lipstick and stared at herself in the mirror. She had to admit, Billy had excelled himself.

When he had initially suggested the idea of a weekend away in Liverpool, she had turned him down on the correct assumption that football would be involved. From the outset of their relationship, given everything that Julie had told her about Billy's past as well as things she'd discovered during late night trawls of the internet, she had taken the conscious decision to keep as far as possible from that side of his life and had stuck to that rule religiously.

However, when he had sweetened the offer with the detail, Claire had relented and as a consequence, had enjoyed the journey north in the leather and walnut interior of a Bentley

Continental borrowed from his garage stock and savoured a sumptuous dinner in the 5 star luxury of the Titanic Hotel. She was even looking forward to watching football tomorrow given that Billy had lined up a full corporate package for the two of them at Goodison Park.

More importantly, despite her fears, she had seen nothing to suggest that far from being a football hooligan, even a former one, Billy was nothing other than a warm, funny and generous man who was still recovering from over a decade in a self-imposed emotional wilderness.

Yet whilst she was in no doubt that her growing feelings for him were reciprocated, his history continued to haunt her thinking and Claire knew that she would only be able to move past that once she had addressed it head on. Maybe this was the perfect opportunity to do it.

She checked herself in the mirror again and after taking a deep breath to calm her nerves, headed for the bar.

Billy stared at the message which filled the screen of his telephone and after a few seconds, closed his eyes and uttered a silent prayer of thanks as months of angst and frustration melted away leaving him wrapped in the warm blanket of satisfaction.

It was done. Now he could move on.

'Can I get you anything sir?'

Billy opened his eyes to see a young waitress standing in front of him. Her Eastern European accent slightly at odds with the fact that she looked like the stereotypical Scouse bird.

'Yes sweetheart,' he said. 'I'd love a bottle of champagne if you could manage that.'

'Of course, sir,' she replied. 'Would you like anything in particular?'

'The one closest to £50.'

She smiled and headed off, passing Claire coming in the opposite direction.

'What're you up to Evans?'

'What makes you think I'm up to anything?'

'Two things,' she said as she sat down beside him. 'One, you're awake and two, because you look like a cat that just stole a shit load of cream.'

Billy slid his phone back into his pocket and smiled as he sank back into his chair. 'I'm just happy,' he replied. 'Very happy,'

Claire looked at him and smiled. 'I'm glad to hear it.' She paused, wondering how best to broach the subject which had been causing her so much angst over recent weeks. 'Listen, I need to say something,' she began. 'I...'

Before she could continue, the waitress returned and placed the bucket on the table in front of them before proceeding to open the bottle and pouring.

'What's this for?' Claire asked.

'I told you, I'm happy.' Billy said as he handed her a glass before lifting his own. 'Absent friends.'

Claire hesitated for a second and then clinked her glass against his before taking a sip. 'And to us,' Billy said with the same disarming smile Claire had seen a thousand times but which she never tired of seeing because it melted her heart, 'and whatever the future has in store for us. Sorry,' he continued after a short pause, 'you were about to say something.'

At that very moment Claire realised that whatever questions she might ask and whatever answers he might give, nothing would change how she felt. She didn't care about Billy's past or what he did when he wasn't with her. She just cared about the here and now and however life with Billy Evans unfolded, she would deal with it if and when it happened.

'I just wanted to say,' she said softly. 'That if you think a bit of flash is going to get you into my pants, you are seriously mistaken.'

Billy raised an eyebrow in response. 'You're forgetting the pièce de résistance, West Ham versus Everton tomorrow. That's got to be worth a bit of second base action at least.'

Claire kept her expression blank for a second before she allowed it to dissolve into a warm, cheeky smile. 'It might.'

Gary Williams reached down and lifted Charlie into his arms as the ambulance pulled away. The flashing blue lights illuminating the houses and faces of the crowd gathered on the opposite side of Cartwright Avenue.

'Poor bastard,' he said to the policeman standing next to him. 'He ain't gonna be running the London marathon any time soon.'

'Save your sympathy,' said the policeman in a voice which contained not an ounce of emotion. 'Hospital's an occupational hazard for his sort. Like the nick and the morgue.'

'What d'you mean, his sort?'

The policeman hesitated for a second, suddenly aware that he was talking to a member of the public and in grave danger of saying something he might regret. 'He's not exactly unknown to us,' he replied as calmly as he could.

'Oh, so d'you think it was a gang thing?'

'We'll know more once we talk to him. Assuming he'll talk to us of course.'

Gary sighed. 'What a bloody shame. What was his name? I'd like to send some flowers or something.'

The policeman looked Gary up and down and wondered if he was stupid or simply naive. He'd just basically told him that the kid they had carted off with his knees smashed and his fingers crushed to a pulp was the kind of filth who were infesting the inner cities across the country and he wanted to send him some fucking flowers.

'Yes,' he sighed with not a little irritation. 'His name's Bennett. Ashley Bennett.'

PART TWO

Chapter Eight
Sunday 25th June 2019

14.30

Jamie Brown stepped from the air-conditioned comfort of the cab and stared up at the Victorian Terrace he called home. It wasn't just good to be back; it was a blessed relief.

The all-inclusive luxury of an Egyptian hotel was all well and good but when the outside temperature was hitting a skin peeling 35 degrees, it was too much. North London with its paltry 25 degrees was far more comfortable and if he was honest, preferable in pretty much every sense.

This was not a sentiment shared by his partner, Lisa. Whereas for him holidays were akin to short-term banishments from his life as a celebrity newspaper journalist, for her, as a detective sergeant in the Metropolitan Police child abuse team, they were cherished and highly valued escapes. As a consequence, returning home didn't just mean an end to the sunshine she relished, it meant stepping back into the gutter. It also meant that the period between leaving the hotel and returning to work were tough. Not just for Lisa, but for Jamie who had to bear the brunt of her post-holiday decompression.

Thankfully, having lived with her for over seven years, he was well versed in the process and whilst not unsympathetic, had learned to deal with it through the simple process of letting her get on with it whilst he acted as normally as possible.

He watched Lisa disappear into the house and with a sigh, set about paying the cab driver and carrying the cases in. It was going to be a long 24 hours.

'Don't even think about touching that!'

Jamie looked up to see Lisa staring at him from the kitchen door. 'I mean it,' she added. 'You're not due at work until the morning and I'm not in until tomorrow night so until then, we are still on holiday. Whatever's on there can wait until morning.'

Jamie stared at his outstretched hand. His forefinger less than 5 centimetres from the blinking light on the answerphone.

'But what if it's your mum?' he said. 'She might be lying on the floor, dying. Desperate for help. Or your sister, telling you that she's left whatsisname and needs a…'

'Go to the shop and get some milk,' she said in a tone more sergeant major than doting partner. 'I'm gagging.'

'Why me? What happened to sexual equality?'

'OK,' she said calmly. 'Well I'll leave this lot and I'll go to the shop. But by the time I get back, you'd better have a load of washing on and most of this stuff unpacked and put away. Deal?'

Jamie wasn't even tempted to call her bluff. He'd been on enough holidays with her to know that within a few hours, the only evidence that they'd been away would be her dark mood and a line full of damp clothes.

'And get some bread as well,' she called as he closed the front door behind him.

It took barely ten minutes to reach the small supermarket which was ample time for Jamie check his messages and discover that he had an early start in the morning. Normally a drive to Birmingham would have been the stuff of nightmares but not even the impending horror of a morning negotiating the traffic on the M1 and M6 was enough to temper his excitement at getting back amongst it.

His only problem was that whilst normally he'd have been eager to tell Lisa that he was going to be interviewing one of her favourite actresses, he was more than aware that the mere mention of work would start her off. Then again, if he didn't tell her and she found out afterwards, she'd kick off about that. 'Bloody women,' he muttered to himself as he began loading his basket with supplies.

'Jesus, you look like you lost a tenner and found a quid. Good holiday then?'

Jamie looked up to see his neighbour and occasional drinking partner Warren standing in front of him. The usual grin on his face and an overflowing basket hanging from his left arm.

'Just got back,' Jamie replied. 'It was hot. Too bloody hot. What have I missed?'

'Nothing much. Same old bollocks,' said Warren. 'Oh, you won't have heard about Keegan.'

'Who's Keegan?'

Warren shook his head and sighed. 'Jesus wept. You're a bloody journalist. How can you not know what's going on under your nose?'

'I don't do news do I,' said Jamie. 'I do, well, crap. Who is he?'

'Perry Keegan, he's that scumbag who was in court for beating up old Teddy Miles and his wife. Remember?'

Even as he was speaking, Jamie did indeed remember. The attack on Teddy and Betty Miles had been huge news when it happened, not least because of the ferocity of the violence used but also because it had happened in their own home. The whole thing had been made even worse when Betty Miles had died shortly after the trial collapsed.

'He got off remember?' continued Warren. 'Lack of evidence.'

'Only 'cos that bastard Keegan threatened Teddy and made him drop the charges.'

Jamie turned and was shocked to find an elderly woman standing behind him. He vaguely recognised her but for the life of him, couldn't put a name to her clearly angry face.

'Bloody coppers are useless,' she added gruffly.

'So, what happened?' asked Jamie, turning back to Warren and ignoring the woman who showed no sign of moving.

'Last Friday, these geezers burst into Keegan's flat and gave him a right battering. Smashed all his fingers and broke both his kneecaps.'

'Good,' interrupted the woman. 'Little bastard deserved it. He terrorised that poor couple for years. Not just him either.'

Jamie threw her a look and then turned back to Warren. 'They got anyone for it?' he asked?

'Course not. They're saying it's a gang thing.' Warren paused foe effect and then added, 'but it wasn't. Word is it was proper villains, y'know, pros.'

'What, like a hit?' replied Jamie. 'Leave it out.'

'I'm telling you. Someone saw 'em, and they weren't no kids.'

'Well I don't care who they are,' Jamie turned back to face the old woman again who, if anything looked even angrier. 'As far as I'm concerned, they're bloody hero's'.

She pushed past them and headed up the aisle and away. Jamie watched her and turned to Warren who shrugged his shoulders.

'Well, it's an opinion,' he said. 'And to be honest, it's bloody hard to argue against.'

'Where the bloody hell have you been? I'm gasping!'

Jamie dumped the bag on the kitchen table and switched on the kettle in one almost fluid motion.

'Sorry, I got talking to Warren. Here, guess what he told me.'

'I don't give a shit. I'm still on holiday until tomorrow evening.'

'But…'

'Beep,' she said, holding up her hand. 'Lisa isn't in right now. Please do not leave a message because she won't care until TOMORROW evening!'

'Smart arse.' he replied as he sat down opposite her. 'Just for that, you can make the tea. Oh, and just so you know, I'm off to Birmingham first thing.'

'Is that work?'

'Yes,' he replied. 'I…'

'Beep…'

Jamie looked across at her. His face blank. 'You're such a dick. Still, at least it saves me having to ask for an autograph.'

Lisa threw him a look. Much as she hated to admit it, she'd always had a fascination with the world of celebrity and was permanently envious of the fact that Jamie got to mix in those circles on a daily basis. She also had a weakness for autographs which had resulted in numerous books carefully packed away in her wardrobe. Jamie, naturally, fed that weakness on an almost daily basis although she wasn't naive enough to think that it was purely for her benefit. As bargaining tools for use during the confines of their relationship, the promise of a signature from an A-lister was as good as gold.

'And you really like the woman I'm interviewing,' Jamie added. His voice laden with smugness.

Lisa stared at his smirking face and inwardly cursed. She'd backed herself into a corner and if he wasn't to become unbearable for the rest of the day, there was only one thing she could do.

'Beep. Lisa isn't in right now.'

'Suit yourself,' he replied. 'Fancy some toast? Or shall we have a takeaway?'

'You're such a twat.'

'Why am I a twat? I'm just asking what you want for tea!' Jamie paused for a second and then smiled knowingly. 'Or am I a twat because you really want to know who I'm meeting but because you're doing your beeping thing to prove a point, you can't ask me who it is so you think I should just tell you anyway? That way you save face.'

'Neither,' she smirked. 'You're just a twat.'

'Sarah Lockwood,' replied Jamie as he slotted some bread into the toaster. 'She was in that movie you liked about the…'

'Beep,'

Jamie laughed and turned to find, as expected, a smug smile spread across Lisa's face and her arms folded across her chest. Victory.

'You're like a bloody child,' he said. 'Now make the tea.'

Chapter Nine
Monday 26th July 2019

20.45

Jamie climbed into his car, drove one hundred yards and then pulled over to the side of the road. Only then did he pull his phone from his pocket and begin sifting through the numerous emails and texts he'd received whilst he'd been with Sarah Lockwood.

It was, on the face of it, an odd thing to do but one of the first things Jamie had been taught when he'd moved to the celebrity desk was that fame and insecurity went hand in hand. It was therefore, important to remember that if you wanted to build a relationship with someone you waited until you were out of their eyesight before using your phone lest you triggered their paranoia and they thought you were on the phone slagging them off.

He had stuck to that rule rigidly from day one and as a result, had developed a reputation for being both trustworthy and honest. Two things that had earned him access to some very famous names over the last few years but which, he was only too aware, were a single phone call away from being destroyed. Hence, he recorded everything which is why he not only carried various recording devices but had installed three dash cams in his car. One facing forward, one rearward and the third pointed at the interior. Over the top maybe, but a necessary evil.

Once he'd finished with his work stuff, Jamie sat back and took a deep breath. He was physically and mentally knackered not to mention a bit pissed off. Thanks to Sarah Lockwood putting back their meeting until late afternoon even as he approached the outskirts of Birmingham, he was now facing a three-hour drive rather than falling asleep on his sofa. He'd also missed seeing Lisa off to work which always annoyed him.

Jamie glanced at his watch and then started his car. It was just after 9.00. Traffic permitting, he should be home by midnight.

Two hours later, thanks to a Ford Focus wiping itself along the central reservation and then collecting a BMW as it slew across the M1, Jamie hadn't even reached Northampton. Instead, like hundreds of other motorists, he'd been crawling along at single figure speeds and only now, having passed the scene, was he back up to normal cruising momentum. Home was still two hours away and tiredness was beginning to take its toll. So much so that he almost jumped out of his skin when his phone rang, and 'Lisa' let up his media screen.

'Hey,' he said. 'How's work?'

'Shit,' came her voice from the speakers dotted around his Kia saloon. 'Where are you? Are you home yet?'

'Northampton, I've been stuck in traffic.'

'Oh Christ. Well you know the drill. Stop and take a kip if you need one. No falling asleep at the wheel.'

'Yeah, I'm going to, I'm shagged out,' replied Jamie even as the sign for Watford Gap Services hove into view.

'Good. How was she? Did you tell her I'm a massive fan?'

'She was nice. Really nice actually.' As he talked, Jamie checked his mirrors and moved into the left-hand lane as he prepared to leave the motorway. By the time they'd said their goodbyes, he'd parked, reclined his seat and was ready for sleep to take him.

It was well after 1.00 when Jamie awoke, and he lay staring at the headliner for a few moments as his brain struggled to catch up with where he was and how he'd got there. Having done that, it turned its attention to his physical needs. Coffee or toilet? Decisions, decisions.

He leant forward, moved his seat into the upright position and turned on the ignition to check if he needed fuel or not. He did, so would grab a coffee there rather than trek into the services. His bladder could wait.

However, before he could start his car, his attention was drawn to three men standing beside a BMW SUV parked about fifty feet in from him. They were all dressed in black clothing and even as he watched, a second car pulled up beside them and two similarly dressed men got out. They high-five'd the others and talked excitedly amongst themselves for a few minutes before climbing back into their cars and heading toward the exit.

Jamie watched them disappear and shook his head as he turned the key and the car burst into life.

'They all come out at night,' he said out loud as he pulled the lever into drive and headed for the fuel station.

Chapter Ten
Tuesday 27th June 2019

11.30

Jamie finished reading through the text of his interview with Sarah Lockwood and having fully satisfied himself that it wasn't only editorially and grammatically correct but would keep her publicist happy, he hit save and then emailed it to his editor for approval.

With that completed, he pulled his headphones from his ears and with the music induced isolation ended, allowed his consciousness to return to the chaos of the newspaper office.

And chaos it was. But Jamie loved it. Every single moment.

He sat for a moment watching his colleagues scurrying around and then returned his attention to his computer and the numerous emails sitting in his inbox. As usual, most were from publicists trying to gain exposure for clients and the rest a mixture of invites, gossip, the odd bit of abuse and notes from his editor all of which were marked urgent even though he knew full well that none of them would be.

Gripped by a sudden urge for coffee, Jamie set off across the office toward the small kitchen at the far end of the large open plan room. He was almost there when his attention was grabbed by the ringing of a telephone. Normally, he'd have avoided answering anyone else's phone like the plague only this one sat on the desk of his office sparring partner, Katie Marshall and the opportunity to potentially score a point or two off her was not to be missed.

'No, she's not here,' he said into the handset as he sat down and began glancing his eyes over the notes strewn across her desk. 'Yeah, her mobiles best,' he continued. 'No, I don't have it, sorry. No, I'm not taking a message. Because…' He placed the phone back on its receiver. 'Twat' he muttered.

His eyes continued to scan the papers on her desk until something caught his eye. Not for the reasons he was hoping for, but something else. However, before he could read it properly, he felt a slap on the side of his head.

'You know what curiosity did.'

Jamie spun around in his chair to find Katie standing over him, arms now crossed and a smug smile on her face. He smiled back in return. Early 20's, slim, pretty and utterly ruthless, she'd been at the paper for almost 18 months and they'd hit it off immediately. Not in any sexual sense, but because they had exactly the same sarcastic sense of humour. But equally, each knew the other to be brilliant at what they did and as such, they had the utmost respect for each other.

'Yeah, it finds stories,' he replied. 'That was assault. I could have you fired for bullying.'

'Go for it. *The Times* are after me anyway.'

'Makes sense, I've read some of your stuff. Oh, you mean *The* Times. I thought you mean *The Fortean*.'

'You're funny. You really should do comedy. Oh wait, I've read some of *your* stuff. You already do.'

Jamie laughed. 'I have a gift, what can I say.' He took the piece of paper he'd been reading and held it up. 'Can I take this?'

Katie took it from him, glanced at it and handed it back. 'Why?'

'I need something to read in the loo. Why d'you think?'

'I don't mean that,' she said sarcastically. 'I mean it's a local news feed. All this stuff is online if...' She paused and clicked her fingers. 'That's right, you wouldn't know that because you're not a proper journalist any more.'

'You're hilarious. Seriously.'

'So how is life on the z-listers desk?' Katie added.

'Stress free,' Jamie replied with a smile. 'Look, no wrinkles. Judging by those crow's feet, you should think about trying it.'

'Fuck off,' she laughed in response before returning her eyes to the paper Jamie was folding in half, as if to protect some dark secret. 'What's got you interested in actual news?'

'Nothing,' said Jamie as he stood up and smiled.

'So, maybe something then,' she continued curiously.

Jamie gave her a wink and recommenced his journey to the kitchen all the while aware that her eyes were fixed firmly on him.

By the time he returned to his own desk, Jamie had read the two-line news item twice and his brain had already put two and two together. As a consequence, with his interest piqued, he immediately logged on to the website of *The Coventry Express* and searched for the full report. It was short, but it gave him the basics.

A Coventry man was admitted to hospital last night following what police are now treating a hate crime. Carl Mason (19), who was recently cleared of the attempted sexual assault of a Coventry teenager, was at home when five masked men burst into his house and attacked him. He suffered serious injuries to his legs and hands and remains in a serious condition. West Midlands police confirmed that enquiries are ongoing but would not comment further.

After a few moments, Jamie read it again to fully absorb what little detail it gave him then sat back in his chair as he pondered the various pieces of the jigsaw forming in his head. Had these been the five men he'd seen in the car park last night? And what about the similarities with the beating someone had handed out to Perry Keegan? Was it a coincidence? Or something more sinister?

He leant forward again and typed 'attacked in home' into Google and then filtered the responses to News, UK and within the last month. It took a heartbeat for the responses to fill the screen and Jamie leant forward and began to scroll them. However, after a few moments he sat back and clasped his hands behind his neck as he continued to stare at the screen. 'Shit!' he exclaimed out loud, before jumping to his feet and heading for the car park.

Jamie sat nervously in front of his editor and waited as the middle-aged man on the other side of the desk sifted through the various sheets of paper in front of him. He felt like a naughty schoolboy, mostly because Pete Goodwin scared the shit out of him.

He was the stereotype of a newspaper editor in human form. Scruffy, loud, ruthless and a bully. But he was also fiercely loyal. A trait he demanded in everyone who worked for him and which he inevitably received because he was the best at what he did.

Goodwin held up a screen grab taken from Jamie's dash-cam and shook his head.

'You seriously think these are the blokes who attacked this kid in Coventry?' he said abruptly.

'I don't know,' replied Jamie nervously. 'But..'

'It's a coincidence,' interrupted Goodwin as he slid the photo back across the desk. 'That's all.'

'But what if it wasn't? And what about the kid near me? And the six others I found with one Google search? All five men, all masked.' Jamie paused. Not for effect, but because he was nervous about the next few words that were going to fall out of his mouth. 'At least let me have a dig around.'

Goodwin looked up, surprised.

'You? You're celebrity. This, whatever it is, is news.' Goodwin let the words hang for a moment and then added, 'Pass this on to one of them. Katie, she loves stuff like this.'

'Come on Pete,' replied Jamie, almost desperately. 'This is mine. Give us a break.'

Goodwin sat back in his chair and clasped his hands together. 'Let me think about it. Now go.'

Pete Goodwin watched Jamie leave his office and smiled to himself. He genuinely could not remember a time when he hadn't wanted to be a journalist. Even as a little kid he'd amused his parents by writing reports on things going on in the family or at school, many of which he still had stored away in his garage at home alongside some of his favourite work from time spent on university magazines, local newspapers and then the nationals.

Now, at aged 45, as an editor on a national newspaper he was exactly where he wanted to be. For now. For like many in his position he had high ambitions and was ruthless in the pursuit of them. As a result, he constantly demanded the best not only from himself, but from his team. Woe betide those who didn't deliver.

There were two keys to his continued success. The first was that he had the gift of being able to sniff stories out of almost nothing, the second was being able to recognise others who had the same gift and getting them to work for him.

Jamie Brown had that gift; Pete had spotted it the second he'd come in for an interview some three years previous. However, he'd never been fully convinced that Jamie actually realised it himself nor was he satisfied that he had the tenacity to go all the way. As a result, he'd hired him and stuck him on the celebrity desk which, whilst often ridiculed by some of the more serious journalists, was actually one of the best places to develop the skill of sniffing out stories. Primarily because no one gave that much of a shit if you got something wrong.

Yet in truth, Jamie had been a disappointment to Pete. He was clearly a solid journalist and had turned in some great celebrity stories over the years but his potential as a proper news hound had never been fully realised, seemingly because of his own lack of ambition. Now maybe, the moment Pete had been waiting for had finally arrived. For whilst he'd played it cool with Jamie, he'd realised within a matter of seconds that Jamie had stumbled onto something. It might not be the story he'd put together in his head but there was definitely something there. What interested Goodwin was whether he'd find it or not.

He leant forward and picked up the phone. It was answered within seconds.

'OK, you've got two days, but I want something out of it even if it's 'how I pissed off my editor and got the sack.'

Chapter Eleven
Wednesday 28th June 2019

10.15

Having jumped at the chance of being allowed to follow up his story, Jamie had decided that the first thing to do would be to speak with Coventry police and tell them about his encounter at Watford Gap. Whether or not they decided it was relevant was up to them but at least he was covered if it panned out to be a factor. He also wanted to ask them about the assault on the youth he'd seen reported in the paper although he'd purposefully neglected to mention that when he'd called them yesterday primarily because he knew full well that they'd refer him to the press office. Far better to drop it into the conversation whilst inside the station where there was a chance of speaking to an actual copper rather than some glorified media student.

Now, having driven up first thing he'd begun to wonder why he'd bothered. For what felt like the thousandth time, he cast his eyes around the grey interior of the interview room and wondered if he'd ever get out.

He'd always imagined Coventry to be a dull and nondescript place and on the evidence of this room, as well as what little of the city he'd seen since his arrival over an hour ago, he'd been bang on the money. What he hadn't imagined however, and certainly hadn't expected, was the apathy which had greeted him. Not a single officer had shown him even a hint of courtesy and the sergeant who had eventually taken his brief statement was bordering on hostile. Now, having been sitting for over 20 minutes whilst the officer had gone to supposedly copy the short movie clip he'd brought up on a USB stick, Jamie was becoming increasingly irritated.

He was about to take out his phone and check his messages when the door opened, and the Sergeant returned and sat down.

'OK sir,' be began brusquely as he slid the stick and various pieces of paper across the desk. 'I'll make sure this information is passed on to the team. I'm sure someone will look into it.'

Jamie watched across the desk for a moment and then said 'You're sure? That doesn't sound very convincing.'

'I'm not sure what you mean sir,' replied the Sergeant as he snapped his notebook shut.

'I mean you don't exactly sound keen.'

'I can assure you that this information will be handled with the appropriate urgency,' replied the Sergeant in a tone which carried more than a hint of annoyance.

'Could I speak to one of the investigating officers?' asked Jamie. 'Just to clarify a few things with regard to the attack on Carl Mason. I'd hate to get my facts wrong.'

The Sergeant eyeballed Jamie across the table for a moment, and then climbed to his feet.

'You'll need to contact the press office sir. As a journalist, you should know that. Now, if you don't mind, I do have duties to attend to.'

Having cut his own teeth on a regional newspaper, in his case the Watford Observer, Jamie was more than familiar with the office vibe at the Coventry Express.

A mixture of eager youths keen to learn mixed with older hacks happy to teach them until their pensions kicked in, they were fun places to work even though most local papers were struggling under the increasing competition provided by the internet and public disinterest.

However, largely thanks to the efforts of its young editor, Richie Wallace, *The Cov* as it was seemingly known to all and sundry, had managed to buck that trend. Sales were steady, if not spectacular and equally importantly, it had a solid reputation. Not just for news either. More than one national newspaper had poached young journalists from under Richie's wing during the four years he'd been there.

Luckily for Jamie, he and Richie had met on a few occasions which is how he found himself sitting in the editor's office staring at a picture of a young girl. Her face covered in a selection of extremely nasty looking bruises.

'You can see why he isn't popular. He's a proper charmer is our Carl.'

Jamie looked up to see Richie had returned, two coffee's in hand.

'So why did the attempted rape charge get dropped?' asked Jamie as he took his cup.

'The only witness withdrew her statement. Without that, it was the victim's word against his, so the CPS had to drop it. Poor kid.'

'But he did it?'

Richie took a sip of coffee and nodded. 'Nailed on. The little shit was even bragging about it the week after.'

'So why aren't the police doing anything?'

'Nothing they can do,' said Richie. 'But it's not for want of trying.'

'Well that's not the impression I got this morning. It was like they didn't give a shit.'

'You couldn't be more wrong,' replied Richie. 'The girl he tried to rape, the one in the picture there, her dad's on the force.'

'Ah,' said Jamie softly. 'Well that explains the frosty reception.' He paused for a moment and then added, 'So who do you think attacked this Mason then? Not coppers surely?'

'No chance,' said Richie flatly. 'They've played this by the book from day one. Not that it did them any good.'

'Could it have been a gang thing then? Or some kind of vigilante attack?'

'No idea. But word is that they told him not to talk about it to anyone or they'd be back.'

'Good incentive,' said Jamie. 'I'm gonna give it a shot though. You never know right?'

'Good luck with that,' laughed Richie. 'But I tell you what, if you ever find who did it the locals will throw a street party in their honour. And the local plod will supply the beers.'

'Popular lad then?'

'Oh, it's not just him, the whole family are proper scum. Honestly, be careful Jamie. They don't take kindly to outsiders, especially after this.'

With visiting hours in full swing, Jamie had no difficulty gaining access to the ward where Carl Mason was recovering and was further relieved to find the teenager alone and fast asleep in his side room.

Reluctant to enter without an invitation, he stood in the doorway and after quickly glancing around, took a short video of the teenager who lay on top of the bed. Only once he'd stuffed his phone back into his pocket did Jamie start to relax a little and actually take in the scene for himself.

Clearly, Mason had suffered serious injuries. His legs and hands were both heavily bandaged but as far as Jamie could see from across the room, his face was untouched. Something which reinforced the idea that it was a deliberate assault.

'Who the bloody hell are you?'

Jamie spun around to find a middle-aged woman staring at him. She somehow managed to look tired, angry and scared all at the same time.

'I'm Jamie,' he said holding out his hand. 'I'm a reporter.'

The woman glared in response before pushing past him and placing herself between Jamie and the bed.

'Yeah, well I'm his mother,' she barked, 'and you can fuck off. We got nothing to say.'

'I understand how you feel but I'm on your side,' said Jamie calmly as he handed her his card. 'Honestly.'

'I said fuck off,' she growled. 'Or d'you want me to get my boys here.'

'OK,' said Jamie, 'but would it help if I told you that I think I might have seen the men who attacked your son.'

The woman froze as the blood seemed to drain from her face and fear entered her eyes.

'We're not interested,' she gasped. 'Get out.'

'But…'

'Get out!' she screamed. Her voice rank with fear. 'Get out!'

Jamie backed away from the door and as her desperate shouts continued and nurses hurried in his direction, he turned and fled.

Having decided to head home rather than go back to the office, Jamie had arrived in time to spend some time with Lisa before she left for work. He was pleased to find that her mood had softened markedly, and she was back to her normal, loveable self.

Having enjoyed a catch up and some food, Jamie had retired to his study whilst she showered and sorted herself out. He was busily typing notes on his laptop when she walked in and moved behind him.

'What're you up to?' she asked as she kissed the top of his head.

Jamie turned and looked at her. A wry smile on his face. 'You tell me,' he said.

'How would I know?'

'Piss off,' he laughed. 'How much of that did you read when you were kissing my head?'

'I don't know what you mean,' she said, feigning innocence.

'Like fuck,' Jamie replied. 'Anyway officer, how can I find out who owns a car?'

'What car?'

Jamie handed her a copy of the screengrab from his dash cam.

'What's this?' she asked.

'Just something that fell into my lap. An actual story no less! So?'

'DVLA are your best bet,' she added as she handed the picture back to him. 'There's a form, V888 I think. You need a good reason though.'

Jamie looked pleadingly at her.

'Oh no, not a chance. Even if I wanted to, I couldn't. Have you any idea of the trouble I'd get into if I got caught using PNC for personal stuff?'

'What's the point of having a girlfriend who's a copper…'

'Don't even think about going there,' she said. 'Anyway, you know the rules Brown. Work is for work, home isn't. And on that note, I'm off.'

Jamie stood and embraced her.

'Be careful out there,' he said sweetly. 'I love you.'

'I love you too,' she replied. And with a smile, she was gone.

Jamie waited until he heard the front door close and then returned his attention to his laptop.

Chapter Twelve
Thursday 29th July 2019

09.30

For the second time in as many days, Jamie sat staring at the walls of a police interview room.

If anything, it was even grubbier than the one in Coventry although at least he'd only had a short cab ride to get to this one, and he had a cup of tea sitting in front of him. Albeit tea in name only.

He was about to risk another sip when the door opened and a plain clothed officer walked in carrying a blue file. Jamie immediately sized him up as early 30's and not just battle hardened but battle weary. He looked like he'd seen it, done it and was tired of it.

'Mr. Brown,' he began. 'I'm detective constable Hartly. I'm handling the investigation into the attack on Perry Keegan.'

'Thanks for seeing me at such short notice,' said Jamie. 'I know you must be incredibly busy.'

'You said you might have something for me,' replied Hartly. His voice backing up Jamies opinion of him as being tired.

'Yes,' said Jamie as he slipped a copy of a still from his dashcam from his bag and placed it on the desk. 'I took this at Watford Gap service station earlier this week. I think these men were involved in an attack on a man in Coventry.'

Hartly took the picture and examined it. 'Have you given this to Coventry police?'

'Of course.'

'What's it got to do with us?'

'I think these might have been the same men who attacked Perry Keegan.'

Hartly eyeballed Jamie across the desk and then slid the picture back toward him. 'It wasn't,' he said abruptly.

'How can you be so sure?'

'Because the five men in this picture are white,' replied Hartly. 'I can't really say any more than that.'

'Oh, I see,' said Jamie. 'I guess there's no point in me asking you if you'd check that number plate for me?'

'Since it has no relevance to my case, no. None at all. Is there anything else?'

'Yes,' said Jamie who was becoming increasingly irritated at the officer's attitude. 'Could you give me a briefing on your investigation?'

'We're pursuing a number of lines of enquiry.'

'That's a bit vague.'

'Well since Mr. Keegan is refusing to talk to us, we don't really have much to go on.'

'So how many officers do you have working on it?'

Hartly returned Jamie's stare. His expression totally blank.

'So basically, no one then.'

'Mr. Brown, as I'm sure you can appreciate, we're extremely busy at the moment so we do have to prioritise.'

'And the fact that Keegan is black, and a serial offender has no baring on that prioritising?' Jamie snapped back. He could almost see the hackles rising on the man sitting opposite him.

'The Metropolitan police uphold the law without fear or favour Mr. Brown. So, I'd suggest that if you hold those opinions, you keep them to yourself. We take allegations of that nature extremely seriously.'

'Is that a threat?' asked Jamie.

'No sir,' replied Hartly. 'It's information. Now,' he continued as he got to his feet, 'if you'll excuse me, I have work to do.'

Half an hour later, Jamie was still bristling from his encounter with DC Hartly as he made his way through the corridors of Paddington Hospital and located the wing where Perry Keegan was recovering.

He found him, like Carl Mason, in a side ward and as he knocked on the door frame, he was shocked by the similarity of the various dressings on his legs and hands.

'Who the fuck are you?' asked Keegan without tearing his eyes from the television bolted to the wall.

'My names Jamie,' he replied before walking in and sitting down. 'I'm a reporter.'

'Close the door on your way out.'

'I want to help, I'm on your side.'

Keegan tore his eyes away from the television and looked Jamie up and down. The distain was obvious. 'You wanna help me? Then piss off.'

'I'm getting that a lot.'

'Then maybe you should start to listen,' replied Keegan before returning his eyes to the screen.

Jamie pulled a copy of the screen grab from his bag and placed it on the bed.

'Are these the men who attacked you?'

Keegan glanced at Jamie and then at the photograph. His face remained calm but his eyes registered panic. 'Where'd you get this?'

'I took it,' said Jamie calmly. 'So, was it them?'

'I ain't saying nothing,' Keegan replied. A slight trace of anxiety in his voice. 'Now fuck off.'

Jamie sighed and stood up. 'Oh well,' he said. 'The police told me it wasn't them anyway.'

Keegan's head snapped around. 'The filth? What they saying?'

'That it was a gang thing.'

'Bullshit!'

Jamie smiled inwardly and sat down. 'Who was it? I'm on your side. Honestly.'

Keegan eyeballed Jamie. 'I don't know.'

'Well were they young, old, black, white?'

'White geezers. Late 20's I reckon.'

'All of them?' asked Jamie, desperately trying to hide the excitement in his voice.

'Yeah.'

'And you told the police that?'

'They don't give a shit. They hate me as much as I hate them.'

'But you told them?'

'Yeah. Course.'

Jamie took a deep breath to calm himself. 'Anything else you can tell me?'

Keegan shrugged his shoulders. 'They talked funny. Like on that Peaky Blinders.'

'They were Brummies?' asked Jamie.

'Where's that?'

'Birmingham.'

'If that's it, then yeah.'

Jamie continued to scribble in his notebook as his mind raced. 'Would you recognise them if you saw them again?'

'You shittin' me, right? You think I ever wanna see them again? Look at me! I'm fuckin' wrecked man!'

Jamie looked up from his notebook and was shocked to see tears in Keegan's eye's. He was clearly terrified.

'What the hell is going on?'

Jamie turned toward the door to find an angry looking woman glaring at him. 'You must be Mrs Keegan, I'm Jamie Brown. I was just…'

'You police?'

'No, I'm a reporter. I was just…'

'I don't care what you were doing,' she blazed before turning her attention to her son. 'What you doin' talking to these people? You stupid?'

'I wasn't. Christ, chill out woman.'

Jamie turned back to the youth on the bed. All trace of fear and vulnerability had vanished. He was back, acting the hard man.

'Get… out,' growled Mrs. Keegan, hate burning in her eyes. 'We got nothing to say.'

Pete Goodwin finished reading through Jamie's notes and smiled to himself. He knew he'd been right to let Jamie run with this although he wasn't going to let him know. Not yet anyway.

'You've had two days and you've still got nothing,' he said without looking up.

'Other than the fact that both attacks involved five men, both sets of injuries were the same and both the victims are arseholes, no.'

Pete looked up from the notes and threw Jamie a look which said 'be careful'. He returned his attention to the notes. 'If we're thinking that it's the same group of men, who are they? What are their motives?'

'That's what I'm starting to think about. Both victims escaped charges after witnesses withdrew statements.'

'So, these are revenge attacks?'

'It looks like it,' said Jamie. 'But they're linked somehow, they have to be. Why would five Brummies come down to London just to batter some no mark like Perry Keegan? And why did that copper lie to me about them being white?'

'Could it be a far-right thing?' asked Pete. Well aware that stories linked to right-wing extremism were like money in the bank for any newspaper.

'Mason's white,' replied Jamie.

'Shit. What about these other cases you mentioned?'

'I've spoken to a few local papers and the basics are similar, but details are all sketchy. My big problem…' Jamie hesitated.

Pete looked up to find Jamie staring at him with a pleading expression on his face. 'I'm out of time.'

Pete hesitated and leant back in his chair. More for effect than anything. 'How's your desk?'

'Covered,' replied Jamie a little too quickly

'It better be. OK, I'll give you another two days but that's it. And you still owe me.'

Having spoken to Lisa on the phone to discover that she'd gone into work early, Jamie had decided that rather than go home he'd do some more digging which is how he found himself standing on a door step less than a quarter of a mile from his own front door. It was opened by an elderly bulldog of a man, Teddy Miles.

'Mr. Miles?' asked Jamie. 'My names Jamie, Jamie Brown. We spoke earlier.'

The old man looked him up and down. 'You the bloke from around the corner?'

'Yes,' replied Jamie. 'Here.' He handed a business card to the old man who looked at it and then gestured him inside.

'Call me Teddy,' said the old man as he led Jamie through to a neat and polish scented dining room which immediately brought back memories of his own grandparents.

'I'll get some tea,' said Teddy as he vanished into the kitchen.

Still reeling from the reminders of his youth, Jamie hesitated to sit down and instead, remained standing. His eyes scanning the room and taking in every tiny detail. From the trinkets which clearly held precious memories to the photographs which held many more. One in particular caught Jamie's eye and he walked silently across the room to stare at it. A middle-aged woman and a smiling man stared back at him. Their faces full of joy and hope.

'That was Betty and me in Spain in 1996,' said Teddy as he placed two mugs down on carefully placed coasters. 'We used to go all over the place.'

'She was pretty,' said Jamie.

'She was beautiful,' replied the old man. His voice already creaking slightly. 'Really beautiful.' Jamie smiled and then at

Teddy's invitation, sat at the dining table behind his tea. The old man following his lead but instead of sitting opposite Jamie, he sat at ninety degrees to him. It was a small thing, maybe even an unconscious one, but it meant that he didn't have to look directly at the man asking him questions. Jamie noticed it immediately. This was going to be tough, for both of them.

In truth, he had hesitated to visit the old man because his initial thought had been that it would be of no value to his investigation. However, the more he'd thought about it, the more he'd begun to realise that whilst Mason and Keegan were victims, they were victims by design. Teddy Miles and the young girl in Coventry were the real victims and he needed to get that mindset fixed firmly in his head. He took his phone from his pocket, placed it on the table and pressed record.

'Can I just start by saying how sorry I was to hear about your wife. I can't even begin to imagine…'

'That bastard Keegan killed 'er. Sure as shit smells that piece of filth killed my Betty.'

Jamie was taken aback by the malice in the old man's tone. He wasn't just angry, he was raging.

'If you've come around here expecting me to feel sorry for him 'cos someone did what the old bill didn't have the bollocks to do,' he continued. 'Then you're wasting your bloody time.'

'I'm just trying to find out what happened that's all,' replied Jamie. 'I'm not judging anyone.'

Teddy leant forward and eyeballed Jamie. 'Not judging? Do you actually know what he did?'

'As I said, I'm just…'

'You don't do you!' Teddy thumped the table and jumped to his feet. 'Fuck me, you come round here…' He paused, struggling to contain himself. 'That bastard broke into my house while we were sat there watching telly. He knocked me about then Betty and tied us to them chairs. Then he…'

'It's OK,' said Jamie calmly. 'You don't have to tell me. I understand.'

'He stood there and molested her,' continued Teddy. His eyes fixed firmly on the empty chair opposite Jamie. 'Right there in front of me until I told him where everything was.'

'I'm sorry. I didn't know.'

'He fucking stood there,' Teddy continued. His voice faltering with every syllable. 'He stood there with his hands down her blouse and…'

Teddy stopped talking. It was too much. They sat in silence for a few moments as Jamie watched him, the old man, trying to compose himself. It was all he could do to stop himself from standing up and hugging the old boy.

'That's why we couldn't go to court see,' said Teddy sadly. 'Poor Betty, she couldn't face the shame of people knowing what he'd done to her and he was threatening to tell everyone. It was too much.'

The old man's eyes filled with tears and he walked out into the kitchen to hide his embarrassment.

Jamie sat, unsure of what to do. Should he leave Teddy alone to gather his own thoughts or go after him? He had no idea, but he did know one thing, he felt ashamed. Ashamed he'd put an old man through this experience when he was clearly still struggling to come to terms with it and when he, as a journalist, should have known better.

Jamie took a deep breath and picked up his phone. He stopped the recording and deleted what he'd saved. It was the least he could do.

It was a full fifteen minutes before Teddy returned. He started to apologise but Jamie stopped him and told him that he had absolutely nothing to apologise for.

'I'll leave you to it,' he said. 'But if you ever need anything, a chat or a beer even. I'm only around the corner. It'd be my pleasure.'

'Thanks,' said Teddy. 'I'll see you out.' He led Jamie out into the hall and pulled open the front door before the two men shook hands.

'Thanks for speaking to me,' said Jamie. 'I genuinely appreciate it and again, I'm so sorry if I…'

'Forget it,' replied teddy softly. 'I just hope it helps.'

Jamie smiled but as he turned to leave, he noticed a wooden plaque hanging on the wall.

'You were in the Army?' he asked.

'National service,' said Teddy proudly. 'Got called up just in time to go to Korea.'

'The forgotten war.'

'Not by us it ain't,' he replied. 'Bloody savages they were.'

Jamie nodded. His own grandfather had often talked about his time in the Army and Korea was a subject which had always been a source of some angst whenever it had been raised.

With a smile, Jamie turned to leave but then stopped. 'One final thing, he asked. 'You don't know anyone from Birmingham, do you? Or Coventry?'

'No. Why?'

'Just a long shot. Bye Teddy. And thanks again.'

Jamie had almost reached home when his phone rang, and he looked at it to see the name Pete Goodwin on the screen.

'Yes boss,' he said. 'Norwich? no I've not seen it. Yes, of course. Text me the address and I'll get up there first thing.'

Jamie stuffed his phone back into his pocket and continued his walk home. His pace markedly increased.

He was surprised to see Lisa's car still parked outside their house and even more surprised to find her sitting in the living room wearing a dressing gown and with a towel wrapped around her head.

'Well you're a sight for sore eyes,' he said as sat down beside her. 'Shouldn't you have left by now?'

'I've got a few hours owing so I thought I'd go in a bit later. You complaining?'

'Not at all,' he said as he took her hand and kissed it. 'You're just what I needed to see.'

'Tough day dear?' she said sarcastically. 'Salad in the Groucho soggy?'

'I know you think you're funny, but you're really not.'

Lisa laughed. 'I am. I'm bloody hilarious. It's a gift. Oh, I've got something for you.' She jumped up and retrieved her rucksack from which she pulled an A4 sized envelope which she held to her chest. 'I took a big risk doing this, so you owe me. Right?'

'What is it?'

'I mean it,' she repeated. 'You owe me, big time.'

Jamie looked at her for a second and then realisation dawned. 'You didn't?'

'I did,' she replied smugly. 'What's it worth? I was thinking West End, show, nice meal.'

'Deal.'

'I'll hold you to that Brown. Here.'

She handed him the envelope and he tore it open. Inside was a single A4 sheet on which was a crudely drawn picture of a vagina.

'What's this?' he asked.

'It's a twat,' she laughed. 'Which is what you are. I love you to bits, but don't ever ask me to break the law again.'

'You're such a dick,'

'You know what I do, you know why I do it and you know why I have to leave it at work.'

Jamie held out his arm and she snuggled into him.

'I know, sorry.'

'I was thinking a musical, expensive seats obviously. Then a nice curry somewhere. Or a Chinese in Chinatown.'

'I've got a better idea,' said Jamie as he let his hand slide inside her dressing gown. Lisa retrieved it immediately.

'No chance. You smell of the tube.'

'That's how you like it.' He reached down again, and this time cupped her breast but even as he did so, an image of Betty Miles jumped into his head and a chill ran through him. However, before he could withdraw his hand Lisa pushed him away, sat up and pulled her dressing gown tight around her.

'No! I've got to go to work.'

Jamie sat watching her for a second and then slumped back on the sofa. His hand reaching for the TV remote even before he'd got comfortable. 'OK,' he said. 'You best get ready.'

Lisa stared at him from the other end of the sofa. A slight smile on her face. It had been almost a week since they'd had sex and she suddenly felt incredibly horny.

She stood up, took the towel off her hair and then moved slowly toward the door. By the time she'd walked through it, the dressing gown had slipped from her shoulders.

'Well?' she said over her shoulder. 'What are you waiting for?'

'I thought you had to go to work?'

'I will if you want.'

Jamie watched her feet through the bannisters as they vanished up the stairs and then waited for a few seconds before he followed her as silently as he could.

'You're like a bloody hippo on those stairs,' she laughed from the bedroom before he was even half-way up. 'You bloody stink like one as well so if you want to come near me, shower first!'

Jamie smiled to himself and began to undress as he walked up the stairs. Five minutes later, still damp from the shower, he was in her arms.

Chapter Thirteen
Friday 30th June 2019

10.15

'At the next junction, turn right. You have reached your destination.'

Jamie turned off his satnav and looked to his right as he drove slowly past the entrance to Bushell Avenue and took in as much detail as he could.

From what he could see, it was a typical council estate street. The pock marked tarmac lined on each side with parked cars and lines of different coloured bins filling the paths. However, what caught his eye was the top of a white Transit parked on the left about fifty yards down. The light bar on the roof clearing signifying it as the property of the Norfolk Constabulary.

He found a parking space and after grabbing a coffee from a cafe, wandered back to Bushell Avenue and walked slowly toward the Transit.

The closer he got, the more detail he took in. The front door of the house was taped off with yellow crime scene tape whilst a single policeman sat in the van obviously staring at his phone.

Opposite the house, three women stood talking and so he crossed the road and walked toward them.

'What's that all about?' he asked.

'What're you then?' one of them asked. 'Another copper?'

Jamie laughed. 'No, I'm a reporter.'

'Telly or paper?'

'Both,' Jamie lied. 'I'm just sniffing to see if there's a story or not. What's happened?'

The three women eyed him up silently for a moment and then the first one spoke. 'Family who live there. Proper shits all of them. They should've been kicked off this estate years ago.'

'Why? What've they done?'

'You name it,' said the second woman. 'Drugs, threatening behaviour and the bloody noise. Music and cars coming and going all hours. They were a pain in the arse.'

'So, did no one ever complain?' asked Jamie in a voice which suggested he actually cared.

'All the time,' said the first woman. 'But that lot were too scared to go near 'em.'

Jamie followed their gaze toward the Transit where the policeman was still absorbed by his phone.

'Useless tossers.'

'What are they doing here now then?'

'Well,' said the third woman who clearly didn't want to be left out of the conversation. 'We heard that the other night, Wednesday, these men burst in and beat the crap out of the dad and the son.'

'We had paramedics, ambulances, the lot down here,' added the first woman.

'What men?

'Dunno. Someone said there was five of 'em but it might have been more.'

'The more the merrier I say,' said the second woman brusquely. 'Shame they didn't do all of them.'

'How big's the family then?'

'Mum, dad and three sons. One of them's inside though.'

'Where are they?' asked Jamie.

'Council finally moved them out this morning, replied the third woman. Good bloody riddance as well. This place'll be a lot nicer now they've pissed off. Oh, look out.'

Jamie followed her gaze to see the policeman had climbed out of his van and was approaching them.

'Can I ask what you're doing sir?' he asked.

'He's talking to us,' said the second woman. There's no law against that is there?'

Jamie ignored her and handed the policeman his card. 'I'm just asking around officer.'

'OK,' said the policeman calmly. 'Would you mind coming with me?'

'You're in trouble now,' laughed the first woman as Jamie followed the policeman toward the Transit. 'Don't forget, say no comment!'

Jamie smiled to himself as the policeman led him to the other side of the Transit away from prying eyes.

'Sir, if you have any questions might I ask you to direct them at the press office? That is what it's for.'

'Understood,' said Jamie. 'I was just getting some background that's all.' He paused for a second and then reached into his pocket. 'Could I ask you a couple of questions, off the record, look.' He showed the policeman his phone. 'Look, I'm not recording or anything.'

'I'm sorry sir,' said the policeman. 'You know…'

'I just want some background. General stuff. Just nod, yes or no. Please, it'd really help me out.'

The policeman looked around and shrugged his shoulders. Jamie smiled in response.

'This family, the…'

'Corbett's'

'Great,' said Jamie. 'Were they known to you?'

The policeman nodded.

'Have they ever been involved in any crimes of a sexual nature?

The policeman shook his head.

'So, it's drugs, violence, anti-social, that kind of thing. Did any of them have criminal records?'

The policeman nodded again then held up his hands before drawing them apart.

'Long records. OK. Have any of them recently been in court but got off something on a technicality?'

Jamie waited for an answer, but the policeman stared back at him.

'That's a bit specific,' he said. 'What's going on?'

'Nothing. Just an idea I had. One of the women said there were five attackers. Is that right?'

'That's not been confirmed, but it appears so.' The policeman paused. 'Now, I think if you need any more...'

'Press office,' said Jamie. 'I know. One last thing, and we're still off the record I promise. Do you have any leads at all?'

'I'm just a local beat copper sir. But whoever did it could be anywhere in the country by now.'

'You don't think they're local?'

The policemen stared back; his face blank.

'Press office. I know.'

Jamie called the Norfolk police press office the moment he returned to his car but their response to his questions was simply to stall him with the classic 'someone will get back to you' line.

For a second, he considered visiting the two men in hospital but decided against it primarily because he didn't think he'd learn anything new but also because his encounter with Teddy Miles had left its mark and he wasn't sure if he'd be able to remain wholly impartial.

Having made that decision, he decided to return to London and within minutes, was heading toward the capital.

He was five minutes into the journey when his phone rang and Pete Goodwin told him, rather abruptly, to turn on Radio 5 before hanging up.

Jamie hit the radio button and voices filled the car. He recognised one immediately, Ian Foster. Conservative MP for West Hertfordshire and as right-wing as it got without being classed as a total nutter.

'Obviously I am disappointed to see yet another tragic murder on the streets of Hertfordshire,' he said. 'But as I said in the house only last week, we are clearly not doing enough to combat this growing menace.'

'What more can the police be doing given the lack of resources available to them?' asked the reporter.

'Their job,' he replied bluntly. 'I don't blame them, but I'm sick and tired of seeing our police being hampered by political correctness and I have no doubt that the vast majority of the country agree with me.'

'Are you suggesting that there are elements of the British public who have lost faith in the police?'

'I'm not suggesting it, I'm saying it. We have policing by consent in certain areas of this country and that isn't right. We need to see a more robust and proactive enforcement of the law.'

'That was Ian Foster MP speaking to me following yet another knife related death in Britain. What do you think? Is he right? 0345 20 20 64 to have your say.'

Jamie settled back in his seat and smiled to himself. This was going to be interesting.

Pete Goodwin sat reading through a blue folder full of notes whilst a nervous Jamie sat opposite him.

'You know what you've got here?' Pete said as he closed the folder and dropped it on the desk. 'What you've got, after almost four days, is fuck all.'

Jamie took a deep breath. He knew Goodwin was right; he'd known it even as he was writing up his own notes. He just hadn't wanted to hear it.

'It's all speculation,' continued his editor. 'Christ Jamie, you know the drill. Who, why, what, where, how. Where's the why and the who? Without those there's no story.'

'So, what're my options?' Jamie asked. 'More time?'

Pete laughed and threw him a look which effectively said 'in your fucking dreams' without using any actual words.

'What do I do?' continued Jamie. 'Just dump it?'

Pete stared at him and said nothing for a moment. Jamie wasn't sure if he was thinking, letting him stew or winding up to give him a bollocking. He was about to say something to break the silence when Pete leant forward and slid the folder back across the desk to him.

'Write me an opinion piece,' he said. 'How you stumbled on the story, bigger picture, victims, vigilantes, anarchy, state of the nation. Crap like that.'

'You sure?' asked a shocked Jamie.

'Why not? Knife crime's big at the moment. And get some Brexit and far-right stuff in their somehow. That always gets them fired up.'

'OK,' said Jamie, not a little stunned by this turn of events. 'I will. Er, thanks boss.'

'Who knows,' added Pete as Jamie got to his feet. 'If it's any good I might even print it.'

It was just after 5.30 by the time Jamie made it home only to discover that Lisa had already left for work.

He made himself a cup of tea, stuck the pizza she'd left out for him into the fridge and ate the fish and chips he'd brought from the cafe by the tube station.

Once he'd consumed those, he took the blue folder from his bag and headed across the hall into his office.

It was another seven hours before he would come out again.

Chapter Fourteen
Monday 2nd July 2019

11.30

After a weekend spent working and sleeping around Lisa's shift pattern, Jamie had headed for work on the Monday morning earlier than normal to make sure that his article was on Pete's desk ready for when he arrived.

He was as pleased with it as he'd ever been with any piece of work he'd ever done and whilst he could just as easily have emailed it, he wanted to enjoy the physical act of hand delivering it.

Having done that, he headed for his desk and began the process of catching up whilst at the same time worrying himself sick with the thought that his article wasn't good enough and he'd blown his big chance. A fear that grew with every agonising minute that passed.

By the time Pete finally summoned him it was close to 11.30 and Jamie headed through the chaos of the office almost totally convinced that he'd be pushing stories about z-list no-marks for the rest of his life.

'Come in, sit down and close the door,' muttered Pete gruffly.

Jamie inwardly cursed and closed the door as instructed. Pete rarely closed his door for anything so whatever was coming, was serious. Maybe even terminal.

'This is good. Bloody good.'

Jamie frowned as he struggled to take in what Pete has said. 'It is?'

'Yes. Why?' asked Pete. 'Don't you think it's good?'

'Well, of course I do,' Jamie stumbled. 'But, well, you know. It's a new thing for me.'

'You do know the flak you're gonna get if I run this don't you. You ready for that?'

Jamie nodded eagerly although in truth, he hadn't considered any such thing. 'Isn't that part of the job?' he added.

'OK then,' said Pete. 'I'll let legal take a look and if they're happy, I'll run it. Might be fun.'

'Thanks boss. Thanks a lot.'

Pete held up his hand. 'No need to thank me,' he said. 'Now get back to what I'm actually paying you for.'

As he watched Jamie make his way across the office back to his own desk, Pete allowed himself a wry smile. He knew exactly how the young journalist was feeling. The adrenaline rush that came with your first published column was one no journalist ever forgot and would only be bettered once he actually saw it in print.

More than that, he was feeling a buzz of his own. The one that came from being proved right. The piece Jamie had handed in wasn't just good, it was solid gold and he was going to make sure that he milked it for every column inch he could.

Still buzzing from his encounter with his editor, Jamie decided to escape the office for a while and spend his lunchtime by himself.

He'd desperately wanted to call Lisa to tell her his news but knowing she'd be asleep until at least three, he'd sent her a text asking her to call him as soon as she woke. At least her week of nights was over, and she'd be at home tonight. Maybe he'd take her out to celebrate if she was up to it.

He was nursing a coffee and pondering where to take her when his phone rang. Instinctively, he glanced at the screen to check the number in the hope that it was Lisa, but it had been withheld. Not unusual in his line of work.

'Jamie Brown. Who's speaking?'

He listened intently to the voice on the other end for a few moments and then, without uttering a word of reply, stuffed his phone back into his pocket and headed for the tube.

After making his way up a flight of stairs which reeked of piss, weed and poverty, Jamie made his way nervously to flat 122 and knocked on the door.

He knew this estate of old and it was a genuine shit hole. So much so that he didn't just feel out of place, he felt in danger and it was huge relief when he heard a chain being slid back and the door swung open.

'Mrs. Keegan,' he said by way of greeting. 'Hello again.'

The women ushered him in and without a word, led him through to the living room where her son lay on the sofa. His hands still heavily bandaged and his legs in casts.

Jamie glanced around the room. It was as clean and tidy as it could possibly have been, yet he didn't get the impression that it was for his benefit. More that it was always like this. Mrs. Keegan was clearly a proud woman; God only knows how she managed to cope having a son like Perry. She must be in a state of eternal shame. Indeed, even as Jamie looked down at him, all he could think of was what Teddy Miles had told him and there was a very real part of him which wanted to deliver a punch in the mouth.

'I'll make some tea,' said Mrs. Keegan.

'No,' barked her son. 'No tea. He ain't stayin' long.'

Jamie half smiled at the woman who glared back at him then vanished into the kitchen, so he turned back to the sofa. 'What can I do for you?'

'Some cop came to see me, asked if I'd talked to you.'

'A cop?' asked Jamie, slightly taken aback. 'What was his name?'

'I dunno.'

'Did he show you his warrant card?'

'My mum answered the door. Mum!' he called. 'Did that cop show you a badge?'

Jamie turned as she appeared in the doorway. Arms folded across her chest.

'He showed me something,' she said. 'I think he did anyway.'

'But he didn't give you his name?' asked Jamie.

'He said something, I don't remember.' She looked disapprovingly at her son. 'You not told him yet?'

'Give us a chance,' he growled in response. 'He's just got here!'

Jamie looked at them both, confused. 'What's going on?'

'You got to forget everything I told you,' said Keegan.

'Why?'

'Cos the copper, he asked me if I'd talked to you then warned me that if these geezers find out, I ain't safe.'

'He mentioned me by name?' asked Jamie.

'Yeah, he told me to tell you.'

Jamie's mind was racing. He'd expected Keegan to give him more information about the men who'd attacked him not drop this bombshell on him. 'But how did they know you'd talked to me?'

'I dunno,' said Keegan. 'Maybe 'cos they're the fucking police.'

Mrs. Keegan grunted disapprovingly. A sound which had a marked effect on her son who suddenly switched from being irritated to contrite.

'Look at me man. I'm proper messed up. I don't want no more grief. You get me?'

'You best go now,' said Mrs Keegan from the doorway.

Jamie looked at her but seeing the look on her face, thought better than to debate the point. 'OK, but call me if you ever want to talk,' he said.

'I won't.' came the blunt reply.

Jamie shrugged his shoulders in response and then followed Mrs. Keegan to the door.

'Don't come back, you hear me?' she said as he stepped out onto the landing. 'You've done enough damage.'

She slammed the door in Jamie's face, and he stood there as he heard the chain being put back on.

'Maybe if your son weren't such a little shit,' he said to himself.

'Who you talking to?'

Jamie spun around to find an elderly black man staring at him. He didn't look best pleased.

'Just myself. Sorry.

'You police?'

'No,' replied Jamie who was suddenly starting to feel nervous. 'I'm... It doesn't matter.'

He forced a smile and then headed for the stairs as quickly as he could.

By the time he made it to the tube, Jamie's mind was racing. It wasn't simply what Keegan has said which bothered him, it was the fact that he'd made him trek all the way to South-East London when he could have said it all on the phone. That made no sense.

He was still wrestling with this when he noticed a man staring at him from the other end of the carriage. Much of his face was hidden behind a large, well-groomed beard but Jamie had no doubt that he was under scrutiny and he began to feel uneasy at the unwanted attention. So much so that when the tube came to a halt, he waited until the last possible moment and then jumped off even though it wasn't his stop.

He glanced nervously back along the platform as the doors closed but his initial relief at the sight of the half empty platform vanished when the doors opened again, and the man stepped off. Seeing him, Jamie turned and hurried toward the exit. His heart racing.

He was almost at the ticket barrier when he heard his name being called. At first, he ignored it but when it was shouted for the third time, he stopped and turned to find the bearded man almost upon him.

'Jesus Christ, are you deaf?'

Jamie stared at the bearded man for a moment and then relaxed as he recognised his former colleague, Craig Ratcliffe. 'For fuck's sake, you scared the shit out of me,' he gasped. 'What's with that fucking beard? I didn't recognise you.'

'Like it?' asked Craig as he stroked it lovingly.

'You look like a bloody Uber driver.'

Craig laughed. 'I get that a lot. So, what's going on? You look spooked.'

'Paranoia. Comes with old age.'

'Tell me about it. How's life at the sharp end of celebrity gossip?'

Jamie had just returned to his desk when Pete appeared.

'We're running your piece in the morning,' he said. 'Lawyers loved it.'

Jamie's heart leapt. 'Jesus, thanks.'

'Don't thank me, it's bloody good. We're using a still from your dash-cam as a header photo.'

'That'll look great,' said Jamie.

'Right, go and brief the social media team and stick your head into PR as well. I think they're going to be busy.'

Having arrived home to find the house empty and no note informing him where she'd gone, Jamie had naturally assumed Lisa had simply popped out and would be back in a matter of minutes. He was hardly surprised when he heard the front door open.

'I'm in here,' he called out. 'I have big news.'

He sensed a presence in the door and turned to find a man standing looking at him.

'Who the fuck are you?' he blurted out as he jumped to his feet.

'I'm Lee,' said the man desperately. 'I work with Lisa.'

'Where is she?'

'Up here!' came a voice from upstairs. 'I'll be down in a minute.'

'Sorry, I didn't mean to startle you,' said Lee. 'She told me to stick my head in.'

'It's fine,' said Jamie as he walked over, and the two men shook hands. 'I'm a bit jumpy today. You want a drink? Tea, coffee, beer?'

'Nothing for me thanks. I'm not sure we'll have time.'

Jamie looked at him, puzzled. 'Time? What d'you mean?'

Lisa burst into the room. A rucksack over her arm. 'I'm really sorry,' she said.

'What's going on?'

'Did you not get my message?'

'Obviously not,' said Jamie.

Lisa walked over to the answering machine and pressed the button. 'Hey, it's me. I've left a message on your mobile but just in case you don't get it, I've got to go to Manchester tonight. I've had to go into work but will pop in about 6.00 to grab a bag so don't cook. Love you. Beep.'

'I didn't get those,' said Jamie.

'Because you didn't check,' Lisa replied before walking over and pecking him on the lips. 'Sorry but we've got to go. Call you later OK?'

She was gone before he could answer and as the door slammed, Jamie took a deep breath and let it slowly drift from his lungs.

'Hey Lisa,' he said out loud. 'Guess what. The paper's publishing my article tomorrow. Are they Jamie? That's great. Yeah, it's a big deal. My first ever column. I thought we'd go out to celebrate.'

Chapter Fifteen
Tuesday 3rd July 2019

08.30

It was with a sense of trepidation that Jamie entered the newsagent by the tube station and purchased a copy of the newspaper that paid his wages. He was no stranger to seeing his name in the paper, but this was something else entirely. This was proper journalism.

He found it on page 7. A full-page spread with the banner headline 'Is This British Justice?' above the now familiar picture of five men standing beside two cars in the half light of a motorway service station.

Even though he knew every single syllable, Jamie read through it again before texting Lisa and his parents with instructions to buy the paper and then headed for work. A self-satisfied smile fixed firmly to his face.

As soon as he stepped from the tube and his phone latched onto a signal, it began to ping with notifications. Not just emails, but voicemails and texts.

Sifting through them as he walked toward the office, he was pleased, and not a little relieved, to note that all the ones that related to his article were congratulatory. There was also a voicemail from his mother telling him she was proud of him and another from the PR office asking him to get in touch as soon as possible. To his disappointment, there was nothing at all from Lisa although that wasn't unusual when she was away working.

'Morning,' came a familiar female voice and he looked up from his phone to find Katie walking alongside him. 'Love the piece,' she continued. 'We'll make a journalist of you yet.'

'I'll take that as a compliment,' he replied with a grin.

'You should. Have you seen Twitter? It's gone crazy. Everyone's talking about you.'

'Not yet, I was just catching up on stuff.' Jamie logged onto the social media site as she continued talking.

'I better warn you, not all of it is exactly complimentary.'

'Bloody hell! Have you seen how many responses it's had? Over 3000, and over 1500 retweets. That's massive!'

Katie patted him on the shoulder as they entered the office building. 'Remember the golden rule, don't bite. The trolls will have a field day with you.'

'Holy fuck,' he gasped as he continued to stare at his screen. 'Have you seen some of these? It's crazy.'

'The price of fame,' she said. 'I reckon you're in for a fun day.'

By the time he arrived at his desk, Jamie was almost worn out from the sheer quantity of abuse he'd been receiving on Twitter. From accusations that he'd fabricated the whole thing to direct threats against his health, he'd received the whole range and they were still coming.

He put his mobile phone down and logged onto his emails only to find a message that his account had been locked and that he was to contact the social media team immediately. With a sigh, he picked up his phone. However, before he could even dial, a young plump brunette appeared, grabbed a chair and sat down beside him. She was as excited as he'd seen anyone at the paper in ages.

'I'm Penny,' she gushed. 'From social media.'

'I was just about to call you,' Jamie replied. 'Why's my account locked?'

'Sorry, but we had to take it over, as it's gone ballistic. We've just locked your twitter account as well.'

'Why?'

'To stop you posting. Your article's troll food.'

'Oh, sorry.'

'Don't be sorry.' she replied, her excitement level actually managing to ramp up a notch. 'Have you any idea of the click through's we're getting today? This is brilliant.'

'What about my emails?'

'We'll filter out the rubbish and the nutters and pass on any important ones. I've just sent a few through.'

'Thanks. I best get on then.'

'I've also sent a few through to the PR people. You've had a few requests for interviews already.'

'Have I?' he asked, slightly shocked. 'Who from?'

'Radio mostly. There was one for TV, but you best speak to PR about that.'

Jamie took a deep breath as Penny glanced at her phone. He'd written a few stories over the years which has caused a stir but nothing like this. This was madness.

'Jesus, you're actually trending. Good work!' She jumped to her feet, reminded him to call the PR team and headed into the chaos.

Having spent much of the morning doing interviews locked in the newspapers own radio room which until 10.15 he hadn't even known existed, Jamie had returned to his desk and was trying to get his head back in the game.

Being soundproofed, the atmosphere in the radio room had been oppressive and what air available, stale. Yet that paled into insignificance when compared to the bombardment he'd received from various journalists and members of the public he'd had to speak with.

The debate had been more considered than the one he'd seen on Twitter, but it was still fairly heated at times and he felt emotionally and physically drained as a result. It had taken two cups of coffee to get himself back to anywhere near normal.

He looked up to see Pete Goodwin approaching, his face an indication that he wasn't in the best of moods. Jamie consciously sat up in his seat to give the impression that he was 100% on it.

'Why the fuck did you turn down the BBC?'

'Oh,' said Jamie as his brain caught up. 'I didn't think...'

'Are you fucking shitting me? You turned down a chance to promote this newspaper on national television?'

'Sorry. I...' Jamie instantly regretted opening his mouth. His reply seemed to make his editor even angrier.

'You NEVER turn down a chance to push this publication through other press outlets. NEVER!' he raged. 'Fuck me, I thought you wanted to be a journalist!'

'I do, I mean I am,' Jamie pleaded. 'I've got more radio stuff booked for this afternoon. LBC and Talk Radio from upstairs and I've got to go to the BBC.' he added in the hope that it would appease the anger being directed at him.

'Then you best piss off then.'

'I've got a few hours yet. It's only in Portland Place.'

'Get out of my fucking sight,' replied Pete who continued glaring at Jamie as he gathered his things together.

'Oh, and my phones been off the hook this morning with people complaining about you. I like that, good job.'

'Thanks,' said Jamie. 'I...'

'Go!' growled Pete.

Jamie forced a smile and headed for the lift.

He might well have been in a building which was known and respected the world over, but with the words of his editor still ringing in his ears, Jamie was entirely focussed on the job in hand.

With him in the BBC Radio 5 studio sat the host, Sarah Connolly, Chief Inspector Tony Davies of the Metropolitan Police and opposite, right-wing MP Ian Foster.

Despite his years of working with celebrities, Jamie had been nervous when initially introduced to two such powerful and influential figures, but both had been friendly and Foster in particular, had been quite charming. Like most successful politicians, he had a charisma you could almost touch.

In the studio however, things had fairly quickly changed with the policeman on the defensive and the MP instantly on the attack.

'I absolutely refute the allegation that the police do not pursue criminals to the full extent of the law,' said Davies calmly. 'That is simply untrue.'

'All criminals?' asked Sarah.

'If there is a reasonable chance of conviction, of course. But that's decided by the Crown Prosecution Service.'

'So that's actually a no,' scoffed Foster. 'Remember, last year we saw huge increase in reported crime figures pretty much across the board and goodness knows how many go unreported.'

'We've certainly had victims call in to say that they hadn't reported the crime,' said Sarah.

'That's because people have lost faith in the police,' replied Foster, clearly warming to his task.

Sarah glanced across at Jamie. 'Did you find evidence of this lack of faith when you were researching your story?'

'Sad to say, but yes,' said Jamie calmly. 'People across the country are angry and they feel let down. They want justice and they're not always getting it. And that's not just the victims, but the communities.'

'Is that what you think is driving these vigilante groups?'

Jamie glanced nervously at the senior officer who was glaring at him. 'I'd hesitate to call them vigilantes. To be honest, until we can establish some kind of motive, we can't really say what they are.'

'And it's the job of the police to establish that motive,' seethed Davies. 'Not the tabloid press.'

Sarah threw a look at the policeman and turned back to Jamie. 'Do you think that the communities where these crimes took place view these men as hero's?'

'No,' he replied. 'Not in my opinion. I think they regard them as more of a necessary evil in the sense that they are the second layer of a two-tier justice system which seems to be operating in some parts of this country.'

'That's a dangerous and worrying allegation,' said Sarah.

'Yes, of course it is,' responded Jamie. 'But I can only talk about what I found whilst visiting these people. They feel badly let down by the justice system.'

'Who are these men? Have you any idea?'

Jamie glanced around the desk; all eyes firmly fixed on him. 'None whatsoever. I wish I did.'

'Chief inspector, I assume that the police are investigating these incidents?'

'Of course. These men are violent criminals and they will be apprehended at some point soon. But I have to say that effectively glorifying them in this manner is not helping.'

Sarah nodded at him and turned to the MP sitting beside her.

'Ian Foster, you're an outspoken critic of the police and the justice system, how do you react to what you've heard?'

'I'm not a critic of the rank and file police,' he said. 'I support them 100%. However, I am a critic of the fact that as an institution, they are increasingly driven by political correctness and quotas that encourage them to chase the easy arrest rather than the real criminals.'

'That is not true,' interrupted Davies angrily.

'Really? Try telling that to people who are effectively prisoners in their own homes because the police are too busy chasing motorists to come out and actually police their area.'

Davies glared daggers at the MP. 'So, are you saying we should ignore crimes such as drink driving?'

'No, not at all. The job of the police is to uphold AND enforce the law,' said Foster confidently. 'However, there is clearly an issue with priorities. Is online crime for example, really comparable to burglary?'

'The victims would argue that it is,' said Sarah.

'Then the victims need educating on the subject of personal responsibility,' replied Foster. 'They have the power to turn off a computer, a victim of burglary or sexual abuse has no power whatsoever.'

'The issue of online crime is a growing problem which we have to take seriously.'

'Why?' bristled Foster in response to the police officer. 'In 90% of cases it's nothing more than sticks and stones.'

'Try telling that to a child who is being driven to the brink of suicide,' said Sarah, barely able to disguise the disgust in her voice.

'I would say exactly that to the parents,' said Foster gruffly. 'And I'd also question them as to why they aren't monitoring what their children are doing online.'

'You can't blame the parents surely,' said Sarah.

'Why not? Do the police ever talk to the parents of these children? Not just the victims, but the bullies as well.'

'You can't lay all the problems at the feet of the police,' replied Sarah angrily as Jamie watched on, bewildered by the ferocity of the exchange taking place around him.

'And nor would I want to,' said Foster. 'As politicians we also have to take some responsibility for the situation we find ourselves in because what Jamie has written about is evidence of the beginning of a backlash.'

'A backlash?' asked Sarah. 'From whom?'

Foster smiled and Jamie suddenly realised that the MP had led the discussion to exactly where he had wanted it to be and now, he was clearly going to take full advantage. Jamie almost smiled at both the audacity and obvious power of the man.

'From the silent majority,' said the MP. 'As we've seen with the whole Brexit debacle, for far too long the political classes have ignored their concerns and history has shown us that we do that at our peril.'

'Ian Foster MP, Jamie Brown, Chief Inspector Davies, thank you,' said Sarah in her perfect radio host voice. 'Judging by the response on social media I think it's safe to say that we'll be returning to this subject very soon.'

By the time he arrived home, it was after eight and having given a succession of interviews to various news outlets, Jamie was feeling exhausted, but thrilled. It had been quite a day.

His article had done exactly what Pete Goodwin had hoped it would and created a shit storm. Not just on social media where he'd had everything from high praise to death threats but in the mainstream media who had jumped onto what was clearly a major public interest story of his creation.

Yet if today had been manic, tomorrow would be worse. Keen to keep the momentum going, the paper had lined up another round of interviews whilst Pete had demanded a follow article within the next 48 hours. It was exciting, but draining and as he stepped through his front door, the only thing he could think of was that he needed a shower, food and sleep and he wasn't particularly bothered about what order they came in.

He was disappointed to find the house in semi-darkness and not for the first time that day, glanced at his phone to see if Lisa had made contact only to find that she still hadn't. Whilst it wasn't unusual for her to go silent for a day or so when she was off with work, it was incredibly frustrating when he had so much he wanted to tell her.

Jamie dropped his bag by the door and after gathering up the mail walked into the living room only to find Lisa sitting on the sofa.

'Jesus!' he gasped. 'You scared the shit out of me! Is everything OK?' He moved toward her, but she held up her hand to stop him.

'What's wrong?' he asked as he began to realise that the mood in the room wasn't just frosty, it was arctic cold.

'D'you know where I went last night?' she asked.

'No, I…'

'I went to Stafford,' she continued, ignoring his interruption. 'And at 6.00 this morning I was arresting four men who have been sexually abusing a 12-year-old girl for over a year and selling the films of it online. One of them was her father.'

Jamie sat down opposite her. 'Shit,' he said. 'Are you OK?'

Lisa didn't even acknowledge his words but as she spoke, her mood began to darken and instead of speaking to him, she was soon speaking at him. 'That's what I do, you know that. You also know that I have to watch those films and once I've seen what these bastards do, I have to talk to those kids about it.'

'I know,' said Jamie softly.

'That's why I don't ever bring work home with me. Once I walk through my front door, I don't talk about it, I don't think about it.'

Jamie simply watched her, his eyes locked on hers and his mind trying to work out how he should react to what was clearly some kind of unfolding drama.

'But I do the job,' Lisa continued. 'because I know that thanks to me, that 12-year-old will wake up in the morning and not have to think about what some piece of filth is going to make her do today.'

Lisa took a deep breath and then reached into her rucksack to pull out a copy of Jamie's paper. 'So how do you think I feel when I pick up a newspaper and read an article written by the man I live with which slags off…'

'Hang on,' said Jamie. The words bringing a glare of such ferocity that he didn't even contemplate continuing.

'Which slags off,' she repeated angrily. 'My job and my colleagues?'

'I didn't say that.'

Lisa got to her feet and began to pace like a caged Tiger. 'Then, to add insult to injury, I have to listen to you on the radio with that dick of a fascist MP taking pot shots at what I do and how I do it.

'Look, I know…'

'But,' continued Lisa without even looking at him.

'Oh Christ,' Jamie said to himself.

'As if all that wasn't bad enough, you then go on to almost endorse these bloody vigilantes! I mean, what the fuck Jamie?'

'I didn't do that,' he said

Lisa lowered her eyelids before retrieving a slip of paper from her bra. 'Quote,' she began. 'they regard them as more of a necessary evil in the sense that they are the second layer of a two-tier justice system which seems to be operating in some parts of this country. Unquote.'

She held out the slip of paper. 'I had to write it down because I didn't believe what I was hearing coming out of your mouth.'

Jamie was about to speak when his phone rang and he instinctively reached for it.

'You answer that fucking phone,' Lisa growled. 'And I swear to God I will walk out that door.'

Jamie pulled his hand from his pocket, got to his feet and held out his arms in apology. 'Look, he said. 'I didn't mean it like that. I…'

'I haven't finished,' Lisa said, cutting him stone dead. 'Sit down.'

Jamie sat down; his phone rang again but this time he ignored it.

'To top it all off,' she continued. 'I've had people I work with taking pot shots at me all day because I live with the person responsible. D'you know what someone called me today?' Lisa paused for a moment as she struggled to keep her emotions in check. 'A traitor. Me. I do one of the toughest jobs any copper has to do, and I get called a bloody traitor. And it's going to be the same tomorrow, and the day after that. So, thank you darling. Thank you very, very fucking much.'

Jamie stared at her unsure if he should speak or just let her stew. Before he could decide, his phone rang again.

'I'm sorry Lisa,' he said apologetically. 'I've got to, it must be important.' He reached into his pocket as she stormed out without another word and listened to her walking up the stairs as he answered the call.

'Hello, he said. 'Yes, that's me. When? Oh Christ. OK, I suppose so. What time?'

Jamie gave Lisa half an hour to cool down before heading after her. He found her in bed, but still wide awake.

'So d'you want to talk about this?' he said as he sat down on the armchair in the corner of the bedroom.

'Not really,' she replied without looking up.

'Look, I'm sorry OK?' he said anyway. 'But what am I supposed to do? Ignore a story because it might impact on you?'

Lisa sat up instantly. Her eyes wide. 'Impact on me! Jesus, you just don't get it do you?'

'Get what?' Jamie protested. 'Look I know you're pissed off but...'

'Oh my God! I'm not pissed off,' she blurted at him. 'I'm bloody terrified!'

Jamie froze for a moment and then moved to the bed. He tried to hold her, but she pushed him away.

'I don't understand,' he said desperately.

'This house was my safe zone. It was the only place in my life where I could switch off mentally and emotionally from all the shit I have to deal with at work.' She stopped speaking and her face crumbled. 'And now it's gone.'

'Of course, it hasn't,' said Jamie. 'Nothing's changed.'

Lisa looked up at him with an expression he'd never seen before. It wasn't simply blank, it was empty.

'Yes, it has,' she said. 'Because you made me bring work through our front door and now it's just another place full of little desperate faces and the sound of their screams. The fact that you don't get that actually makes it worse.'

The two of them sat in silence, each wrapped in their own desperate thoughts. Suddenly, Lisa climbed out of bed, retrieved a small suitcase from the top of the wardrobe and began to fill it with clothes.

'What the fuck are you doing" asked Jamie desperately.

'I don't feel safe here anymore. I need to get out,' she said as she closed the case. 'I'll call you tomorrow.'

Jamie sat in silence until the front door slammed shut and he'd heard her car pull away from the kerb outside.

'Bollocks.'

Chapter Sixteen
Wednesday 4th July 2019

07.45

After a sleepless night, mostly spent sitting in the living room wrestling with guilt and hoping Lisa would return, Jamie had showered and eaten a slice of toast before a car collected him at 05.45 to convey him to the Sky News offices on the outskirts of West London.

Now, he sat listening as Ian Foster speak to the host via a large screen between them although in truth, he was struggling to take any of it in such was the turmoil going on in his head.

'As I've said previously,' continued Foster in the background, 'in any democracy the people have ultimate control of the legal process because they have the power of rebellion.'

'But if people are taking the law into their own hands, that can only lead to anarchy surely,' replied the host.

'Absolutely,' replied Foster. 'And what Mr. Brown has done with his article is to fire a much-needed warning shot in the direction of the establishment at the prospect of that. Hopefully, coming on the back of the mess they're making of leaving the European Union they'll take note and react accordingly.'

The host turned and smiled. 'How do you respond to that Mr. Brown?'

'Well, I agree up to a point,' said Jamie. 'There are certainly some fundamental questions to be asked about the law and how it fails people.'

'Victims you mean.'

'Yes, victims. Of course. But we must also remember that these cases are extremely rare and for the most part, the police do an outstanding job. Often in extremely challenging situations.'

With the interview complete, Jamie had his makeup removed and after confirming to the producers that he'd be available for the rest of the day just in case they wanted him again, he headed for the exit.

He was expecting to find the Asian driver who'd collected him earlier waiting to take him to work but found instead a tall well-dressed white man.

'Mr. Brown,' he said with a disarming smile. 'I'm Paul. I'm here to take you to your office.'

'What happened to the guy from earlier?'

'He finished at 7.30 Sir. If you'll follow me.'

Jamie shrugged his shoulders and followed Paul out to a black Mercedes. Once inside, he checked his phone and began to sift through his various messages as the car headed for central London.

'I saw you on the show sir,' said Paul. 'Very good if you don't mind me saying.'

'Thanks,' said Jamie without looking up.

'You made some good points. Middle England and all that. I totally agree with you.'

Jamie looked up from his phone and stared at the eyes in the mirror. They were seemingly fixed on him.

'You do?' he said.

'I think if you scratch the surface, most people do.'

Jamie smiled to himself and placed his phone on the seat beside him. 'Thanks,' he said. 'This TV stuff is all new to me.'

'Well you'd never have known it. You were very professional. Feel free to close your eyes if you want to sir. We have about 30 minutes,' continued Paul.

Jamie smiled again then settled back into his chair with his eyes closed as his mind returned to the problem of Lisa.

However, before he could fully drift off, he became aware of the car slowing to a halt. Expecting it to be nothing more than traffic or lights, he kept his eyes tightly shut but suddenly, a door opened, and he felt someone climb in beside him.

Even before Jamie could fully work out what was happening his phone had been spirited away and the car had pulled back into the moving traffic.

Jamie stared at the man beside him. Like his driver, he was white, well-groomed and smartly dressed whilst his face wore an expression of assured calmness. 'What the fuck's going on?' Jamie gasped.

'No need to panic Mr. Brown,' said the man. 'We just wanted a word that's all.'

'A word? What about?'

'The things you've been writing about us,' he said before holding up an admonishing finger. 'Naughty, naughty,'

Jamie stared at him, terrified. 'Where are we going?'

The man smiled and settled back into his seat. 'Not far,' he said. 'Just relax and enjoy the ride. There's a fresh bottle of water in the door if you're thirsty.'

Jamie leant back against the door as he struggled to get a handle on that what was happening. Twenty minutes ago, he'd been on live television and now he'd been kidnapped by what he assumed were violent criminals. It was like something out of a shitty gangster movie.

He took a deep breath and tried to calm himself. It was fairly safe to assume that whatever was waiting for him at the end of this journey wasn't going to be pleasant, so he had to either escape or put up some kind of fight however futile that might be.

'By the way,' said the man beside him calmly, 'please don't try to open the door. The child locks are on so it can only open from the outside.'

'Who are you?' asked Jamie desperately. What's going to happen to me?'

The man looked at him and smiled. 'Nothing's going to happen to you. You're not in any danger whatsoever.'

'Why the hell have I been kidnapped?'

'Kidnapped!' exclaimed the man. 'That's a bit strong.'

'Well what else would you bloody call it?' asked Jamie. 'I'm in a car I don't want to be in being taken to a place I don't want to go to by people I don't know!'

'I can see why you're a journalist,' laughed the man. 'You're very clever with words.'

'Let me out of this fucking car!' growled Jamie. 'I want to get out!'

'Why?' said the man calmly.

'What d'you mean why? Why the fuck d'you think?'

'But this is your story Mr. Brown. You wanted to know what's going on and you're about to find out. Or maybe you don't actually want to know at all.'

The man looked at Jamie for a second as if waiting for an answer and when none came, he leant forward and tapped the driver on the shoulder. Almost instantly, the car pulled over and stopped.

'Well?' said the man. 'The choice is yours. If you want to get out, I'll let you out.'

Jamie eyeballed him and then looked at the rear-view mirror to see the driver's eyes staring back at him. Both sets wore the faintest hint of a smile. Not kind, but knowing and confident. The man was right of course. Why on earth would he not want to find out the background to his story when it was, if anything, an even bigger story. It had to be worth the risk.

'OK,' he said nervously. 'I'm in.'

The man nodded in reply and without another word, the car pulled away.

'Can I at least ask where we're going?'

'Of course,' replied the man sitting beside him. 'We're on our way to Slough.'

'Slough!' said Jamie nervously. 'What are we going there for?'

'Because there's someone who wants to meet you.'

Just over thirty minutes later, the car slowed to a halt in a nondescript housing estate and almost instantly, Paul exited the car and opened Jamie's door to allow him out. Never had air smelt so fresh.

'So, what now?' he asked as the second man climbed out and walked round to stand beside him. 'Or is this it?'

Before Jamie knew what was happening, he was being expertly frisked and having removed the dictaphone from his jacket pocket, the man smiled and pointed across the road.

'The gentleman over there,' he said, 'will tell you all you need to know. When he's finished, we'll be here to take you to your office.'

Jamie turned to see a man watching them. Unlike the two in the car, he wasn't wearing a suit but was dressed in smart dark clothing. In many respects, he looked fairly nondescript and as Jamie walked across the road toward him, he struggled to pick out anything other than the fact that he was medium build, short dark hair under a baseball cap and looked to be late 30's, early 40's.

'So,' said Jamie as confidently as he could. 'Here I am. They told me that you're the person who's going to fill in all the blanks.'

The man stood, arms folded across his chest as he looked Jamie up and down like a boxer in a ring sizing up an opponent. His facial expression somehow managed to convey absolute indifference yet at the same time, there was something about him that radiated not merely strength of purpose, but power.

'Possibly,' he said. 'That depends.'

'On what?'

'On what I think of you.'

The hint of sarcasm in the voice made Jamie feel uneasy and he began to consider the possibility that far from uncovering the next chapter of his story, he was about to become another victim of it.

'Do I at least get a name?' he asked in a thinly veiled attempt to disguise his growing anxiety.

The man continued to stare at him for a few moments before a slight smile crept across his face.

'My name's Billy, he said. 'Billy Evans.'

PART THREE

Chapter Seventeen
Wednesday 4th July 2019

09.20

Billy scrutinised the man standing nervously in front of him. He looked different from the pictures he'd seen on the internet but to be fair, in most of those Jamie Brown had been smiling alongside some celebrity or other whereas here, he was probably shitting it. Billy knew from experience what that did to people.

He also knew that as a journalist Jamie Brown was both smart and sharp, so he'd have to be on his guard throughout their exchange. The best way to do that was to drive it from the outset whilst maintaining the possibility of a threat.

'I'm guessing that's not your real name,' said Jamie nervously.

'Why wouldn't I use my real name?' Billy replied confidently. 'What'd be the point in that?'

'But surely…'

Billy held up his hand to stop him. 'Listen, don't make the mistake of thinking I'm some kind of mug OK? D'you really think you'd be standing here if I hadn't covered my back with a cast iron alibi?'

Jamie shrugged his shoulders in response. The man standing in front of him was either incredibly arrogant or staggeringly stupid but as yet, he had no idea which.

'So why am I here?' he asked.

'Your article,' said Billy calmly. 'Why else?'

'So how close was I?'

'Personally, I'd have preferred to keep things quiet for a while longer but fuck it. It is what it is,' continued Billy thoughtfully. 'I did like the second-tier justice system line you used on the radio though.'

'You didn't answer my question.' said Jamie.

Billy smiled. 'You were close, but you missed a couple of things.'

'Such as?'

A sly grin spread across Billy's face. 'Come on,' he said. 'Let's have a little wander.'

He turned and walked along the road toward a small corner shop which occupied a small plot on a junction. Jamie walked beside him listening intently as Billy talked.

'See that shop?' he said without slowing down. 'Six times in twelve months that place was robbed and always when the old woman was behind the till.'

Barely fifty yards further along the road Billy pointed to a neatly kept terraced house opposite them. He stopped and faced Jamie. 'A young woman and her baby live there,' he said. 'She was burgled twice in three months by the same bloke. The second time she woke up in bed to find him standing over her. Luckily he fucked off when she screamed.'

Without another word, Billy started moving again as Jamie followed on. They had barely got into their stride when he pointed to another house. 'The old couple who live there had their shed burnt down and used to get dog shit smeared on their front door and shoved through their letterbox. The Muslim family next door would get rashers of bacon tied to their gate.'

Jamie stopped walking. 'OK,' he said, 'It's a dump. I get it.'

Billy stopped and walked back toward him, the smile gone, the expression stern. 'No, you don't,' he said brusquely. 'You don't get it at all. Come on.'

Billy headed off again, this time with Jamie walking behind him and in silence. A short distance along the road, they turned into an alleyway and followed it until it spilled out onto a small green surrounded by seven small, but neatly kept bungalows. Outside one sat four elderly women who looked up from their gossiping to stare at the two men who had suddenly appeared in their little oasis.

Billy lifted his arm and waved at them. A gesture that was immediately returned before the women returned to their chat.

'Who are they?' asked Jamie.

Billy ignored him. 'Half the gaffs in this square have been turned over in the last two years,' he said. 'Four of the residents have been assaulted and all of them have had their lives made a bloody misery. They're old age pensioners, it's shameful.'

'I'm guessing there's a point you're leading up to,'

Billy looked at Jamie and shook his head dismissively. 'You know the one thing you got wrong?' he said. 'Motive. You assume that what's going on is about revenge, it's not.'

'So, what is it about?' asked Jamie.

'It's about them,' said Billy gesturing toward the women. 'Simple as that.'

'I don't understand,' said Jamie.

'I know you don't,' replied Billy. 'People like you never do. You're too busy moralising to see what's going on under your fucking noses.'

'That's not fair.'

Billy laughed at the suggestion. 'Fair! I'll tell you what's not fair. D'you know how many people were responsible for most of the crap going on around here. Three?'

'You can't know that for sure,' said Jamie.

'I don't, but they do because they live round here,' replied Billy as he gestured toward the women. 'So did the old bill. Yet every time they got one of them into court some smarmy fucker of a lawyer got them off. So, they came back even cockier and life for the people round here got worse. It was a vicious circle and the same thing's happening all over the country.' Billy paused and smiled. 'Even where you live.'

Jamie froze. 'How do you know where I live?' he asked.

'You'd be surprised at what I know,' said Billy calmly.

'That sounds like a threat.'

'What possible point would there be in threatening you?' scoffed Billy.

Jamie stared at Billy as he tried desperately to get a handle on him. He'd rarely met anyone so supremely confident in his life.

'So, what gives you the right to act as judge, juror and executioner?'

'Me personally? Or the collective me?'

'Either.'

Billy raised an eyebrow in admonishment and thought for a moment. 'Have you ever been let down by the law?' he asked. 'I mean really let down?'

'No.'

'So, what gives you the right to judge people who have?'

'I'm not judging them, I'm judging you. You can't just simply sidestep the system because...'

'The system!' scoffed Billy. 'I could give you 17.4 million reasons why that's fucked and as for the law, ask them if they've got any faith in it,' he said gesturing toward the old women. 'Or the owner of the shop. While you're at it ask them how many times they called the police when they were getting burgled or harassed and then how any times they actually turned up. Then ask them how many times they've had to call them since we came along and stood up for them. I'll answer that for you, it's zero.'

'And you think that justifies what you're doing?'

'No,' Billy said calmly as he glanced across at the old women who were now laughing riotously at something or other. 'That does. Look at them and tell me what's happened here is wrong.'

'And that's thanks to you I suppose?'

Billy laughed. 'I had nothing to do with this.'

'So, you're not one of these vigilantes?' asked Jamie.

Billy smiled a wry smile in response. 'You mean do I go around putting people in hospital? No, I don't.'

'But you are involved somehow?'

'You say it like it's a bad thing.'

'Because it is,' said Jamie.

'How can standing up to bullies and making communities safer be a bad thing?'

'What you're doing is anarchy,' said Jamie. 'However, you dress it up, that's what it is.'

'That depends on your definition of anarchy,' said Billy thoughtfully. 'Although when did a little rebellion ever hurt anyone? Anyway, you've got about ten minutes left so if you've got any questions, fire away.'

'OK,' replied Jamie. 'How many of you are there?'

'At the last count, just under 100 across England but that's growing.'

'Why just England?'

'Because we're English.'

'That's not what I meant.'

'I know what you meant,' said Billy with a disarming smile. 'But this has nothing to do with race or religion so don't go down that road.'

'But it is right-wing?'

'I voted Tory at the last election. Does that count?'

'But…'

'For fuck's sake. Why are you so desperate to label this? We don't. It's not about right or left, it's about right and wrong, that's all we care about. Now move on before I get bored.'

Jamie nodded but logged Billy's response just in case he had actually touched a nerve. 'How are these groups organised?'

'With secrecy,' said Billy. 'It's better for everyone's sake.'

'And how are the victims selected?'

Billy frowned. 'Victims? They're not victims, they're targets.'

'OK, so how do you pick these targets?'

'We listen. Simple as that. It's not hard to get to the root of a local issue if you listen hard enough.'

'And what happens if you make a mistake?' asked Jamie.

Billy smiled knowingly. 'We don't make mistakes,'

'Everyone makes mistakes,' said Jamie.

Billy smiled at him and then said bluntly. 'We don't, we can't. Next question.'

'So how many of these targets have been dealt with?'

'To date, 47. All being well, that'll be 49 by tomorrow morning.'

Jamie balked. Shocked both at the number and the matter of factness of the announcement that two more people would end up in hospital tonight. 'And who are these 47 people?'

'They're criminals who have managed to dodge justice as handed down by the system you're so fond of,' said Billy. 'So, we educate them in the only way they actually understand.'

'Violence you mean.'

'Absolutely,' said Billy. 'And d'you know what happens once the first one has been given a taste of proper justice? The rest just fade away. Happens every time.'

'But what happens when they come back?'

'D'you think we just abandon people?' laughed Billy. 'How else do you think I know where you live?'

'Teddy Miles,' exclaimed Jamie. 'He told you. Was it you who visited Keegan as well?'

Billy smiled confidently 'Not me, but someone keeping an eye on him. Now you answer a question for me. Why do you think it's wrong to want to bring a sense of right and wrong back to local communities?'

'I don't,' replied Jamie. 'But I certainly don't agree with the way you're trying to do it.'

Billy smiled and pointed at the women sitting across the square. 'I don't give a fuck whether you agree or not,' he said, 'what they think is all that matters. Come on. Time's up.'

Billy led Jamie back along the alley and within a few minutes, they were standing opposite the Mercedes where Paul and the second man were still waiting patiently.

'One last question,' asked Jamie.

'OK. Ask away.'

'Why am I here? It makes no sense.'

'It makes perfect sense to me,' said Billy.

'It doesn't to me. I mean, you've got to know I have to write about this.'

'As long as you don't mention my name, I don't give a fuck what you do.'

'And why wouldn't I do that?'

'Because you're not stupid,' said Billy.

'Another threat?'

Billy smiled. 'If you and your paper want to be sued into oblivion for defamation, that's fine by me.' Billy paused for a moment before continuing, his expression and tone more serious. 'But that'd be a shame.'

'A shame?' said Jamie, puzzled by the change in Billy's manner. 'Didn't you know that there's no such thing as bad publicity.'

'Try telling that to Rolf Harris.'

Billy glanced across to where Paul was waiting and raised his hand, a signal that their meeting was over. 'You want to know what it's all about? Start thinking about the bigger picture.'

Jamie thought for a moment and then smiled. 'Oh, so that's what this is all about,' he scoffed, 'you want publicity for some kind of cause. The right are on the rise, is that it?'

'There you go again, taking me for a mug and missing the point,' relied Billy with a sigh. He gestured toward the waiting car. 'Safe trip back to the smoke.'

'So, what if I need anything else?' asked Jamie, more out of habit than anything. 'Can I get hold of you? Or anyone else?'

'Oh, I'm pretty sure we'll speak again soon,' replied Billy. 'Be lucky.'

Billy waved at the men opposite and walked away. Jamie watched him until he was almost out of sight and only then did he walk slowly across to the waiting Mercedes.

Billy sat in his Range Rover and waited until the Mercedes sped past him. Since no one had called to tell him otherwise, he assumed that the journalist was inside so picked up his phone, found the number he wanted and texted 'It's done'. Once he'd sent that, he started his car and headed for the M4.

He was not however, heading for work but to Brentwood and the increasingly familiar confines of *The Top Of The World*. Jamie Brown was not the only meeting Billy Evans was due to have that day.

Chapter Eighteen
Wednesday 4th July 2019

11.00

Having been dropped outside of his office building, Jamie hurried up to his floor and headed directly for Pete Goodwin's office. Even as he approached, he could see from the look on his editors face that he wasn't best pleased.

'Where the fuck have you been?' he roared. 'And why haven't you been answering your fucking phone? D'you know how many people are after you?'

Jamie collapsed into a chair. 'I've been to Slough,' he said. 'I got kidnapped.'

'You what?'

'Kidnapped,' repeated Jamie. 'After the Sky interview two men took me to Slough to meet this guy. He pretty much gave me chapter and verse about what's going on. It was surreal. He even…'

Jamie jumped up and moved around to Pete's computer, opened a fresh page and typed Billy Evans into the search bar. 'Jesus!' he gasped as the screen filled. 'That's him. That's the guy!'

'Hang on,' said Pete. 'He actually told you his real name?'

Jamie gestured at the screen. 'Obviously,' he said as he began reading what was on the screen. 'But….'

Before he could continue, Pete eased him away from his desk.

'This can wait,' he said calmly. 'Before you do anything else, go and write up everything that happened this morning. And I mean everything. OK?'

Jamie nodded in agreement.

'Do you want the police involved?'

'No,' replied Jamie with a shake of his head. 'They took my phone and I've no way of proving anything. Besides, he did this for a reason. I just need to work out what it is.'

'Now you're thinking like a reporter,' said Pete with a smile. 'So, get that written up and get back here. You've got half an hour.'

The second Jamie had left his office, Pete picked up his phone and dialled. 'Katie, drop whatever you're working on. I'm about to email you a name and a photo. I want every single thing we have on this guy.'

Even as his photograph was flying through cyberspace toward Katie Marshall's computer, Billy was cruising in the left-hand lane of the M25 at a steady 65 miles per hour. He was in reflective mood and inevitably, his mind had turned to a familiar place.

Whilst he would be the first to admit that he still missed Hawk terribly and had struggled to come to terms with the grief that at times had almost dragged him into the darkest of places, Billy was utterly convinced that his old friend was still around. Not just watching and listening but guiding him. That wasn't merely a help and a comfort, it was something Billy continually drew strength from. 'What would Hawk think or do?' had become his mantra and like his gut instinct, it had never let him down.

Yet Billy was also well aware of the irony to be found in the fact that his friend's murder had been the catalyst for almost everything that had happened to him over the last eight months. He would almost certainly never have met Claire who had now become a permanent fixture in his life, nor would he have ever been recruited into what had become known as 'the firm'. Not least because had Hawk still been alive, the two of them would have almost certainly laughed off the very idea of getting involved in anything so ludicrous. However, within a few minutes of meeting the two men at *The Top Of The World* the day after Hawk's funeral, Billy had known that he'd wanted in.

Their pitch to him had been simple. They represented a small group of ex-military policemen who had become so disenchanted with the law that they were prepared to step outside of it to deliver justice for people who had been failed by the courts. And by justice, they effectively meant revenge. Violent revenge.

The idea had come about after the elderly mother of one of their number had been attacked and sexually assaulted. The police had arrested someone fairly quickly but the courts had failed to convict him on a technicality and so her son had understandably sworn to extract his own kind of justice. However, before he could act, some of his former colleagues had offered to do it for him and so with the son and his family ensconced in a hotel at the other end of the country, his friends had visited the guilty man at home and delivered a serious beating.

Having covered their tracks using their experience of criminal investigations, they were effectively uncatchable. Not that the local police were that bothered about trying to find them anyway since most had been pissed off that the victim hadn't been locked up.

That had been two years ago, and their little group had grown to 19 highly trusted men who had used the same tactic a number of times over the intervening period. Yet they had been increasingly frustrated by a lack of new members and with the military police veteran community so small, their fear was that sooner or later someone would be approached who would not only reject the idea but report them to the authorities.

That's when they had started to think about involving people from outside and whilst the initial plan had been to recruit solely from within the veteran community, it had proven to be too complicated. That's when they'd had the idea of looking at the football hooligan community.

It was in many ways, the perfect fit. Small, tightly knit and highly organised groups of men who were not only used to violence but were adept at avoiding attention from the police. More importantly, they were spread across the country and by virtue of following football, highly mobile. The problem the ex-MP's faced was gaining access to the kind of people who might be willing to work with them.

Even as they were looking into how they might achieve that, one of the group had stumbled across a news item about the failure to convict anyone for Hawk's murder and that had led them directly to Billy. With his history and contacts, he was the ideal candidate to approach and so the question they had for him was simple, was he interested?

However, rather than ask him for an answer, they had instead played their trump card. For how better to prove to him that they were serious than by providing an example of how they worked.

So, whilst Billy and Claire had been in Liverpool enjoying a weekend away and obtaining a cast iron alibi into the bargain, Ashley Bennett had been visited by five former Military Policemen who had proceeded to batter him senseless. By the time Billy had been contacted again and asked the question properly, long dormant feelings of wanting to be involved in something questionable had been awakened and having never shied away from exploiting his hooligan past, not only was Billy ready to give them an answer in the affirmative but he had already begun to put feelers out to carefully selected people who he suspected might be willing to follow him.

However, Billy hadn't simply been looking for people who could deliver a beating, they would have been easy to find. He was instead looking for solid lads who would help him both organise and recruit. For even as he'd been driving back from Liverpool, Billy had begun thinking about the longer term.

Like many, he'd been watching the country tear itself apart over Brexit and whilst he'd never had any real interest in politics, it was fairly clear that the growing social tension was not only fuelling resentment and division, it was creating a political vacuum. If Billy knew one thing, it's that any kind of vacuum equalled opportunity and whilst he'd had no idea how that might manifest itself, he'd suspected that working with the veterans and having a group of lads at his beck and call might well prove advantageous at some point. All he had to do was make sure that whatever form that opportunity might take, he had to be ready to grab it with both hands when the time came.

As a consequence, he had thrown himself into this new project with gusto and had fairly quickly found not simply willing participants, but actual groups from amongst the darker side of the football community.

He hadn't however, recruited anyone from within *The CSS*. Not because he didn't trust them but purely on the basis that it was too close to home and the risk of someone saying something when they were together was potentially too great. Far better and safer to keep everyone involved at a distance from everyone else.

That was the ethos which forged the basis of the communication network Billy had developed which ensured that with a few exceptions, he being one, no one involved had any contact with more than two people outside of their small group. Even that was via texts to untraceable pay as you go phones which he had provided. Even the few veterans Billy liaised with directly were known to him only by their Christian names.

It was a setup designed solely to protect everyone involved and thus far, it had worked seamlessly. More importantly, by insisting that the veteran and football side of things be kept entirely separate, primarily to ensure that he kept control of his side of the firm, he had placed himself into a position where as the only link between the two groups, he was indispensable. This immediately afforded him a degree of power, and power meant control.

Yet despite that, Billy had always remained mindful that he'd been a piece in someone else's jigsaw although in truth, it had been a role he'd been happy to play. He had never once felt the need to question how the targets were selected, although it didn't take a rocket scientist to work out the involvement of a rogue serving copper or two, nor had he concerned himself with thoughts of who was pulling the strings. Instead, he had contented himself with the buzz of plotting, organising and even waiting for news of attacks. That had been more than enough to keep him interested and for the first time since Sam's death, Billy had begun to feel alive again. He'd even began to feel comfortable in his burgeoning relationship with Claire.

Equally, he had drawn strength from seeing how things improved for people when they suddenly realised that after years of being ignored, there was actually someone on their side. It didn't matter that they were effectively invisible or even violent men, just knowing that they were there had empowered both people and communities.

Things had changed dramatically with the publication of Jamie Brown's article for as soon as it had hit the internet it had resulted in a flurry of phone calls both from concerned lads and an angry Paul who had suggested in no uncertain terms that either he or his mob had messed up and were obviously unreliable.

Whilst Billy had quickly realised that the men mentioned in the article had been the Chelsea lads he'd tasked to deal with Carl Mason, he certainly couldn't apportion any blame to them for what had after all, been nothing more than a bizarre coincidence and he definitely wasn't going to let anyone else slag them off. As a consequence, he had demanded an immediate meeting to clear the air but even as he'd been on his way to that, Billy knew that the time had come to address an issue that he'd been keeping on the back burner for a while. For as the only person with a foot in both camps, it was fairly obvious that he was the most vulnerable to exposure and that meant that if old bill were coming after anyone, it was going to be him. With the bare bones of their activities now laid bare, that clearly could not continue and so by the time an irritable Billy arrived at the meeting with Paul and Tom, he had decided that he wanted an introduction to the men at the top. If he didn't get what he wanted, he was going to walk and take his lads with him.

He had however, been somewhat taken aback when not only had they immediately agreed to his demands and apologised for any offence caused, but had outlined the details of a plan of action which, if it worked, would not merely neutralise the impact of the article but could actually help them benefit from it. Initially, given the brazenness of it and the fact that their idea required him to put himself directly in the firing line even before he met the main faces, Billy had baulked at it but the more he'd listened to them talk, the smarter it had seemed. So much so that Billy had agreed to go for it and whilst the encounter with Jamie Brown had been a risk, albeit a calculated one, both his gut, and Hawk, were telling him that it was a gamble that had paid off. If it hadn't, then he'd knowingly opened himself to the kind of scrutiny that he had spent his entire life avoiding and the consequences of that were unthinkable.

But even as Billy pondered that potentially nightmare scenario, an idea of his own began to take shape.

It was ambitious, dangerous even, but it potentially gave him both an edge and an escape route. Two things that were always useful to have in the back pocket, even when dealing with people who were supposedly on your side. However, if it was going to work, Billy would need to gather information because information was power. And as he turned off the M25 and began the last leg of his journey to *The Top Of The World*, that thought was uppermost in his mind.

12.30

Having scanned through the sheets of A4 notes and press cuttings Katie had handed him, Jamie did exactly what he'd always done when checking or proof-reading articles, he took a deep breath and read through it all a second time. Only when he finished did he look up to find Pete and Katie staring at him.

'Holy shit,' he said.

'And that's him?' asked Pete. 'That's the guy you met this morning?'

Jamie returned his attention to the scan of an article that his own newspaper had published in 1997. It showed Billy standing on the steps of an Italian courtroom as he spoke to journalists following the conviction of an undercover police officer for murder. Despite the two decades that had passed there was no mistake. 'Yes, he said. 'That's definitely him.

'So, how the fuck did a known football hooligan end up running the security at West Ham? Or was it a case of better the devil you know?' asked Pete jokingly.

'I don't know, but I could find out. There's something else.' Katie paused for a moment as she struggled to find the right words.

'Just spit it out,' barked Pete.

'The car accident his wife was killed in might not have been an accident.'

'Jesus,' groaned Jamie. 'Don't tell me he murdered her?'

'No, but when I saw the stuff about West Ham, I called a mate who used to cover them for the old Standard to ask him if he'd heard of him. Well, he had, obviously, and he told me a few things including that there were strong rumours at the time that it was a revenge killing.'

'Revenge? Revenge for what?' asked Jamie.

'He didn't know,' Katie replied with a shrug.

'And he didn't say who by?' asked Pete.

Katie hesitated for a second and then said as calmly as she could, 'Irish Paramilitaries.'

Jamie's blood ran cold. 'What?'

'Sorry Jamie, that's what he said.'

Pete took a deep breath, picked up the sheet of notes and quickly looked through them. 'That was 18 years ago, so what's he been doing since then?'

'Well,' Katie began. 'He sold his security business in 2003 and since then...'

'That was a rhetorical question,' said Pete firmly as he handed the sheet of paper to her. 'Find out.'

'And what d'you want me to do?'

Pete looked down at Jamie and then glanced up at Katie with a look that said 'leave'. Only once she had closed the door did Pete sit down and return his gaze to Jamie.

'This is your story. You sure you want to run with it?'

Jamie nodded. 'Absolutely.'

'Good. 'Cos if you'd said no, I'd have fired you.'

'Thanks.'

'Look Jamie, your piece kicked off a shitstorm yesterday and I'll be fucked if I'm gonna let another paper steal it off us, right?'

'I know.'

'Besides,' Pete continued, 'this could be bloody good for you.'

'I know that too,' said Jamie.

'So, what's your gut telling you?'

Jamie forced a smile. 'To be bloody careful.'

'Your reporters gut.'

'That is my reporter's gut,' said Jamie thoughtfully as he settled back in his chair.

'Have you got enough to get something else out today?'

Jamie shook his head. 'I don't think so.'

'That was another rhetorical question.'

'Oh, right. Well as I said, this Evans character is no mug. He knew exactly what he was doing this morning and he knows that I can't prove it actually happened.'

'Just go back and get some quotes from the locals, that'd give you enough for a follow-up'

'They wouldn't talk, and they certainly wouldn't want to be named,' said Jamie with a shake of his head. 'On top of that

I'm betting he'd know about it almost immediately so that'd kill any chance of him talking to me again.'

'Which begs the question, why the performance this morning?'

'I dunno,' said Jamie with a shrug of his shoulders. 'He as much as told me to investigate him so he obviously wanted me to find out what kind of person he is.'

'Intimidation?'

'Scare me off you mean? No, I don't think it's that.' Jamie thought for a moment and then looked at Pete. 'What if he's testing me?'

'For what?'

'He said some things at the end,' continued Jamie thoughtfully. 'He said think about the bigger picture and talked about bringing back a sense of community. And he always said we, never I.'

'So, he's another football hooligan with a crazy political agenda. That's tabloid fodder,' said Pete dismissively.

'No, it's more than that. I think he's trying to find out if he can trust me.'

'Why would he want to trust you?'

'Because there's a bigger story and he needs someone to tell it for him.'

'OK,' replied Pete after taking a few moments to mull over the idea, 'you've got 24 hours to convince me. In the meantime, work with Katie and get me something for tomorrow. I don't care what, just make sure we keep this momentum going. Didn't he tell you that there'd be two more attacks tonight?'

'Yep.'

'Then make sure the overnights are keeping a watch and the second anything pops up, get on it OK?'

Jamie nodded.

'Good, now sod off. Publicity were looking for you earlier which probably means you've got media stuff to do. It's all about the paper, remember that.'

'Yes boss,' said Jamie as he got to his feet.

'And Jamie, be careful OK. No stupid risks.'

The two men stared at each other for a few moments and then without another word, Jamie pulled open the door and headed for his desk.

Chapter Twenty
Wednesday 4th July 2019

12.45

Billy pulled into his customary parking spot at the far end of the car park and turned off his engine.

Although slightly late, his first action was to check Jamie Brown's social media accounts for any mention of the morning events. Once he'd done that and found nothing, he pushed open the door and moved to climb out. However, before his foot touched the ground his phone rang, and a familiar voice came over the speaker.

'Mr. Evans.'

'Paul,' Billy replied. 'I've just parked.'

'I know, I can see you. Could you follow us please?'

The phone clicked dead and Billy glanced around until he spotted the now familiar Mercedes moving slowly toward the car park exit. 'All this cloak and dagger bollocks is starting to get on my tits,' he muttered to himself as he started his car and slowly headed through the rows of parked cars toward it.

By the time he arrived at the exit the Mercedes had come to a halt forcing Billy to pull up behind it as it sat silently purring away. He waited patiently for a few moments until he suddenly became aware that a man was standing by his passenger door. Billy stared at him for a moment, not because he was concerned but because he was genuinely stunned. 'Holy fuck,' he thought as he reached down and unlocked the door allowing the man to slide in beside him. 'Holy fucking fuck!'

'If we could er…,' said the man with an accent that immediately marked him out as a cut above pretty much everyone Billy had ever met, '…follow.'

Billy nodded and followed the Mercedes out into the traffic.

'I'm delighted to finally meet you Mr. Evans,' said the man. 'Or may I call you Billy?'

Billy stole another glance across his car as he struggled to calm himself. In all the scenario's he'd played out in his head over the last couple of days, nothing like this had featured and so he needed to refocus, and quickly. 'Billy's fine,' he replied after a few moments. 'And what should I call you? Sir? Or the right honourable gentleman?'

The man smiled. As much to himself as anything. 'I'm sorry to disappoint you but I'm not who you think I am.'

'Really,' scoffed Billy sarcastically. 'So, who are you then? An Ian Foster lookalike?'

'Yes actually,' said the man. 'Although technically, I'm the older one so he's the lookalike. I'm Major Christopher Foster, Royal Military Police. Ian Foster MP is my twin brother.'

Billy drove in silence for a few moments as he tried to compute the information he'd just been given. It would be easy to confirm of course, but only once he'd stopped and logged on to the internet. However, there was one question which had appeared in his thought process almost immediately and it was one which begged to be asked. Primarily because it could impact on pretty much everything, not least the idea Billy had been fermenting for the last 24 hours.

'So,' said Billy as confidently as he could. 'Does brother Ian know that you've got people running around battering members of the public?'

Foster settled back in his chair but even without looking at him, Billy could sense that his passengers mind was working at full pelt.

'We'll discuss that once we get to where we're going,' he replied. 'In the meantime, why don't we talk about you?'

Billy looked across at Foster and smiled. 'Talk to a copper without a brief?' he said. 'Fuck that.'

Foster laughed. A genuine, hearty laugh. 'I knew I was going to like you,' he said. 'I think we're going to get along just fine.'

Having spent much of his life skirting with the concept of right and wrong, very little shocked Billy Evans. However, it was fair to say that having listened to Christopher Foster talking for almost half an hour straight, Billy was genuinely taken aback. 'You're not serious?' was all he could come up with.

'Deadly,' replied Foster calmly. 'Thanks to this journalist we have an opportunity to take this onto the next level and we'd be foolish to let it pass. But we can only do it with your help, so the question is, are you with us?'

'Us?' asked Billy curtly. 'I thought it was already us.'

Foster smiled. 'Sorry, bad choice of words. You don't need me to tell you how important you are to this whole operation.'

'I don't. I don't need smoke blown up my arse either.'

'Of course,' said Foster. 'My apologies.'

Billy took a deep breath, leant back in his chair and looked at the ceiling of the hotel room they'd taken residence in. In truth, whilst he was attempting to look both cool and thoughtful, he was actually trying to contain his excitement. For what Foster had proposed went way beyond anything he had even considered. But was it too far? That was the question that suddenly begun to tug at Billy's gut. And had the brief exchange about 'us' been a flash of Foster's true ambitions slipping? Maybe, maybe not. But it had certainly reinforced one thing to Billy and that was that whatever Foster had ultimately planned, he was an outsider and as such, was only being given the bare minimum of information. As a consequence, whatever he decided to do it was absolutely vital that he protect himself at all costs.

'Let me get this straight,' he said, leaning forward to look Foster in the eye. 'You genuinely think this government are going to screw over 17.4 million people and try to keep us in the EU?'

'I've no doubt about it,' said Foster. 'And that will cause a backlash in this country which will cause a huge swing toward the right.'

'You mean the far-right?' asked Billy.

'I mean the right,' repeated Foster softly.

'Funny, this reminds me of something my grandad used to talk about,' said Billy sarcastically. 'Germany, 1930's, bloke with a tash.'

Foster laughed. 'We're not the bloody Nazi Party Mr. Evans. We just want a return to old values. Right and wrong, respect for the elderly and our armed forces and good old-fashioned patriotism. What's wrong with that?'

'I refer the gentleman to the answer I gave a moment ago,' replied Billy sarcastically. 'And where do the law fit into all this?'

'You'll have to trust me when I ask that you let us worry about that,' said Foster.

Billy scoffed. 'Once a copper, always a copper eh?'

The room fell into an uncomfortable silence but whilst Foster was clearly trying to work out a way to handle a situation that was seemingly drifting away from him, Billy was doing the exact opposite. He'd decided almost immediately that whatever was unfolding, he wanted a part of it. Not because of the politics, he had no real interest in that, but because he could sense that something big was on offer. All he had to do was work out how best to play Foster to maximise his slice of whatever it turned out to be.

It was Foster who blinked first. 'Look,' he began, 'nothing's going to happen overnight but believe me it's going to happen. When it does, things will move fast so we need to be ready.'

'So, what do you want me to do?' asked Billy. 'Other than put myself into the frame obviously.'

Foster slid a copy of Jamie's article into the middle of the table. 'Talk to your lads, they trust you and they'll have seen the reaction to this just as we all have. People are on our side, let's take the next step.'

Billy looked at him, his face expressionless but his brain almost fizzing with thoughts and possibilities. 'OK,' he said after a few moments. 'I'll ask them. But I've got three conditions. First, if any decide to duck out, there'll be no consequences. Agreed?'

'Agreed,' said Foster.

'Second,' continued Billy, 'if I decide to walk, it'll be game over and I'll shut my stuff down within an hour. Don't think I'll be handing any names over either.'

'Understood,' said Foster. 'And the final thing?'

Billy smiled and then brought himself into a proper upright seated position. 'If I do stick around, I call the shots when it comes to my lot. No one else, just me. That's non-negotiable.'

'Everything's negotiable surely?' said Foster.

'Not this. They'd never trust you anyway. You're Old Bill, remember.'

Foster smiled and nodded. 'OK,' he said as he got to his feet and held out his hand. 'Whatever you say.'

Billy remained sitting for a few moments before he stood and took Foster' hand. 'Then I'll ask them' he said. 'And we'll see what they've got to say.'

Having left Foster and the others in the hotel, Billy headed for his garage in thoughtful mood.

The truth was that he had absolutely no intention of talking to anyone about what had unfolded that morning, least of all the lads who were effectively working for him. To ask their advice about something that Billy was pretty sure was nothing more than borderline fascist fantasy would do nothing but increase the chances of someone blabbing and him ending up inside.

Equally, there was only really one opinion Billy really valued and that was his own. If, and it was a huge if, something did begin to happen along the lines Foster had outlined, he would be the one calling the shots and he'd only act if he was totally convinced it was the right thing to do. At that point, he'd have a proper conversation with his lads but even as he considered this, Billy couldn't imagine a point where he'd have to do it.

He was however, more than satisfied with the outcome of the meeting. Not just because he had new information and had been able to lay down his marker in terms of what he would and wouldn't accept, but because he had discovered who was pulling the strings. Foster might not be an MP, but his brother was and that would certainly give him some leverage if push somehow came to shove. The only problem would be proving it.

Billy was still considering how he might do that when he suddenly realised that he was rapidly approaching an all too familiar location and just as he always did when he reached that point on the A12, he moved into the right hand lane and much to the annoyance of the drivers behind him, began to slow to a steady 30 mph.

Irrational it might be, but even after all these years Billy refused to drive over the spot in the road where he had held Sam's hand as she'd died. If that pissed off a few motorists who happened to be behind him as he drove slowly past it, he didn't give a fuck.

Normally, once past the point Billy would immediately indicate and pull over to the left where, depending on how he was feeling, he would either acknowledge or simply ignore the audible or even visual protests of the drivers overtaking him. Not once had he ever responded with anything other than a nod and an apologetic wave and in truth, had never felt the need or desire to. His thoughts, understandably, were always elsewhere.

On this occasion however, Billy had just started to move into the left-hand lane when a blue van appeared on his inside. The middle-aged drivers' face twisted with hate as he screamed what was fairly obviously a string of obscenities in his direction before accelerating forward.

Billy shook his head and tucked in behind him but even as he straightened his steering, the driver slammed on his brakes forcing Billy to do likewise. 'Twat,' he barked angrily.

For a fleeting moment he considered chasing the driver down and giving him a kicking but even as he was weighing up the pro's and con's, another thought jumped into his head. He leant forward, reached up behind his rear-view mirror and pulled down the discreet dash cam that he'd had installed before he'd taken delivery of the car only a few months previous.

'Well, fuck me,' he said out loud as he cradled it in his palm. 'I forgot all about you.'

Billy hurried up the stairs and strode purposefully toward his office. Within a few moments, he'd turned on his laptop and was busily connecting the camera.

'Have you had an accident?'

Billy looked up to see Lauren, his secretary, standing in the doorway. A cup of coffee in one hand and a stack of notes in the other. 'No, nothing like that. I was just hoping I'd recorded something that's all.'

He finally connected the camera and within seconds, a page full of files had opened up.

'So, did you?' she asked.

'It better, or it's going out the fucking window.'

Lauren watched Billy as he stared at the screen watching God knows what. Having worked for him for over six years she was well versed in his ways and as a consequence was well aware that there were some things he got up to that were best ignored. 'I didn't expect to see you today,' she said as she placed the cup and the various papers on his desk. 'It's gone three.'

'Sorry,' he replied without looking up from his laptop. 'I should have called. Everything ok?'

'Nothing drastic. Just...'

'Bollocks!' barked Billy. 'Shit, wank and bollocks. £200 that cost me and there's no bastard sound.'

'You want me to open the window?' asked Lauren sarcastically, ignoring the colourful language.

'Sorry,' said Billy, blushing slightly, 'I was hoping I'd recorded something but there's no sound.'

'Why not?'

'I don't bloody know.'

Lauren picked up the camera and stared first at it and then at Billy. 'You know you've got your headphones plugged in,' she said.

Billy looked down and noticed the lead poking out from the side of his computer. 'Shit,' he mumbled. 'Thanks.'

'Any time,' she said before turning and heading for her desk whilst Billy retrieved the camera, plugged it back in and stuffed his earpiece in.

'Technically, I'm the older one so he's the lookalike. I'm Major Christopher Foster, Royal Military Police. Ian Foster MP is my twin brother.'

Billy hit stop and smiled to himself as he remembered Jamie Brown and how it had been his dash cam that had kicked off this whole series of events.

Irony didn't come close.

20.10

Jamie kicked his front door closed and stared down at the small pile of envelopes and junk mail on the mat. As evidence that Lisa not only wasn't home but hadn't been home, it was pretty damning.

'Bollocks,' he muttered before walking through to the kitchen where he grabbed two beers from the fridge and then headed for the relative sanctuary of his sofa.

After downing the first beer, Jamie pulled his phone from his pocket and dialled Lisa's number only to be met, as he had been on every one of the numerous times he tried to speak to her that day, by the answering service. 'Hi, it's me yet again,' he said. 'Just letting you know I'm home. I really need to speak to you. Please call soon as you can.'

He held on to the phone for a moment, unsure if he should say anything else but then with a sigh, ended the call, dropped the phone on the sofa beside him and cracked open the second beer. Considering the day he'd had, the consumption of alcohol seemed a far more sensible use of his time than trying to work out how to appease a stroppy female. After all, this wasn't exactly the first time she'd stormed out and whilst Jamie understood the immense pressures of her job, he had learned long ago that one of her coping mechanisms was to have the odd emotional collapse and clear her emotional cache.

Normally, that was fine, and he'd be there to bear the brunt, clean up the inevitable mess and enjoy the post-melt down spoils. This time however, things were different for the crisis wasn't hers, it was his and she was nowhere to be seen.

Jamie took a swig from his second bottle and forced his attention away from Lisa and onto the subject of Billy Evans. He still couldn't quite get his head around the fact that someone he hadn't even known existed barely 14 hours ago had been able to make such a huge impact on his life. Yet here he was, embroiled in an unfolding drama he had no control over because his destiny was firmly in the hands of a crooked car dealer from Essex.

To make matters worse, the article he'd been forced to cobble together for tomorrows paper wasn't exactly Pulitzer prize quality journalism. Instead, devoid of anything relating to Billy Evans, it was merely a rehash of the original article, albeit with a bit more detail added in for substance. Still, if it kept Pete and the lawyers happy, he could hardly complain, especially with the issue gaining traction in other papers. Of course, the real hope was that it had passed whatever test Evans had set for him and that he'd be encouraged to make contact again. Then he might start to formulate some idea as to what this was all about.

If it hadn't, then Jamie would have no choice but to hit the streets and go after Evans personally. A not exactly enticing prospect given everything he'd learned about him already. Then again, since he was pinning much of his hope on the possibility of two people being put in hospital over the next 12 hours or so, he could hardly complain.

'Jesus,' he thought to himself, 'that could be happening right now!'

Jamie took another swig from his bottle and let his head fall back against the sofa but then the thought struck him that maybe he was coming at this from the wrong angle. Rather than wondering what might happen shouldn't he be focussing on what already had? More specifically, how had this whole thing begun and more importantly, where did Evans fit in? Judging by everything he'd read that day he certainly had form and was clearly not lacking in either confidence or arrogance so was Billy Evans actually the story he should be focussing on?

But why the cloak and dagger stuff this morning? There was no sensible reason why anyone involved in criminal activity would knowingly introduce themselves to a journalist unless they had a very specific reason. Yet try as he might, Jamie couldn't come up with a single scenario where that made sense other than the notion that he was being played in an effort to keep him silent for a while. Either that, or he was going to be exploited in an effort to unfold a bigger picture at some point although what that might be, eluded him.

One thing Jamie was certain of however, was that he was absolutely knackered and after sending Lisa a goodnight text and draining what was left in his bottle, he lay down on the sofa. Within a few moments he was fast asleep.

At the same time as Jamie Brown was drifting into unconsciousness, Billy was enduring the closing stages of yet another episode of *Game of Thrones*.

He looked down at Claire who was lying with her head in his lap and sighed. 'What did I ever do to you?'

'Shut the fuck up,' she replied without moving her eyes from the screen.

'Utter crap,' he grunted.

Claire moved her hand up to between Billy's legs and he felt a finger poke his balls. 'If you don't shut up, I swear to God these are going to get it.'

'That's not very nice.'

Claire pulled her hand away from his crotch, grabbed Billy's phone from the coffee table and handed it to him. 'Here. Text, read, play. I don't care, just shut up!'

Billy thought about sliding his hand inside Claire's dressing gown, but he dismissed the idea. Primarily because experience had taught him that for some reason he had never been able to fathom, her obsession with watching *Game of Thrones* seemed to be accompanied by a massive sense of humour failure.

He unlocked his phone and sifted through the various emails and texts that had been waiting for his attention but there was nothing much of interest. The texts he was waiting for wouldn't come for at least another hour and even then, they'd be on his other phone which was on charge in the kitchen.

Billy closed his email app and typed his own name into Google but nothing new appeared and so he entered 'Jamie Brown' into the search box. Other than a couple of mentions of the journalist in other news articles relating to the attacks, it was the same stuff he'd seen earlier and most of those were little more than fabricated bullshit. Billy clicked on the images tab to reveal a variety of images of the man he'd met only that morning appeared and smiled to himself. It had been a while since he'd fronted someone up like that and it had been a nice buzz. In truth, the whole day had.

'There,' came a voice from his lap. 'Now you can speak.'

Billy looked down at Claire who was now staring up at him. 'You do know that when the football season starts, I'm going to make you watch every game,' he said. 'That'll be my revenge.'

'Big deal,' she replied. 'I'm a nurse, I can fall asleep at will.'

Billy smiled down at her then stroked her cheek lovingly. 'Tea?'

'Always.'

Claire sat up and Billy headed for the kitchen. He was retrieving the milk from the fridge when he looked up to find her standing in the doorway watching him.

'One of the girls at work was telling me about something she'd seen on telly this morning.'

'Oh yeah?' replied Billy as he poured boiling water into two cups. 'What was that?'

'They were talking about vigilantes.'

'Yeah, I heard about it,' Billy replied as he handed her a cup.

Claire stared back at him and then calmly took a sip of tea. 'Anything to worry about?'

Billy looked back at her and smiled. 'Nothing at all sweetheart. It's under control.'

'Good,' she replied with a knowing smile. 'Now why don't we take these up to bed?'

Chapter Twenty Two
Thursday 5th July 2019

06.20

Jamie Brown woke with a start and grabbed his mobile phone which seemed to be ringing even more persistently than normally.

'What?' he grunted before listening, eyes closed, to a voice on the other end which rattled off a series of words which Jamie could only barely form into a coherent thought. 'Hold on,' he said, 'Who called me? When?' Forcing open his eyes to look at the clock and silently cursed that it was so early. 'OK, stop! Can I call you back? Ten minutes, yes I promise.'

With the phone call done, Jamie dropped the handset onto the sofa and sat up as he tried to work out if it was the hunger, the grubbiness or the stiff neck which was worse. A task he was still struggling with when he heard a key being inserted into the front door.

'Shit,' he hissed to himself as he grabbed the empty bottles and headed for the kitchen, dumping the empties into the recycling as quietly as he could.

'Hiding the evidence?'

Jamie turned to find Lisa standing in the doorway. 'Christ, you look like shit,' she continued.

'I had a tough day,' he replied as he stared at the woman he'd spent most of the previous day trying to talk to. Normally, he could read her like a book but this time there was something about her that was different. 'So, are you home or passing through?'

'That depends. We need to talk.'

'OK,' he said calmly, 'but it'll have to be later. Duty calls. Sorry.'

Lisa nodded thoughtfully in response and satisfied that she was sufficiently happy with his reply, Jamie headed for the bathroom.

By the time he had showered, shaved and dressed, Lisa had made him a bacon sandwich and filled his travel mug with coffee.

'I can drive you if you want,' she said.

'No thanks,' he said as he took a bite of the sandwich. 'The tube'll do.'

'OK, if you're sure.' She hesitated for a few moments and then added, 'I'm off tonight.'

Jamie looked at her, slightly puzzled. They'd had plenty of arguments over the years and she'd stormed out more than once, but she'd never behaved like this before when she'd come back. The usual tactic was to act as if nothing had happened, this was almost unnerving. 'OK, I'll try and be home by seven,' he said. 'Maybe we can do something.'

'Yes, talk. Now go, I'll see you later.'

Jamie forced a smile and headed for the front door. By the time he was at the end of the path, he was on the phone to his office.

'Yes, I know I said 10 minutes, but something came up. Now start again.'

At the exact moment that Jamie Brown was heading for the tube, Billy was in ebullient mood. Having seen Claire off to work, he had checked his phone to discover that the two visits arranged for the previous night had both gone entirely to plan with the result that two more vermin had been taken off the streets.

He had then searched the news sites to discover that Jamie Brown had published a fresh expose on the subject of vigilantes. Headlined 'The Toxic World of Britain's underbelly'. First sight of it had driven Billy's heart into his mouth but once he'd realised that it didn't contain a single reference to the events of yesterday, he'd relaxed and read it properly.

Light on detail, it was understandably better than most of the crap being pumped out by those rival papers who had jumped on the bandwagon but that wasn't saying much. What did interest Billy, however, were various mentions of attacks that he knew nothing about and which he could only assume had been carried out by the Army lads. Initially, that had irked him slightly as it highlighted the fact that things were going on outside his control. Still, Brown wasn't to know that and if, as seemed likely, he had shied away from mentioning him because he'd understood what yesterday was all about, then that meant that they could start thinking about the next phase of the plan Foster had outlined. Billy was actually looking forward to that.

He fired off a message to his lads to let know that he'd seen the article and that they had nothing to worry about and then after noticing that the time was rapidly approaching 8.30, headed for the shower.

There was work to do.

'Did she say anything else? asked Pete Goodwin as he stared at the sheet of paper in his hand.

'Nothing, just that,' replied Jamie.

'And she's adamant that her husband isn't responsible?'

'Absolutely.'

'OK, so who else knows about this?'

'No idea. I've no way of knowing if she called anyone else.'

'So, what the fuck are you sitting here for? This is the first actual bloody name you can link to this story and you're sitting here scratching your arse!'

The two men eyeballed each other for a moment before Jamie jumped to his feet and without another word headed for his desk only to find Katie waiting for him.

'He looks pissed off,' she said, her eyes fixed on the editor's office.

'He is,' sighed Jamie as he began gathering his things together.

'So, what's going on?'

'A woman called the paper last night trying to get hold of me. Seems that her husband is being threatened by a local gang.'

Katie frowned. 'So?'

'One of the gang leaders was put in hospital by masked intruders three weeks ago.'

'Ah, gotcha. And they think he was responsible.'

'Apparently.'

'So, was he?'

'That's what I'm hoping to find out this morning, but I spoke to her earlier and, well she just seemed, normal.'

'D'you need some company? Female touch and all that.'

'Jamie looked at her and smiled. 'No, I'll be fine. Can you keep digging into Evans for me? I think he's going to turn out to be our best angle of attack, but I need something concrete to run with.'

'Consider it done,' Katie replied as she handed him a sheet of paper. 'Oh, and this just came through. A 22-year-old male was seriously assaulted in Lincoln last night. Five men, injuries consistent with the others.'

Jamie glanced at the paper and smiled. 'You bloody legend!' he gasped. 'I owe you one. Now I gotta go before Pete has a stroke.'

'Where are you going anyway?' she asked.

Essex,' he replied as he threw his rucksack over his shoulder. 'Where else?'

An hour later, Jamie was sitting in the living room of a neat, well-kept three bedroomed house in the outskirts of Brentwood. In front of him a young woman, probably no more than 30, sat nervously twisting her fingers as she spoke. To say she looked stressed was an understatement. At times, she looked plain scared.

'So, Mrs. Sanford, can I just go over the details,' said Jamie calmly.

'It's Alison,' she said nervously.

Jamie smiled reassuringly at her. 'Alison, OK, so can I make sure that I have it right?'

Alison nodded and Jamie began reading from his notes.

'Your daughter Carrie was knocked over in May last year and suffered from a broken leg and fractured arm. The car didn't stop but was identified by various people as being owned by this Darren Carter who was arrested. Police charged him with various offences, but he denied being the driver and the case was eventually dropped.'

'After witnesses were threatened,' said Alison abruptly. 'But it was him, definitely.'

'Darren Carter is involved with this gang, G12. Yes? And your husband threatened him.'

Alison nodded again. 'Andy, yes. Outside the police station. But he was angry, he's not really like that, honestly.'

'But he was in the Army?'

'Yes, but he was medically discharged. He was injured in Afghanistan. He lost a leg.'

Jamie looked up in surprise. 'I'm sorry,' he said as he added that detail to his notes. 'So, he's at work now, yes?'

'He's a shift manager at one of the supermarkets in the town.'

'And he knows I'm here?'

Alison looked nervously at the floor. 'No. But I saw you on the TV and I didn't know who else to talk to. The police are…'

'OK, don't worry we'll come to that,' said Jamie calmly. 'Now, let's get back to this. Three weeks ago, Carter was attacked by four men who beat him with baseball bats. Yes?'

'No,' she replied. 'It was five. There were five men. The police told me.'

Jamie smiled knowingly. 'Good,' he said, 'five men. And he's claiming that your husband was involved so this gang have sworn revenge.'

'Yes,' said Alison as she stared at the floor. The desperation in her voice almost heartbreaking.

'And was he? Involved I mean.'

Alison looked up from the floor and stared at Jamie. 'No,' she said flatly. 'I told you, he's not violent.'

Jamie took a deep breath and pondered for a few moments. 'Tell me about this gang?

'Everyone around here knows about them. Drugs, burglary, stabbings, you name it. They're animals, all of them.'

'So, you think they're serious about Andy?'

'Oh, they're serious,' she said. 'I woke up the other morning and there was a knife stuck in the front door. We've had the tyres on our car slashed twice and they're always hanging around whenever either of us leaves the house. You know, like they're watching us.'

Jamie stared back at her for a few seconds and sighed. 'Sounds like a nightmare. So, what about this Carter? Has he been seen around here?'

'Hardly. They smashed his legs to bits. The police told me he'll probably be in a wheelchair for the rest of his life. That's why they're dead set on getting Andy. They've got to be seen to save face. It's pathetic.'

'What have the police said?'

'Aside from move?' scoffed Alison. 'They've installed a panic button and said that they'll keep an eye on us, but that's it.'

Jamie snapped his notebook closed. 'What do you think I can do?'

'I don't know,' she replied softly. 'I just thought... I don't know what I thought. I just hoped, you know, that you might be able to help us somehow. We don't have anyone else.'

'All I can do is tell your story. But if I do that, I'm going to have to name you and I can only do that with your permission. I'd need Andy's too. Would he agree to that? I mean, it might make things worse, you do know that?'

Alison took a deep breath and stared into space, deep in thought.

'I think he will, but I'll have to ask him.'

Jamie smiled in agreement and handed her a business card. 'There's no pressure,' he said. 'I totally understand your situation, just call me when you decide OK?'

Having said his goodbyes, Jamie walked to the end of the street and turned back to survey the scene. On a whim, he took out his phone and took a picture.

'Poor bastards,' he thought. 'What a fucking nightmare.'

For a moment, he considered speaking to some of the neighbours but mindful of the fact that Alison might decide not to go into print, decided against it. However, as he stood and wondered about his next move, a thought entered his head and after considering it for a few moments, Jamie took out his phone and searched Google for a number. When he found it, he hesitated for a moment and then dialled.

Billy had just finished talking to a customer on the phone when his intercom buzzed.

'Yes Lauren,' he said.

'There's a call for you. Someone called Jamie. He said you met him yesterday.'

For a brief moment, Billy was taken aback but then he smiled to himself. 'Let the games begin,' he muttered.

'Pardon?' asked Lauren. 'Shall I put him through or tell him you're not available?'

'Tell him I'm on a call and get him to leave a number,' replied Billy slowly. 'I'll call him in a few minutes.'

'Will do.'

Jamie ended the call and cursed to himself. He couldn't help but think that he'd just made a massive mistake. Not least because by knocking him back, Evans had brought himself some time to get his head together for when he called back. That's assuming he was actually going to talk to him at all.

However, even as that thought was rattling around in his head, his phone rang although it wasn't Billy, but Katie.

'Hey,' he said. 'Just to let you know, I might have to cut you off, I'm waiting for a call.'

'No worries,' she said. 'I've just spoken to one of the policemen who investigated Evans. He's happy to talk to you whenever you like. Seemed quite keen actually.'

'Brilliant,' replied Jamie. 'Can you text me his number and I'll... Shit. Gotta go.'

He glanced at his phone to see 'number unknown' on the screen so cancelled the call from Katie and answered.

'Jamie Brown speaking.'

'Mr. Brown,' came a familiar voice, albeit one which was speaking in a more deliberate and considered manner. 'My name's Evans, I'm returning your call.'

'Thank you,' said Jamie as calmly as he could. 'I have a question for you, if you don't mind.'

'Why would I mind? I don't even know who you are.'

Jamie smiled to himself. He knew exactly what was running through Billy's head and why. 'I give you my word that I'm not recording this if that's what you're wondering,' he said.

'I wasn't wondering anything,' came the considered reply. 'Although I'm not really sure why you'd want to record me anyway?'

'OK,' said Jamie. 'I get it.'

'Er, OK. So, what do you think I can do for you?'

Jamie paused for a moment. He had to think quickly if he was going to have any chance of pulling this off. 'I have something to tell you,' he began, 'and it would be useful if you could just let me speak. Would that be OK?'

'Go ahead.'

'Darren Carter, he's a gang leader from Brentwood. He suffered some er... injuries recently. He claims to know who was responsible and his gang are threatening to take revenge on the family he's blaming. But he's wrong, and the family are in serious danger. Their name's Sanford, they have a young child. I just thought you might want to know.'

Jamie paused for a moment and then without another word, ended the call.

'Fuck,' he thought to himself. 'I've either helped them or I just made things a whole lot worse.'

The moment the phone clicked dead to signal the end of the call, Billy switched off the recorder and listened to the conversation again. The thought that he now had some potentially compromising dirt on Jamie Brown barely registered because what really interested him was the fact that he had absolutely no idea who Darren Carter was.

One thing was certain however, he was going to find out.

After speaking to Billy Evans, Jamie called Katie although given the circumstances, he thought it prudent to keep details of his conversation with Billy Evans to himself. He did, however, learn that a second attack had seemingly taken place the previous night, this time in Sutton Coldfield. Since Katie was already looking into both in the hope of obtaining some pertinent information, he asked her to carry on and then called the number she'd texted him earlier. It was answered within three rings.

'Mr Roberts?' he said. 'My name's Brown. You spoke to my colleague earlier, about a Billy Evans.'

'I did,' said the voice with a hint of excitement in his voice that Jamie couldn't help but notice. 'What do you want to know?'

14.30

Having spent some time thinking about how best to handle the information Jamie Brown had given him, Billy was in cautious mood.

Whilst his first instinct had been to call Foster and give him both barrels because someone from his side had fucked up, he quickly began to consider other options. Not least the fact that he had potentially been handed an opportunity to seize even more control over who did what as well as where and when they did it. But then another thought had struck him, and his gut was telling him that he needed to take this one very seriously.

For whilst a brief search of the internet had revealed some information relating to a Darren Carter from Brentwood, most notably in relation to a hit and run accident on a young girl, Billy had no knowledge of any attack in the town nor was there anything about one on the web. Whilst it wasn't beyond the realms of possibility that it was legit, there was also the chance that Brown was trying to set him up somehow.

Yet, despite the risk, Billy could not discount Brown's assertion that a family were potentially in danger and he knew, not even deep down, that if the journalist were telling the truth and he didn't try to stop it, he would never be able to forgive himself if anything happened to them. The question that left him was how best to handle things without weakening his own position.

With that thought uppermost in his mind, Billy called Paul and demanded to speak to Foster on a matter of the utmost urgency. That brought him some time to think although he had no idea how much. As it turned out, it was but a few minutes.

'Mr. Foster,' Billy said calmly. 'We have a situation.

'Who told you this?' asked Foster after Billy had given him the bare bones of the situation.

'You forget that Essex is my manor. I've got eyes and ears everywhere. Speaking of which, I don't appreciate things happening in my back yard that I don't know about. Especially when they ain't being done properly.'

'We agreed from the outset not to share information about our activities.'

'Yeah, well things have changed haven't they,' said Billy curtly. 'So maybe we need to revisit that.'

There was a silence and Billy smiled to himself as he thought of Foster churning over what was a barely disguised power grab.

'That's a fair point,' replied Foster eventually. 'But first things first, we need to address the matter in hand.'

'Yeah, we do, because your lot have fucked up. Why aren't they keeping an eye on their targets?'

'I don't know,' replied Foster. 'But I'll find out. In the meantime, we need to warn this Carter character off.'

'Leave it to me,' said Billy confidently. 'I can get it sorted tonight. He won't be any more trouble after that.'

'No, this was our mistake,' barked Foster. 'We'll take care of it.'

'You better, and fast,' said Billy. 'Or this could get very nasty very quickly.'

'I'll be in touch.'

The line went dead and Billy almost laughed out loud as he leant back in his chair. God only knows what the man on the other end of the line was thinking, but from his perspective that couldn't have gone any better if he'd have scripted it himself. Not only had he hopefully dealt with the Carter situation, he'd given Foster a verbal slap down and proved that his was obviously the more effective operation of the two. That could only bode well for when the time came to make his next move, and that time was fast approaching.

It hadn't taken long for Jamie to work out that Gary Roberts still harboured a massive grudge against Billy Evans. Indeed, at times it felt like the former police sergeant could barely contain his excitement at the idea that his nemesis was finally being investigated by someone. So much so that Jamie had begun to wonder if some of the tales were being embellished for his sake.

Now, having returned to the office and spent over two hours checking through everything, that thought continued to linger. Primarily because so little of the information Roberts had given him could actually be confirmed. Mostly, it was nothing more than rumour and suspicion and whilst Jamie was in no doubt that Billy Evans was certainly on the wrong side of the law, he couldn't help but wonder why, if even half of what he'd been told were true, had the police never been able to prove any of it? It's not as if they hadn't been motivated, that was clear from the way Roberts had been talking.

Yet as Jamie had seen at first hand, Evans was clearly no fool and he'd certainly given the impression that he had the confidence and arrogance to pull some of the stunts that Roberts had told him about. Was it really beyond the realms of possibility that he'd been able to run rings around the police? The answer, fairly obviously, was no. So, what chance did he have?

'Fuck!' he groaned out loud as he fell back in his chair and turned his gaze to the ceiling. 'Fuck, fuck, fuck.'

'Going well I see?'

Jamie turned his eyes to Katie and shook his head. 'I'm beginning to long for the days when I was covering Big Brother,' he groaned.

'Well,' she said, perching herself on the edge of his desk. 'I have good news and I have bad news.'

'Bad news first. Gives me something to look forward to.'

Katie smiled. 'OK, I checked out these names you gave me. Jarvis, the copper who led the National Football Intelligence Unit who first investigated your man, he's retired and lives in Somerset. I'm trying to get a number for him, the copper jailed in Italy for murder…'

'Porter.'

'Yep, he was released in 2011 and moved to Spain, no idea where. Ian Mirren who ran the security company that covered West Ham before Evans took over, he died of a stroke four years ago.'

'Great,' sighed Jamie. 'So, what's the good news.'

'Well, I called my contact who used to cover West Ham and he put me onto a guy called David Knight. He used to be the club's security officer. I had a quick chat with him, and he said that whatever you're hearing about Evans, if it's criminal, it's probably true.'

'That's no help.'

'Maybe not, but he did confirm what your policeman told you about Evans being a top ten target of the old National Football Intelligence Unit and that he was once the leader of the hooligan element at West Ham. He also told me more about how Evans took over the security at Upton Park, that used to be West Ham's ground in case you didn't know.'

'Cheeky bitch,' laughed Jamie.

'Just checking,' said Katie with a grin. 'Anyway, it was apparently quite a nasty business. Mirren, the guy who owned the original company, he sold up after being threatened.'

'That could be useful. Anything else?'

Katie glanced at her notes. 'Yes, did your policeman mention someone called Graham Hawkins?'

'No,' replied Jamie. 'Who's he?'

'He was apparently Evans right hand man back when they were hooligans and he was involved with a company called St. George Security which was owned by Evans. They specialised in security for the car trade.'

'That was the security company at West Ham.'

'Yep.'

'What's this Hawkins character doing now? Could he be involved in all this?' asked Jamie, his interested piqued.

'I don't know. I've not checked him out yet. I only just got off the phone.'

Jamie fell forward and typed 'Graham Hawkins' into his search engine as Katie pulled up a chair and sat down beside him. Aside from a stream of links to obviously unrelated social media profiles there was nothing obvious on Jamie's screen and so he clicked on the news tab to see if that would give him anything.

'Shit,' he groaned when nothing obvious appeared. 'We don't even know what we're looking for.'

Katie leant across and took the keyboard. 'Then broaden the search,' she said as she typed 'Graham Hawkins West

Ham' into the search box and hit enter to refresh the page and bring up a fresh set of results.

Jamie leant closer to the screen and pointed his mouse at the third link on the screen.

> *Police are investigating after a Chadwell Heath man died of stab wounds in the early hours of Wednesday morning. Graham Hawkins, (51) was attacked when he confronted an alleged burglar at his property and died in Queens Hospital of his injuries.*
>
> *Essex police have appealed for witnesses but confirmed that a male is in custody. However, they refused to comment further saying that enquiries are ongoing.*

The two of them read the entry in silence before turning to each other. 'August last year,' sighed Katie. 'If that's him, then it's a dead end. No pun intended.'

'That's him,' Jamie muttered as he slid the keyboard back from Katie and began typing. 'I'd bet money on it.' He paused for a moment and then smiled. 'There you go. August 4, 2000. I knew it.'

> *The Evening Standard can exclusively reveal that the general manager of the company responsible for match day security at West Ham United has a history of involvement in football hooliganism.*
>
> *Graham Hawkins (33) of Chadwell Heath, Essex, who took over the post with Mirren Events Limited in June, was one of a number of fans held and subsequently deported from Italy last year following the fatal stabbing of an England football fan in Rome.*
>
> *Hawkins, who was not charged with any offence relating to that incident, is also believed to be a member of the notorious hooligan group The Cockney Suicide Squad. A group who ironically, affiliate themselves to West Ham United.*
>
> *After initially refusing to comment when The Evening Standard contacted them yesterday, the club later issued a press release announcing that figures just published by*

the National Criminal Intelligence Service showed that
arrest figures in and around Upton Park fell to amongst
the lowest in the country toward the end of last season.
This confirmed their long-held belief that Mirren Events
Limited was amongst the best in the country when it came
to match day security.

However, it is believed that since those figures were
compiled, the company has merged with St George
Security Limited, which is owned by Essex entrepreneur
William Evans. Unfortunately, we were unable to
contact anyone at the company yesterday to confirm this.

A spokesman for NCIS said that they had been made
aware of the sensitive situation at West Ham and would
be monitoring it over the coming months.

'That stabbing in Rome must be the one that the copper was sent down for,' said Jamie as much to himself as to Katie. 'The plot thickens.'

'How?' asked Katie. 'We don't even know if he and Evans were still in contact. And there's also the small matter of him being dead.'

Jamie leant back in his chair and locked his hands behind his head with his eyes fixed firmly on the ceiling. After a few moments, he sat forward and turned to Katie. 'What if they were in touch and he wasn't stabbed by a burglar but by someone who fought back?'

'During one of these attacks you mean?'

'Why not?' replied Jamie as he grabbed his notebook and began flicking back through the pages. 'The first one we know about took place last March. That's five months before he got killed so they were obviously at it by then.'

'But we don't know if he was,' said Katie.

'Then let's find out. That report said that the police had someone in custody so let's try and talk to them,' he said excitedly. 'Can you find out about his family? If there was a partner, it might be worth talking to her.'

Jamie glanced at his watch and cursed. 'Bloody hell, it's almost 5. I promised Lisa I'd be home by 6.'

Katie shook her head. 'Go,' she said. 'I'll stick around for a bit and see what I can dig up.'

'You legend,' said Jamie as he shut down his computer, stuffed his notepads into his desk draw and got to his feet. I owe you one.'

'One?' Katie laughed. 'And the bloody rest.'

Chapter Twenty Four
Thursday 5th July 2019

19.30

Billy was on the sofa with his laptop when Claire returned from the bedroom. Freshly showered and devoid of the lingering smell of Accident and Emergency, she looked both refreshed and knackered at the same time.

'You mischief making Evans?' she asked as she curled up beside him.

Billy looked up at her and raised an eyebrow. 'As it happens,' he said, 'I'm trying to buy a Bentley.'

'For me?'

'D'you want a Bentley?'

'Depends what it's going to cost me,' she purred.

'Nothing you haven't done before, just lots more of it.' Billy smiled, then paused for a moment before adding, 'then again, there is that one thing…'

Claire raised in eyebrow in mock admonishment. 'There isn't enough alcohol in the world Evans,' she said, 'although if you bumped it up to a Ferrari, I might think about it.'

Billy returned his attention to his computer. 'Nah, it's OK. I've done it before.'

She leant forward and playfully slapped his arm. 'Cheeky twat.'

Billy winked at her in response, but his attention was drawn to her gaping dressing gown and barely concealed chest. 'And you can put those away,' he said. 'They're bloody dangerous.'

Claire looked down and then squeezed her breasts together to make a cleavage. 'They're not dangerous,' she said, 'they're nice.'

'They're fabulous,' replied Billy as he turned back to his laptop. 'Which is why you need to put them away or they're going to cost me a fortune.'

Claire smiled and pulled her dressing gown around herself before settling back on the other end of the sofa. She'd known Billy long enough to know when she was beaten and buying Bentley's trumped boobs every time, even hers.

In truth, she didn't have any problem with this temporary demotion in Billy's priorities. There had been more than enough arseholes in her life over the years and she'd been hurt more times than she cared to remember so having someone who was not only nice and attentive but actually cared about her was making a welcome change. So much so in fact, that she had started to move beyond simply being happy and had started to consider the very real possibility that she was falling in love.

Initially, the very idea of it had terrified her. Not because of the numerous lectures she'd had about Billy's past from Julie, but because of Samantha, his late wife. For whilst he had never once given any hint of comparison between past and present and had always avoided taking her to any of 'their' places for fear of causing upset, he had been quite open about the fact that Samantha was and always would be his great love. In those early days, the thought of a life lived in another woman's shadow had resulted in a degree of caution on Claire's part but as their relationship had begun to develop, she had fairly quickly come to realise that she had nothing to fear. Quite the opposite in fact. Her role wasn't to compete or replace, it was purely to supplement and once she had accepted that and realised that she had no need to be either envious or resentful, things had progressed in leaps and bounds.

Not surprisingly, Julie had been dismayed when Claire had told her what had been happening but whilst she had eventually accepted the inevitable, a distance had since developed between them. Primarily, Claire suspected, because after the funeral she had hoped to be rid of Billy and the memories he held but that wasn't going to happen, at least not for the foreseeable future.

There were probably other reasons of course, not least the fact that Julie hadn't wanted to see her friend dragged into anything untoward yet in all honesty, the darker side of Billy's life had never bothered Claire. She wasn't stupid, she knew as much as she wanted to know and whenever she'd ever asked Billy anything, she had assumed that he'd answered her honestly. That was good enough for her, the rest was his business. Truth to tell, she actually found it all quite exciting.

'Finally!' exclaimed Billy as he snapped his laptop shut. 'Victory!'

Claire smiled at him. 'So, when do I take delivery?'

'Delivery? I've already sold it on,' said Billy with a self-satisfied grin.'

Claire shook her head in feigned disgust. 'So much for romance,' she sighed.

Billy put his laptop on the floor and held his arm out. Claire hesitated for a moment then slid along the sofa and snuggled against him.

'Now,' he said, 'you were saying something about boobs.'

Claire pulled his hand in tighter against her and let herself relax against him. She was happier than she had been in years, and if this was love then so be it.

Nothing was going to get in the way of her from enjoying it.

The mood was far less romantic in North London where having made a sizeable dent in a second bottle of wine, Jamie and Lisa had settled into what had become their normality. Yet it wasn't normal. There was a tension between them as a result of words that needed to be said but were being held back. As a result, the tension had been slowly building until eventually, Jamie could hold back no longer. He was after all, the injured party. 'So,' he said, 'are we going to talk?'

Lisa kept her eyes fixed on the television for a moment and then reached forward and switched it off before turning to face him. 'OK,' she said, her voice heavy with reluctance. 'Let's talk.'

'Right, Lisa, you can't just...'

'No,' Lisa interrupted. 'Me first.' She paused for a second and almost bowed her head. 'You know how seriously I take my job, and you know that I have to switch off. If I didn't, I'd crash. When I read your article and then heard you on the radio, it threw me. I wasn't ready for it, especially the things you were saying,' she said slowly. 'But I shouldn't have stormed out. That was childish of me and I'm sorry.'

'It's OK. I…'

Lisa held up her hand to stop him. 'Let me finish, please.'

Jamie nodded in acknowledgment, but his heart was racing. Something big was coming, he could sense it. 'Is this the end?' he wondered as she took another mouthful of wine. 'Is she going to leave for good?'

'I don't know how to say this,' she began, 'so I'm just going to come out with it. This thing you're investigating, you need to drop it.'

Jamie looked at her, stunned. Of all the things he'd expected to hear, that hadn't even occurred to him. 'What?' he said.

Lisa stared down at the floor. 'I need you to drop it,' she repeated without looking up.

'Why?'

There was a pause and then Lisa looked up at him. Her face devoid of any emotion. 'Because two of the people targeted by these attackers were my cases. I'm responsible.'

'What do you mean, responsible?' asked a stunned Jamie. 'You didn't…?'

'They should have been locked up but… we blew it. I blew it.' She shrugged her shoulders and took another sip of wine.

Jamie sat in silence for a moment as he tried to process the information Lisa had just given him. It was only when she looked at him again that he found some actual words. 'You weren't actually involved in…'

'The assaults?' she said as he let the words tail off. 'No, I don't know who was either. And to answer your next question, no I'm not sorry. They got what they deserved.'

'What they deserved? Jesus Christ, Lisa,' gasped Jamie. 'You're a bloody copper. What happened to upholding the law?'

'Lawyers happened,' replied Lisa bitterly. 'We work our arses off to put these scum away only for some shitty lawyer to get them off on a technicality.'

'So, if you can't put them in prison, you put them in hospital? Is that how it works now?'

'Why not? At least they're off the streets, and the victims got some justice.'

Jamie shook his head in amazement. He barely recognised the woman sitting in front of him.

'Do you know someone called Billy Evans?' he asked after a few moments.

Lisa looked up and frowned. 'Are we talking or are you interviewing me?'

'We're talking. I just wondered if you knew the name that's all.'

'I don't,' replied Lisa. 'Who is he?'

'Someone I met yesterday. He gave me chapter and verse on all this. You're sounding just like him.'

'Is he a copper?'

Jamie smiled at the very idea. 'No,' he said. 'He's a football hooligan who's been linked to everything from car ringing to the conviction of a copper for murder. He's involved in all this.'

Lisa took another mouthful of wine and thought for a moment. 'You need to drop this Jamie. You don't want to make enemies; I know I don't need any more.'

'More?'

'Yes Jamie, more,' said Lisa abruptly. 'There are a lot of coppers sympathetic to what's going on so being the girlfriend of the bloke trying to expose it isn't exactly a career enhancing position. And on top of that, can you imagine the shitstorm if your article kicks off an investigation? Every force in the country will be in the crap.'

'You're actually telling me that there are coppers directly involved,' exclaimed Jamie. 'Jesus Christ, Lisa!'

'Drop it,' she growled as she suddenly got to her feet. 'I'm going to bed. It's late.'

'I thought we were going to talk?'

'So, did I,' Lisa replied angrily. 'Look how that worked out.'

Jamie watched her leave the room and listened to her climbing the stairs. The sound of her stomping hardly the most inviting proposition he'd had recently.

'What happens now?' he thought. Should he drop what could be a potentially career changing story and try to save his relationship or carry on regardless and risk losing Lisa altogether?

As he sat there, Jamie had no idea what to do but one thing he was certain of was that if he didn't go to bed right then, the decision would be taken out of his hands. She would cut the tenuous thread keeping them together and that would be it.

With a sigh, he got to his feet, took the cups into the kitchen and headed for bed.

Jamie was awoken by Lisa shaking him. 'Your bloody phone's ringing,' she hissed. It's one o'clock!'

'Ignore it,' he groaned.

'It's rung three times. Go and answer it.'

With a sigh, he climbed out of bed and headed down the stairs where the screen of his phone was busy half lighting the room. He glanced at it and seeing the name, quickly answered. 'Alison, it's Jamie. What's going on?'

Less than an hour later, Jamie was in a cab pulling up at the end of the road where Alison Sanford's house sat.

As he paid the driver and climbed out, the first thing that struck him was the pungent smell of burning which hung heavy in the air. The second was the police car blocking the entrance to the road beyond which were two fire engines. Their flashing blue lights illuminating the scene in almost perfect flashing unison.

'Fuck,' he muttered as he turned to face Lisa who had climbed out after him. Her face reflecting all kinds of emotions from horror to embarrassment. 'Come on,' she muttered. 'Let's find out what's going on.'

Jamie followed her across the road to where two policemen were standing opposite a small group of locals who had gathered to watch the evening drama unfold. 'I'm DS Cooper, from the Met. Any chance you can fill me in on what's happened?'

The two policemen looked at each other cautiously.

Lisa showed them her badge and they relaxed. 'I'm investigating a complaint,' she lied. 'The Sanford family…'

One of the policemen nodded knowingly. 'Oh right, well it's a murder case now,' he said. The words sending a shiver down Jamie's spine.

'Murder? But I thought they got out,' said Jamie anxiously.

'He's with me,' said Lisa in response to their glances.

'Smoke inhalation, about an hour ago. Poor little mite.'

Lisa glanced at Jamie who looked crushed. 'What's the rumour mill saying about the fire?'

'Don't quote me,' said the policeman, 'but it looks like petrol through the letterbox closely followed by a burning newspaper.'

'Any idea who?' asked Lisa.

'The dad had a beef with a local gang. They reckoned he had one of their main faces done over.'

'He didn't.'

They all turned to face Jamie. Lisa glared at him and shook her head to tell him to be quiet. He was about to speak again when his phone rang. 'Alison?' he said having seen the name on the screen and moved away from the policemen. 'Where are you?'

There was a brief silence and then a female voice came on the line. Jamie realised straight away that it wasn't the woman he'd talked to earlier.

'Who is this?' she asked.

'My name's Brown. I'm a journalist. I was…'

'Where are you?' the voice asked. More insistent this time.

Jamie hesitated and glanced at Lisa who was still talking to the two policemen. 'Who is this?' he asked nervously.

'My name's Detective Sergeant Bowden of Essex police. I'd like a word with you, if you don't mind.'

10.20

Billy had just arrived back at his desk having taken his customary mid-morning stroll around the garage forecourt when his phone beeped to signal the arrival of a text from Claire.

'On a break in 5 minutes, pls make sure you're alone. Need to talk.'

Billy stared at it for a few moments before placing the phone down on his desk. Texts like this weren't unusual and could mean anything from Claire needing a friendly voice because of something shitty at work through to being horny.

After telling Lauren that he didn't want to be disturbed for the next half hour, he pulled his door shut and returned to his desk to wait. However, he had barely got comfortable when his phone rang.

'Hey,' he said. 'Everything OK?'

'Have you seen the news today?'

Billy instantly noticed both the hushed tone and the nervousness in her voice and sat forward. 'No, why?'

'There was a family brought in late last night, they'd had a fire at their house. Their little girl died.'

'Oh Jesus,' said Billy. 'That's bloody awful. Are you OK?'

'Yes, I'm fine but Billy, the police are all over here. They're saying it was arson.'

'Arson? Why do they think that?'

'It was a revenge attack.'

Billy felt his heart thump a little harder in his chest and took a deep breath as a horrible feeling began to grip him. 'Do you know where they lived?'

'Yes, Brentwood.' There was a pause and then Claire spoke again. 'Billy, is this…'

'No,' he said as softly and reassuringly as he could. 'I don't know anything about it, I promise.'

'Good,' said Claire, her voice calmer than before. 'I…'

Before she could continue, there was a knock on the door and Lauren's head appeared. 'I'm sorry Billy,' she said. 'There are some people here...'

'I don't give a fuck,' he replied sharply. 'I'm on the bloody phone.'

Lauren looked at him anxiously then held out her hands in a gesture of surrender. Billy stared back at her for a moment and then, without breaking eye contact, he returned to his phone call. 'Claire, sorry sweetheart but I've got someone here. I'll talk to you tonight OK?'

Billy put the phone down on the desk, his eyes still firmly on Lauren. After a few seconds, he gave her an almost imperceptible nod and she pushed the door open to reveal a man and a woman standing behind her. His instincts told him instantly that they were police.

'And what can I do for you?' asked Billy as Lauren ushered them in and closed the door.

'I'm Detective Sergeant Bowden of Essex Police,' she said, 'and this is Detective Constable Brookes.'

Billy smiled. He'd had enough dealings with the police over the years to know that there was only one way to deal with them and that was with indifference bordering on arrogance. 'That's nice,' he said. 'Are you looking for anything in particular?'

'Yes,' said DS Bowden. 'You.'

PART FOUR

Chapter Twenty Six
Friday 6th July 2019

12.30

Pete Goodwin had seen more tragedy during his career than he cared to remember and seen more than one journalist fall apart in the wake of a story going horribly wrong.

As a consequence, he knew that now, whilst the self-blame game was in full swing, wasn't the time wasn't for trite comments. It was a time to sit patiently whilst Jamie sat opposite him, head in hands, struggling to deal with the torture he was enduring.

'Go home Jamie,' he said calmly. 'Go home, talk to Lisa, get shit-faced and then come back in the morning and we'll work out our next move.'

Jamie looked up and shook his head. He hadn't mentioned his conversations with Lisa the previous evening to either Pete or the police, but the fact remained that the last place he wanted to be right now was with her. Even though he knew how irrational it was, he was certain that she'd shown signs of guilt over little Carrie's death, but he had no idea why. Mind you, they'd been nothing to the amount he apportioned to himself which was almost crippling. 'No, I need to be doing something,' he said.

'OK,' replied Pete. 'What are you going to do?'

Jamie stood up and began to pace. 'Fuck knows.'

'Right, so what exactly did you tell the police?'

'The basics. That I'd met Alison and she'd told me about the threats from this gang.'

'And you told them about Evans?'

Jamie shook his head as he continued to pace. 'Yeah, that was stupid. Sorry.'

'No,' said Pete. 'it was the smart thing to do. If he was involved and it came out later that you'd withheld information, you'd be right up shit street. Anyway, it's done so there's sod all we can do about it.'

'So, what do I do?'

Pete settled back in his chair and thought for a moment. 'I'll get Katie to do a report on the fire, but we can't link it to your stuff, not until you've spoken to the police properly.'

'They're going to let me know when they want to interview me,' said Jamie. 'Probably be tomorrow now.'

'So where are we with this Evans character? You said you talked to him.'

'I did, but it was more a case of talking at him,' said Jamie. 'I told him what Alison had told me in the hope he'd do something.'

'What did you think he'd do?'

'I don't know,' sighed Jamie. 'Something, anything.'

Pete took a deep breath and slowly exhaled as he let his brain compute the various angles that were opening up to his thinking process. 'Have you considered the possibility that it might not even have been anything to do with him?'

Jamie threw him a worried look. However, much he didn't want to admit it, after his conversations with Lisa over the previous evening that possibility had started to make solid inroads into his thinking. He was absolutely certain from her reaction that she genuinely had no idea who Billy Evans was and at times had seemed quite confused about the version of events Billy had given him.

Yet if Billy Evans hadn't been involved in the attack on Darren Carter, who had? Increasingly, only one answer came when he asked himself that question and it was one that genuinely scared him. So much so that he was afraid to voice it to anyone else.

'Well I can't do much until I've spoken to the police,' Jamie sighed. 'I can't risk prejudicing their investigation.'

'Then start digging deeper into his background,' said Pete. 'What was the name of this other guy? Harris?'

'Hawkins,' said Jamie. 'Katie's looking into him.'

'Good. The more ammunition you've got for when the time comes to go to print, the better. If we're gonna take a shot at Evans, then we'd best do it with both barrels. Oh, and Jamie, be careful. If we're right about this character he's not going to be exactly thrilled that you've put him in the frame for murder.'

Far from being unhappy, Billy was buzzing. Proper buzzing.

The visit from the police, whilst certainly unexpected, had been supremely satisfying from a personal perspective. The reaction of DS Bowden to his denial of even knowing who Jamie Brown was let alone ever meeting him had been priceless. Not least because it rendered everything she had planned to ask him totally pointless.

As a consequence, the visit had lasted barely a few minutes and they'd left with the names and contact details of the three men who would testify that Billy was playing golf with them in Watford on the morning that Brown claimed to have met him in Slough. He'd even let them take a photocopy of his signed score card for good measure. It was obviously fake, but they didn't need to know that.

With the police officers gone Billy had sat quietly for a while and reflected on what had happened. Clearly, having grassed him so quickly and seemingly readily, Jamie Brown's integrity was open to question although Billy hadn't really expected anything else. More importantly, tragic though it was he felt absolutely no guilt for the consequences of the arson attack that had killed Cassie Sanford. Given his position, he was confident that he'd done everything he possibly could have to prevent it happening short of going around to the house and camping on the Sanford's doorstep. No, if there were any fingers to be pointed, they had to be at Foster and his group and that was exactly what he intended to do. For the truth of the matter was that the events of the previous night had not only given Billy the ideal opportunity to enact the next stage of his plan they had put him in a far better position than he could have hoped for. The only thing he had to work out was how best to handle it and as with all such things, the only answer he could come up with was, head on.

He was about to pick up the phone and dial when it rang, 'number withheld' displaying brightly on the screen. Billy listened for a few seconds and then replied as calmly as he could, 'I'll be there in an hour.'

Lauren watched from the window as Billy walked across the lot, climbed into his Range Rover and drove off.

She'd become used to the odd encounter with the police since she'd worked for him as it apparently went with the territory. The car trade was after all, rife with villainy. Yet something about this felt different.

Usually the policemen who'd passed through her office had been in uniform, not detectives like these two. And whilst she didn't know much about how the law worked, she did know that if they were involved, whatever they wanted with her boss was probably serious. Then again, Billy hadn't seemed at all concerned at their arrival and had actually been quite jolly when they'd left so if he wasn't concerned, why should she be?

With a sigh, she took another sip of her coffee and stared out at the numerous cars parked out the front. She'd heard all the rumours of course, many of them fed to her even before she'd taken the job. Billy Evans was violent, devious, abusive and the garage was a front for all kinds of criminal activity, plus there was all the stuff she'd read about him on the internet. Yet from the time she'd arrived for her job interview, she'd felt comfortable with him. The fact that she'd been open from the outset about not taking any crap had, as he'd told her many times, been the thing that had secured her the job because that's what he'd wanted and needed.

And in all fairness, other than the odd raised voice on the phone, she'd never seen or heard anything she'd considered questionable. Quite the opposite in fact. Indeed, she genuinely regarded Billy as the best boss she'd ever had so the thought of him involved in anything illegal just didn't ring true.

Lauren took another sip of her coffee and with a shake of her head, returned to her desk. She was worrying about nothing; she was absolutely certain.

Billy glanced around the beer garden of *The Top Of The World* and satisfied that no one was within earshot, returned his attention to Foster who sat opposite him.

'You're fucking kidding me?' he said quietly.

'I'm afraid not,' replied the Army officer stoically. 'The child's death was obviously a tragedy but...'

'Bullshit,' growled Billy. 'You fucked up. I told you what was going on and you did nothing. You could have stopped it. You know you could have.'

'Possibly, but hindsight's a wonderful thing.'

Billy shook his head. 'Yeah, in hindsight you should have let me take care of it.'

'As I said, it's regrettable but we're at war Mr. Evans. Haven't you realised that yet? Casualties are inevitable in war.'

Billy frowned. 'Hold on,' he said. 'Are you telling me that there have been others?'

Foster took a sip of his drink and placed the glass back down on the table. 'Not as serious, but yes.'

'Fuck me,' gasped Billy with a shake of his head. 'So much for the military being a well-oiled machine.'

'I resent that insinuation,' said Foster abruptly.

'I don't give two fucks what you resent, you're not the one with the old bill knocking on their door.'

'I wouldn't worry too much about the police,' replied Foster calmly.

'Don't tell me, you've got the law in your pocket.'

Foster smiled at the sarcastic tone in Billy's voice. 'I didn't have you down as being naive Mr. Evans.'

Billy suppressed a grin. He'd long suspected that given the amount of information they'd had on targets, Foster had to have had a few serving coppers sympathetic to the cause and the man sitting opposite him had just as much as confirmed it. That certainly made life easier, but he had no intention of letting him off the hook just yet.

'Then get them off my back,' he barked.

'I'll do my best,' replied Foster calmly.

'Good, they're bad for business. And don't talk to me like I'm one of your bloody oiks.'

'I apologise. That wasn't my intention.'

Billy nodded an acknowledgment and took a sip of his drink. This was the moment he'd been waiting for and he wasn't going to waste it.

'This, whatever it is, has worked pretty well so far but if it's gonna continue, we need to tighten things up. Do it properly.'

'Agreed,' said Foster.

'I'm not having any more of your lot doing stuff on my doorstep that I don't know about. Not with this bloody journalist sniffing around.'

'OK. So, what do you propose? Better coordination?'

'No, I want total control of operations. I do most of it anyway, so it makes sense.'

'That won't happen,' replied Foster abruptly. 'My men won't work for a civilian.'

'Why not? We're all on the same side, aren't we? And besides, aren't they civilians now?' Billy spotted a slight change in Foster's expression. 'Or are they?' he added.

'I don't want to comment on that.'

Billy gave him a wry smile. His other suspicion that some of Foster's men were still serving in the military was also true.

'So, give me a rank,' he joked. 'Or is that also being naive?'

'Would your lads work for me?' asked Foster. 'Of course not. So, what's the difference?'

'My lads don't let kids burn to death in their beds.' said Billy. 'Because I make sure that they don't have to.'

Foster fell into a thoughtful silence but before he could react, Billy got to his feet.

'I don't want another dead kid on my conscience,' he said calmly, 'either I get control, or I walk, and I'll take my lads with me. Let me know what you want to do, but you ain't got long.'

With that Billy turned and headed for the car park.

As he passed through the bar, Simon called Billy over.

'Here,' he said, slipping him a USB stick. 'Just what you asked for. There's obviously no sound but the pictures are fine.'

'Cheers mate,' replied Billy as he slipped the stick into his pocket. 'I owe you one.'

15.45

Jamie was staring at his computer screen, deep in thought, when Katie appeared and sat on the desk alongside him.

'Jesus,' he gasped. 'I wish you'd stop creeping up on me like that. 'It scares the shit out of me!'

'It's how I get all the best gossip,' she replied with a broad smile which she replaced almost instantly with a concerned look. 'I heard about the fire. Tough break.'

Jamie shook his head. 'I should have done more.'

'Like what?'

'I dunno. I told Evans about it, I thought he might be able to do something.'

'What did the police say? I mean, you told them about him, right?'

'They spoke to him earlier but apparently he told them he had no idea what they were talking about. Never met me, never spoke to me, no idea who I am.'

'And they swallowed that?' she asked incredulously.

Jamie shrugged his shoulders. 'Yep, and I can't prove otherwise.'

'Well, at least they've made an arrest.'

'Have they? When?'

'About an hour ago. Didn't you know? Two local teenagers. Bang to rights apparently.'

Jamie leant back in his chair and ran his hands over his face. 'What a bloody waste,' he sighed. 'So, what are you up too?'

Ah,' she said. 'Well I've been checking into the late Graham Hawkins. I called the ex-copper you spoke to, Roberts, he told me that Hawkins and Evans were proper close, like brothers.'

'So, it's likely they were still in touch,' said Jamie.

'I'd guess so.'

'Is there anyone in his family we could talk to?

Katie held out a slip of paper. 'The widow Hawkins,' she said. 'Her name's Julie. She's a nurse at Queens Hospital in Romford. I called their HR department and asked them to pass on your number, but it might be worth giving them a nudge.'

Jamie took the paper and smiled. 'Have I told you how bloody awesome you are?' he said as he picked up the phone and began dialling only for Katie to take the receiver out of his hand and place it back down.

'I haven't finished yet,' she said confidently. 'The person arrested for killing her husband was a local kid, Ashely Bennett, but he was never charged. The police had to drop it as there were no witnesses. But get this, Hawkins was murdered in the August, that November, 5 masked men burst into Bennett's house and beat the crap out of him.'

'You're fucking joking!' exclaimed Jamie. 'Seriously?'

'Yep. There has to be a link. Either that or it's a pretty crappy coincidence.'

'OK,' said Jamie excitedly. 'We need to speak to some of these people. I'll take Bennett. Can you...'

'I've still not finished,' said Katie almost smugly.

Jamie sat back and looked at her, almost in awe. 'You're kidding?'

'I've also been checking these attacks from the other night. There weren't two, there were three. Lincoln, Sheffield and Milton Keynes. Five men, same injuries, everything.'

'Evans told me that there were going to be two.'

'Which means that there are at least two of these groups operating,' said Katie.

Jamie hesitated. For a second he wondered if he should tell her his suspicions, but he dismissed the idea. He needed more information before he felt confident enough to do that.

'That's what Pete thinks,' he said eventually. 'It'd certainly explain why he didn't do anything about the fire. Maybe he couldn't because he didn't know about the Sanfords.'

'Which potentially gives us an even bigger story.'

Jamie rested his chin on his hands. 'Fuck,' he sighed, 'this is bloody crazy. All this and we've still got nothing concrete to tie it all together.'

'You've got Evans. Maybe you should have a proper crack at him.'

Jamie glanced up at Katie and shrugged his shoulders. 'With what? I've got nothing concrete to throw at him.'

'Then make it up. All you've got to do is get him to compromise himself.'

'He's too smart to fall for anything like that. Honestly, you should meet this bloke. He scared the shit out of me without even trying. Christ knows what he'd be like if he was pissed off.'

Katie stood up and smiled. 'Then go home and sleep on it,' she said. See if anything fires up inside that meagre brain of yours. Maybe Lisa will inspire you.'

Jamie nodded in response and watched Katie as she headed back to her own desk. The last thing he wanted to do was to talk to Lisa about any of this because he was actually starting to wonder quite how much she knew that he didn't. Yet deep down, he knew that after everything that had gone on over the last few days, he had no other choice but to confront her and find out.

Not just for the sake of their relationship, but for the sake of a story that felt like it was rapidly running out of control.

He was about to get to his feet when his phone rang. 'My names Julie Hawkins,' said a voice hesitantly. 'Someone called Jamie Brown wanted to speak to me.'

'That's me,' he replied as he grabbed a pen and notepad. 'Thanks for getting back to me so quickly.'

'That's OK. They said it was urgent.'

'It is, kind of,' said Jamie cautiously. 'I'm working on a story about someone you know and I'm hoping you can give me a bit of background.'

There was a silence for a few moments and then Julie replied in a tone which already suggested that she knew the answer to the question she was about to ask. 'Who?'

'His name's Evans. Billy Evans. I believe he...'

Before he could finish the sentence, the line went dead. Jamie stared at his phone for a few seconds and then put it down on the desk. 'That'll be a no then,' he said out loud. 'Bollocks.'

Claire was sitting nursing a cup of tea in the staff cafeteria of Queens Hospital when Julie appeared, seemingly from nowhere.

'Hello stranger,' she said. 'I haven't seen much of you lately.'

Julie forced a smile and sat down. 'Yes, I know. Sorry about that but, well, you know how it is.'

Claire nodded. Sadly, the wall Julie had built around herself was still very much in evidence. 'What's up?'

Julie glanced around and then returned her attention to Claire. 'I need you to pass a message to Billy,' she said quietly.

'Why don't you call him yourself. He'd love to hear from you.'

'No,' replied Julie abruptly. 'Just tell him that a journalist called me today. He wanted to ask me about him.'

'A journalist? About Billy? Why?'

'I don't know, I didn't talk to him, but I thought he should know. Here's his name and number,' she said handing Claire a slip of paper.

'OK I'll tell him.'

'Thanks,' said Julie. She hesitated for a moment and then gave another half-smile. 'Is everything good with you two?'

'It's brilliant. Honestly, we're really happy.'

Julie looked at her for a moment and then got to her feet. 'I'm glad,' she said with a slight smile. 'Tell him I said hi.'

Claire watched Julie until she was out of sight and then pulled her phone from her pocket.

Having viewed the contents of the USB stick that Simon had given him which included fairly good coverage of his meeting with Foster, Billy had been about to leave his office when Claire had called and now he sat at his desk quietly seething. It was one thing Brown coming after him but trying to do it through Julie was bang out of order. The question he now faced was how best to deal with it.

His initial thought had been to call Brown and warn him off, but the number Claire had given him had been the landline he'd called Brown on when they'd spoken about the Sanfords'. Assuming that was at the newspaper, if he called it again it would potentially leave a contact trail and he'd worked hard enough to avoid doing that to want to risk it now.

His second instinct had been to go and front him up in person. Billy had a rough idea of where Brown lived and having knocked on plenty of doors over the years trying to find the owners of cars, he certainly wasn't averse to doing it again to ask the locals if they knew him. But again, that would also potentially leave a trail which handed him the same problem.

The thought had also occurred to Billy that he could simply put Brown onto his schedule and send some lads round to inflict upon him the kind of retribution that he was seemingly so interested in. However, he had dismissed that out of hand. Not because it didn't appeal or because it would play into Brown's hands, but because he didn't send others to do his dirty work. That of course left him with only one option, to do nothing.

After all, if Julie had refused to talk to Brown then that avenue had obviously been shut off and Billy couldn't imagine who else in his circle would ever talk to a journalist. That surely left him with nothing to write about other than the past which didn't provide a single credible link to what was going on now.

Reluctantly, Billy accepted that this approach made the most sense even though doing nothing certainly went against the grain, especially when someone was coming for him. Then again, he could always go back and address the matter at a later date and if, as he hoped, Foster decided to hand him overall control he'd have plenty of resources at his disposal to ensure that his angst was more than adequately satisfied.

With the decision made and the red mist rapidly dissipating, Billy glanced at his watch to see it was almost six o'clock. Claire was due at his in about half an hour and by the time he'd locked up, he'd just about make it home before she did.

However, he had one call to make first and whilst he'd been putting it off, Billy knew that if he didn't make it now, he'd spend all evening thinking about it. With a deep breath, he picked up the phone and dialled.

'Julie,' he said as soon as it was answered. 'It's Billy. Yeah, she did but I just wanted to let you know that it's nothing to worry about honestly, he's just fishing. Will you let me know if he contacts you again? Great, thanks. How are you?'

Chapter Twenty Eight
Friday 6th July 2019

19.15

Jamie sat on the sofa running the events of the last 24 hours over and over in his head like some kind of nightmare reality binge watch.

Julie Hawkins reaction to his mention of Billy Evans had sewn the seed of an idea in his head and now, having nurtured and tweaked it, he was reasonably confident that he had a plan of action which at least gave him a chance of getting his story into print. It was risky, but it was certainly better than what he had at the moment.

Yet even as he thought about it, nagging doubts kept entering his thought process. Not about Evans, but about the idea that he wasn't the whole story. Fundamental to those doubts were the various conversations he'd had with the woman who at the very moment, was relaxing in the bath above his head. For they had thrown up far too many questions for his enquiring mind to ignore, not least the notion that Lisa might actually be aware of some kind of direct police involvement. Something which if true, was a potentially far bigger story.

He was obviously going to have to ask her about it but however many times Jamie ran the scenario through his head, he knew that however he did it, there were going to be consequences. Potentially, it could even prove catastrophic to their relationship which begged the question, was it worth it? It was after all, only a bloody story.

But of course, it wasn't, it was about much more than that. For Jamie knew that if he didn't confront Lisa with his suspicions, not only would he ever be able to trust her again, but he'd never be able to regard himself as a journalist. At least not one worthy of the name.

That realisation was enough to convince him that he had no choice but if he was going to do it, it had to be now. Any delay would only make things worse.

With a sigh, Jamie dragged himself from the sofa and headed for the kitchen and switched the kettle on. If he was going to destroy his future with Lisa, it might as well be done over a cup of tea.

Having had to work a little late, by the time Claire arrived at Billy's house he was already parked on the sofa watching television.

'Sorry,' she said as she dumped herself on the sofa. 'Work was mental.'

'You don't have to apologise,' said Billy as he got to his feet. 'You want tea or wine?'

Claire let her head fall to one side, her eyes fixed on Billy standing in the kitchen doorway. 'Alcohol,' she said. 'But can I ask you something first?'

'Go for it.'

'What was all that about with Julie today?'

Billy paused for a moment. He hadn't expected it quite so soon, but he'd been fairly certain that she was going to ask him that very question at some point over the evening. He, after all, was used to his life and everything that went with it but it was still all new territory for her and so it was obvious that having a journalist asking about her partner would be cause for concern. As a consequence, he'd prepared exactly what he wanted to say to appease her but now that the time had come, he simply couldn't do it. She deserved if not the whole truth, at least a potted version of it.

'It was the reporter who wrote the articles. I'm guessing that he's fishing for something to link me to what's been going on.'

'I thought you were being careful,' said Claire, her eyes still firmly fixed on him.

'Trust me, I am,' replied Billy as he headed for the kitchen.

Claire continued to stare at the empty doorway as she listened to Billy rattling around in the next room. She had long accepted that when it came to his work, life was always going to involve an element of half-truths and avoidance because that was how he kept control. But the realisation struck her that in her case, it wasn't because he had anything to hide, it was because it was his way of protecting her because he cared about her. Suddenly, for the first time in their relationship, Claire felt a part of Billy's life. A real part.

'I have one last question,' she said as he came back into the room and handed her a glass of wine, 'and I want you to promise me that you'll answer it honestly.'

Billy nodded. 'OK. What is it?'

'Are you worried?'

Billy cocked his head to one side and gave her his trademark cheeky smile. No,' he said. 'Not in the slightest.'

'Good,' said Claire after a moment's pause. 'What's for dinner? I'm starving!'

Jamie took a deep breath and tapped on the bathroom door

'Can I come in?

'Since when have you ever knocked?' came the brusque reply.

Jamie pushed upon the door, walked in and placed a cup of tea on the edge of the bath. 'Here you go,' he said. 'D'you mind if I…?' He nodded in the direction of the toilet.

'No,' barked Lisa with a frown. 'I'm in the bloody bath. Use the one downstairs.'

'I thought we should talk,' he replied.

Lisa sunk a little lower into her suds and closed her eyes. 'Do I have a choice?'

Jamie put the toilet seat down and parked himself. 'So, about last night…'

'You've changed,' she said, interrupting him.

'Have I?'

'Yes. You've gone all serious. I liked you better when you were writing about Love Island and Little Mix.'

'It is serious,' Jamie replied. 'A little kid died last night, remember?'

'Believe me, there are worse things that happen to children than dying,' Lisa said without a trace of emotion in her voice. 'Much worse things.'

Jamie watched her for a few moments then said, 'and that's why we need to talk.'

'No, we don't.'

'Yes Lisa, we do. Look, I know you want me to drop this, but you know I can't.'

'OK Jamie, why don't you tell me what you think, and I'll tell you if I think it's bollocks.'

He hesitated a moment and then Jamie took a deep breath. 'I think that there's more going on than I first thought, and I think you know something about it.'

'I know lots of things,' replied Lisa. 'You're going to have to be more specific.'

'You know what I mean, these attacks.'

Lisa fell silent, her eyes closed. However, Jamie knew her well enough to know that despite the appearance of calm, her mind was working flat out.

'I think that there are policemen involved somehow and I need to know what you know about it,' he continued.

Lisa opened her eyes and looked at him. 'Who said I know anything?'

'You as much did last night. You said that there were coppers sympathetic to what's been going on. So, are there? Or were you joking?'

Lisa closed her eyes and settled back in her bath. 'You're interviewing me again,' she said.

Jamie sighed and got to his feet. 'OK, I give up,' he said. 'But I'll tell you something, if you know any coppers who are involved in this then you need to warn them…'

'Warn them?' laughed Lisa. 'You're not serious?'

'Yes, I bloody am. I'm not giving up on this Lisa, not after last night. And it could get very messy very quickly.'

The bathroom fell into silence. For a few moments Jamie stared down at the bath and his emotionless partner and then, without another word, he turned and headed downstairs.

08.45

With Claire on duty over the weekend, Billy waited until she'd left for work before he made himself a coffee, grabbed his mobile phones and his laptop and took station on the sofa.

It had been less than 24 hours since he'd given Foster his ultimatum and whilst he didn't expect to receive any response until at least Monday a part of him was still disappointed when he switched on his dedicated mobile and nothing came through.

'Twats,' he muttered out loud to himself.

He was however, totally convinced that he'd done the right thing. More so now that it had been pretty much confirmed that elements of the police were not only onside, but actively involved. If Foster agreed to let him take control, having a few old bill in his pocket could prove really useful although he wasn't sure all of his lads would agree. There were some who would refuse to work alongside the Old Bill on principle but there were others who wouldn't give a shit. Then again, Billy had thus far led them all to think that he was the main man anyway so it could be a case of what they didn't know not hurting them.

The thought of it all working out in his favour was proving to be quite a buzz but mindful of the fact that everything was ultimately dependent on his lads being happy, he sent everyone on his contacts list a brief message. Hold fast, weekend off. Keep the faith.

With that done, he opened up his laptop and finding an inbox full of mails relating to either work or West Ham, settled down to deal with business.

As expected, Jamie's bathroom encounter with Lisa had been the precursor to an emotionless evening of silence culminating in a night on the sofa. Much of which had been spent wondering how his seemingly comfortable life had been turned upside down in what had been the craziest few days of his life.

Now, having shifted himself to his office, he had heard the front door slam and not knowing if Lisa was going for a run or for good, had forced his thoughts away from his seemingly doomed relationship and turned his attention to what were rapidly assuming the role of more important matters.

Initially, Jamie had cleared his mind as best he could and read objectively through everything he had in the hope that it would throw up something he'd either missed or not thought of. However, it had been a fruitless task and had effectively left him with absolutely nothing he could tie together that he hadn't covered in his initial two articles. Indeed, he was actually in a worse position because now he had not only Evans and the attacks to consider but the possibility of police involvement. The potential for a story like that was unimaginable. Not just in terms of what it would do for his career, but for the impact it would have on the country as a whole. That was assuming he could ever get it into print but to do that, he'd need a lot more than the minuscule amount of information he had at the moment.

With a groan, Jamie leant back in his chair and stared at the ceiling. He was stuck with a story that was going nowhere, the question was, how was he going to kick it up the arse and get it moving? That was the $64,000 question.

It took only a few moments before he remembered the idea he'd had before he spoke to Lisa. If anything, it was even riskier now that he suspected that the police were directly involved but he didn't see what other choice he had. After glancing at his watch to check it was after 9.30, Jamie grabbed his phone and dialled.

'Hey,' he said. 'I know it's Saturday, but I need help, and fast.'

Katie stared over the rim of her coffee and widened her eyes.

'You're fucking joking?' she gasped.

'Nope. That's exactly what she said.'

'Was she serious?'

'Deadly,' said Jamie earnestly as he glanced around the cafe to make sure no one was listening. 'And d'you know what, the more I think about it, the more sense it makes. Evans told me that they never make mistakes but how could he say that unless…'

'You seriously think the police are feeding him information?' Come on Jamie, that's crazy.'

'And there's something else,' continued Jamie, warming to his task. 'You said there were three attacks, Evans told me there were going to be two. And why didn't he do anything to protect the Sanfords? Because he didn't know anything about them. There are two separate groups. There must be.' He hesitated for a moment and then took the plunge. 'And I think the other group are coppers. That means there could be even more attacks than the 47 Evans told me about.'

'It's 50 now,' corrected Katie. 'But you know you're contradicting yourself. How can he be getting information from the police but not knowing that they're also at it?'

Jamie paused and shrugged his shoulders. 'That's where my thinking stumbles a bit.'

'A bit?' laughed Katie. She took another mouthful of coffee as she considered Jamie's thinking. 'OK, let's assume that you're on to something. What do we do?'

'We need to go back over all of the attacks we've found and find out if there has been a single arrest. My guess is that there hasn't.'

'That wouldn't prove anything.'

'Maybe, maybe not,' replied Jamie. 'But it would indicate a lack of interest in due process which would beg the question as to why.'

'Because all the victims are arseholes?' asked Katie.

'Even arseholes deserve justice.'

'You haven't met my ex,' said Katie wryly. 'What about Evans? What do you want to do about him?'

Jamie took a deep breath. 'I think he's stringing me along to try and keep me quiet.'

'So why meet you in the first place? That makes no sense.'

'I dunno, arrogance maybe. Remember, he doesn't know about Lisa or what she's told me.'

'True,' Katie conceded.

'And the longer we wait around, the more chance of someone else nicking our story.'

'Also true. What's the plan?'

'We need to try and spook him. If we get him rattled, he might fill in some of the blanks and give us our story.'

'And how are we going to do that?'

'We use his mate,' said Jamie confidently. 'We use Graham Hawkins.'

Billy was on his second coffee and had almost cleared his inbox when his phone rang. 'Unknown' displaying on the screen.

'Yes?' he asked curtly.

'Mr. Evans, good morning,' said a familiar voice.

'Morning to you Mr. Foster. I was wondering when you'd call.'

'We need to talk. Are you available?'

'I can be.' said Billy. 'Usual place at say, one o'clock?'

'Well if it's not too inconvenient,' replied Foster calmly, 'I'm actually parked outside your house right now.'

Billy smiled to himself. 'So that's the way you want to play it,' he thought. 'OK, matey, let's have some fun.'

Without answering, Billy cancelled the call and headed outside to find the inevitable black Mercedes parked at the end of his drive. He waited until the electronic gates had swung fully open and then headed for the car, climbing into the back beside Foster.

'Well this is a pleasant surprise,' he said, 'just passing, were you?'

'I was in the area,' replied Foster dismissively. 'You certainly have an impressive home.'

Billy let out a sarcastic laugh. 'What did you expect? A council flat?'

'I'm sorry, that sounded wrong. I didn't mean to cause any offence.'

'Then it's a good job I didn't take any,' said Billy. 'What's so urgent?'

Foster smiled. 'I have some good news for you. The officers who interviewed you the other day are happy that you weren't involved in any way, so you won't be spoken to again.'

'Thanks,' replied Billy. 'But you could have told me that on the phone.'

Foster smiled. 'Well, there is something else,' he said softly. 'We've given some consideration to your proposal and we need you to reconsider.'

'You mean you need me to back down,' said Billy.

'No, reconsider. You must understand that there are certain, er... sensibilities involved.'

'You mean the old bill,' said Billy brusquely.

'In essence, yes. The feeling is that at this stage, there still needs to be a degree of separation.'

'Because I have a bit of a past?'

Foster shrugged his shoulders in agreement. Billy smiled in response. 'No hypocrisy there then,' he scoffed. 'What if I say no?'

'I hope you won't,' said Foster. 'We've all put in a great deal of work to get to this point but it's just the start. If we're going to achieve our objective, we have to keep building.'

'What d'you think I've been doing all this bloody time? I've got over a hundred lads out there.'

'Surely it makes sense to stay amongst the vanguard.' said Foster. 'You've seen the public reaction to the articles, the winds of change are blowing so it makes sense to...'

'What makes sense,' said Billy, 'is no more mistakes. In case you've forgotten, when your lot fuck up, I'm the one in the frame. Not you, not your mates in the old bill, me. I've already had that bloody journalist sniffing around.'

Foster balked. 'When?'

'Yesterday. He contacted someone I know looking for dirt on me.'

Foster looked anguished for a moment. 'That's not good. I thought we had him primed.'

'Obviously not.'

'What did your friend say to him?'

'Nothing,' said Billy. 'They told him to do one.'

'You have to tell me if anything like this happens. It's important that we know everything that's going on.'

'You mean like frying kids?' said Billy, unable to resist taking the dig.

'Touché,' replied Foster. 'I promise you that we're making changes to ensure that we don't see a repeat of that...' Foster paused for a moment. 'But it's as much for your sake as ours that we retain control over our own activities. I'm sure that you wouldn't want it known that you were working directly with the police.'

Billy looked at Foster and smiled. 'You're not trying to intimidate me are you Mr. Foster?'

Foster smiled. 'Would it work?'

'Not for a fucking second,' replied Billy with a grin.

'Then I hope we understand each other. Look, I know what you want, and I think I know why, but it can't happen. Not yet, but down the line, who knows?'

Billy nodded sagely. 'OK,' he said. 'Let me think about it.'

'That's all I ask,' said Foster.

'And one other thing, I want your direct phone number. All this pissing about trying to get hold of you gets on my tits.'

With a grin, Foster pulled out his phone and texted Billy his number. 'There,' he said. 'Call me anytime. But please don't doubt how much we value your involvement. We can only continue the good work we've been doing with your help.'

Foster held out his hand and Billy took it.

'I'll be in touch,' he said before climbing out of the car and heading back towards his house.

Having returned to the sanctuary of his sofa, Billy checked his mobile to see a missed call from Julie which had seemingly been closely followed by a text asking him to call her as soon as possible.

'Julie, everything OK?'

'No Billy,' she said, 'it's not. That journalist has called the hospital again. What's going on?'

'Did you speak to him?'

'No, and I'm not going to. What's going on Billy? Or shall I ask Claire?'

The tone of her voice and the manner of her delivery instantly brought back memories of numerous conversations Billy had overheard her having with Hawk back in the day so he had no doubt that not only was she getting pissed off, but she wasn't to be messed with. 'This journalist, he thinks he has something on me.'

'Does he?' she asked in the same abrupt manner.

'No,' Billy replied as calmly as he could. 'But he's digging for dirt.'

'Then tell him that if he calls again, I'll be talking to the police. I mean it Billy, get it sorted.'

The phone went dead before Billy could respond but even before he could formulate his thoughts his phone rang again.

'Lauren,' he said having answered. 'What's up? Are you at work?'

'Yes, I've just popped in to pick something up. Look, some blokes left a couple of messages asking you to contact him urgently. Jamie Brown, do you know him?'

Billy felt his hackles rising. 'Did he leave a number?' he asked as calmly as he could.

'Yeah, I'll ping it over. I just thought I better let you know, just in case.'

'Yeah, it's fine,' said Billy. 'See you Monday.'

Billy cancelled the call and stared at the screen until the text arrived delivering Jamie Brown's mobile number.

'Right you twat,' he muttered. 'Let's find out what you're up to shall we.'

He started to dial then stopped himself as an idea leapt into his head.

'Fuck it,' he muttered out loud before jumping up and heading for the shower.

Less than two hours later, Billy was parked a short way along the road from Jamie Brown's house.

Having visited Teddy Miles, he'd been given a rough idea of where the journalist lived with the final details being supplied by the local shopkeeper in exchange for a ten-pound note. Now, having also been informed that he lived with a woman called Lisa and had no kids, Billy had begun to wonder if he was actually doing the smart thing.

Tempted as he was to knock on the door and give the journalist the slap he obviously needed, Billy was smart enough to know that this would play right into Brown's hands. More importantly, as Foster had reminded him only that morning, the journalist was potentially a key element of their plan so punching his lights out might not be the best move. Then again, he was obviously digging for something and as Billy knew only too well, there was plenty to find if he looked in the right place. More importantly, the last thing he wanted was grief from Julie and she certainly didn't deserve some arsehole giving her any. That had to stop, or rather be stopped. The question was, how best to do it.

One thing he was certain of was that there was someone in the house because the upstairs windows were wide open. However, he had no way of knowing if it were Brown, his partner or both of them.

After deliberating on this for a few minutes, Billy made a decision and dialled the number Lauren had texted him. If it was good enough for Foster, it was good enough for him.

'Mr. Brown,' he said the moment the phone was answered. 'I hear you want a chat.'

Inside the house, Jamie held the phone to his ear and tried to suppress the nerves that had suddenly gripped him the instant he heard Billy's voice.

'Well do you, or don't you?' asked the voice impatiently.

'Yes,' Jamie blurted out. 'I wanted to run a few things past you.'

'OK. Then we best meet. When and where?'

'No!' said Jamie at a speed which contained a little too much urgency. 'It's fine, I can do it on the phone.'

'Well I can't,' replied Billy. 'So when and where?'

Jamie's heart started racing. He'd never been one for confrontation at the best of times, but this was next level. Worse, he was at home, alone and had no idea when or even if Lisa would be back. He had to try and stall this character so that he could meet him in a public place, preferably with someone else in tow.

'It might be a difficult today, I've just got home and I'm due out shortly, so I won't have time to get to… wherever you are.'

Billy smiled to himself. 'You won't need time,' he said. 'I'm parked right outside. D'you wanna come out or shall I come in?'

Jamie felt his heart stop for a second and instinctively hurried across to the front window to try and see if anyone strange was parked outside. There was nothing, at least not that he could see.

'You're outside MY house?' he said tentatively.

'Not right outside,' replied Billy calmly. 'Just up the road, black Range Rover. So, are you coming out? Or what?'

Jamie took a deep breath to try and calm himself, even a little. 'I'll be out in a second.'

Billy waited until he saw Jamie leave his house and start looking up and down the road before he climbed out of his car. He could see from the journalists demeanour that he was absolutely bricking it and so to compound matters, he stood firm leaving Brown no choice but to walk to him. 'Advantage me,' he thought to himself.

'So, Mr. Brown,' said Billy as Jamie arrived within speaking distance. 'What the fuck are you doing calling my best mate's widow?'

Jamie glanced at the notebook he held in his right hand and tried desperately to conceal his nerves. Despite the fact that he was standing in the middle of a North London street at just gone 3.00 in the afternoon, he'd never felt so intimidated, or alone.

'I have some questions,' he said without looking up, his voice shaking slightly.

'About what?'

'Graham Hawkins,' he said, 'and the circumstances of his death.'

Jamie looked up just as the punch hit him. The force jolting his head back with such force that he was driven back a few steps. Almost instinctively, his hands flew to his face. Not just to protect himself from further blows but in an attempt to stem the flow of blood that was already flowing into his hand.

'What the bloody hell was that for?' he yelped.

'To save time,' said Billy angrily. 'I was gonna smack you sooner or later. It might as well be sooner.'

Before Jamie could respond, Billy bent down and picked up the notebook which lay strewn across the road. 'I'll take this,' he said. 'See what other mischief you've been up to.'

'You can't,' pleaded Jamie as he made a grab for it only for Billy to shove him away. 'That's theft.'

Billy burst out laughing as he began to flick through the pages. 'Well you have been a busy boy,' he said. Suddenly he stopped and looked up. 'You think Hawk was involved in...,'

Even through the pain spreading across his face, Jamie could sense the change in the mood in the man standing facing him. 'It's a theory,' he said quickly.

'You're wrong,' hissed Billy as he stepped forward. 'And if you write that, you're a fucking dead man.'

'What the bloody hell's going on? Jamie, are you ok?' Billy turned to see a blonde woman approaching. Her face like thunder.

'Do yourself a favour and fuck off love,' barked Billy.

'Excuse me?' she replied, feigning indignation.

'It's OK Lisa, honestly,' said Jamie. 'Just a disagreement that's all.

'You must be the Mrs,' said Billy, looking her up and down for effect. 'Your fella's been a naughty boy.'

Lisa eyeballed Billy for a second and then held out her hand. 'I'll take that,' she said.

Billy stared back at her and let a sly smile crawl across his face before turning to Jamie. He'd made his point. He had the notebook. Time to leave.

'Stay away from Julie Hawkins,' he said. 'I'm not asking either.'

'I said I'll take that,' growled Lisa, her hand still outstretched. 'Or d'you want me to nick you?'

Billy turned to face her. His smile growing even wider. 'You're kidding me,' he said incredulously. 'You're old bill? Sorry love, but you're gonna have to prove it.'

Lisa continued to eyeball him for a moment and then reached into her pocket and pulled out her warrant card.

Billy examined it for a second and then with a shrug, handed the notebook to her.

'Now piss off,' said Lisa. 'Before I lose my temper.'

Billy nodded and glanced at Jamie. 'Remember what I said Jamie Brown,' he said before climbing into his car and slowly driving away.

The second he was gone, Lisa grabbed hold of Jamie and started to examine his nose, but Jamie shook her off. He didn't know if he felt embarrassed, angry or a mixture of both.

'Just leave it,' he grunted as he took his notebook from her.

'OK,' Lisa said, holding her hands up in mock surrender. 'What the bloody hell was that all about?'

Billy drove for about five minutes and then pulled over. Taking his phone from his pocket, he took a note of Lisa's details before driving away again.

As stupid as he felt for allowing himself to snap so quickly, the encounter with Brown had given him all kinds of things to think about. Not just about Hawk, but about Police Sergeant 72435 Lisa Cooper.

For what neither she nor Jamie had any way of knowing was that this wasn't the first time Billy had seen her.

Having finally stemmed the flow of blood and been assured by Lisa that his nose wasn't broken, Jamie had taken station on his sofa whilst he waited for the ibuprofen to kick in.

Thus far, Lisa had said almost nothing about the events she'd stumbled across in the street, but he knew it was only a matter of time. He wasn't wrong.

'So,' she said in a manner which suggested that this was her normal work voice, 'what was that all about?'

'Remember I asked you about someone called Billy Evans? Well that was him.'

'OK,' she replied thoughtfully. 'So why are you fighting a football hooligan in the street outside our house?'

'Did you see me doing any fighting?' barked Jamie. 'Seriously? He fucking hit me!'

'Why did he hit you?'

Jamie paused for a few moments. 'I told you, he's involved with this vigilante stuff.'

'That doesn't explain why he's outside our bloody house Jamie. Once again, what's going on?'

'I'm working on another piece and…' he let the words tail off.

'In other words, you provoked him?'

'I suppose,' sighed Jamie.

Lisa fell silent for a few moments. 'What's this new piece about?' she asked. Her voice suddenly terser.

'His best mate was killed a year or so back. I think it was by someone who they'd gone to attack but who fought back. I think that's what started it all off.'

More silence. Jamie could almost hear Lisa's brain churning over although he wasn't sure if it was a thought process or trying to keep calm.

'I asked you to drop this,' she said to finally break the silence.

'I can't Lisa,' Jamie replied. 'You know I can't.'

'Even though it has implication for me?'

Jamie stared at her. 'What implications?'

'I told you, some of his victims were my cases.'

'So what? Why would that come back to you?' Jamie asked before adding 'Or are you worried because you know that there are coppers feeding him information?'

Lisa glared at Jamie in response. 'You're questioning me again,' she barked.

'Then tell me what the fuck's going on!'

'I can't,' she said. 'I don't know anything.'

Jamie threw up his hands in exasperation. 'OK, if that's how you want to play it, fine,' he said. 'But I've got to run this story.'

'Even though it'll hurt my career?'

'How is it going to do that? You're not involved.' Jamie stopped for a moment and eyeballed her. 'Or are you?'

'No,' said Lisa. 'I told you. But…'

Jamie watched her as her mood softened. For a moment, he almost thought she was frightened.

'There are people I work with who… they'll put two and two together.'

'For fucks sake,' groaned Jamie. 'So, you're going to guilt trip me now.'

'If that's what it takes,' Lisa replied without a hint of humour. 'Look, it's not just for my sake. You just got attacked in the bloody street outside our house remember.'

Jamie shook his head. 'I'm not worried,' he said, not especially convincingly.

'Well, maybe you should be. I know I am.'

Jamie shook his head, climbed from the sofa and headed for the kitchen. 'I need a drink,' he groaned.

Even as Jamie and Lisa were arguing, Billy was sitting at his laptop scrawling through a file of photographs. Each one linked to a particular case that Foster had sent to him for action. He'd been at it for almost an hour before he found what he was looking for.

In a newspaper article about a sex offender who'd been released from court after his trial had collapsed, was a picture of a group of disgruntled looking police officers. Standing amongst and looking more upset than most of them was Sgt Lisa Cooper.

'I bloody knew it,' said Billy excitedly. 'You smug bitch.'

He sat back and wondered how best to use this revelation. On the face of it, it was nothing of any real significance but when context was added, it was a different matter. The question was, what context?

If she were helping Brown in any way, then that would obviously be of interest to Foster and his police officer mates. However, if she were one of the coppers feeding information to Foster, or was even directly involved with the other group, then that would obviously be of interest to Brown.

Then again, if Lisa Cooper were involved with The Firm in some way it was highly unlikely that Foster had any idea that she and Jamie Brown were a couple which might also be valuable information.

Either way, the potential implications for her were immense which gave him a degree of leverage although no idea of where to apply it.

On a whim, Billy typed Sergeant Lisa Cooper into Google but nothing came up and so he slumped back in his chair and stared at the ceiling. Given that his primary motivation was killing the story on Hawk, his initial instinct was to use what he had to threaten Brown into not publishing. Coming on top of a punch in the face, the idea of seeing his other half spread across the tabloids might well have the desired effect but Billy knew that he'd only have one shot. If Brown didn't react accordingly, he could actually add to his own troubles and by association, Julie's.

The other thought which began to enter his thinking was to do with Foster. If Lisa Cooper was in his pocket it was only going to be a matter of time before she let someone know that Billy had attacked her partner. That could become a problem very quickly, especially after his morning visit. Then again, if she was keeping her relationship with Jamie Brown a secret, she wasn't likely to tell anyone anything, least of all Foster.

'For Christ's sake,' said Billy out loud. 'Why is everything so fucking complicated.'

He pondered his quandary for a few minutes and then grabbed his phone. Ultimately, there was only one option open to him and the sooner it was done, the better.

'Mr. Foster,' he said as soon as the phone was answered. 'Can you talk?'

Chapter Thirty
Sunday 8th July 2019

11.15

Major Christopher Foster of the Royal Military Police sat opposite Billy Evans in the garden of *The Top Of The World* public house and considered his options. He was not happy.

'I assume that you've realised that he goaded you into doing exactly what you did?'

'I'm not going to sit back and watch my mate's memory dragged through the shitter,' hissed Billy.

'And you think assaulting him was the way to stop that?'

'Probably not, but it made me feel better.' Billy leant forward slightly and lowered his voice to give it a more menacing tone. 'I'll do whatever it takes to protect my mate's family. Don't for one second think that I won't.'

Foster eyeballed Billy for a few seconds. 'Is that a threat of some kind?' he asked.

'Whatever it takes,' repeated Billy.

Foster forced a smile to try and diffuse the tension. 'OK,' he said. 'Well I can't pretend that I'm not disappointed but what's done is done. What do you think I can do?'

Billy hesitated. For all his bluster he didn't actually know what Foster might be able to do about his problem, if indeed, he'd be able to do anything at all. His entire reasoning had been based on the assumption that because of his brother, he must have a degree of influence.

'Stop Brown from publishing,' was all he could think of to say.

'And how am I supposed to do that?'

'You must have mates in high places.'

'I'm not without contacts, that's true. But why should I help you? Only yesterday you were issuing ultimatums and now you're issuing threats.'

'I'm not sure you're grasping what I mean by whatever it takes,' said Billy.

'I grasp it perfectly well,' replied Foster with a smile. 'But I'm not sure you're fully understanding the implication of what you're doing.'

'So that's how you want to play it is it?'

'I don't want to play anything Mr. Evans,' replied Foster calmly. 'What I want is for us to continue working together under the terms I gave you yesterday. If you agree to that, then I'd be delighted to help you resolve your problem in any way I can.'

'And if I don't?'

Foster shrugged his shoulders. 'Then you're on your own.' He paused for a moment and leant forward to emphasise what he was about to say. 'And you'll have made a lot of policemen very unhappy. That could make life quite difficult.'

Billy let out a laugh but he suddenly realised that he'd backed himself into a corner. Much as he hated to admit it, Foster had him by the balls and worst of all, he'd just handed them to him on his own plate.

'OK,' he said. 'Supposing I agree to your terms, can you actually help me stop this arsehole printing this story?'

'I can't make any promises,' replied Foster confidently. 'But I give you my word that I will do my very best.'

Billy stared at him for a few moments and then said, 'I'll hold you to that,' before holding out his hand.

With a smile Foster took it. 'Welcome back to the fold,' he said. 'Now, let's get back to work.' Foster took a USB stick from his pocket and held it out. 'I have some targets for you.'

Billy stared down at it for a moment. 'Before we get to that, there's a Met Sergeant, Lisa Cooper. Is she one of yours?'

'I can't answer that.'

'Can't or won't?'

'Can't, because I don't know. You know how things work; we know as little as possible. Who is she?'

'She's Brown's missus.'

Foster hesitated for a second. 'Are you sure?'

'She flashed her warrant card at me after I smacked her old man.'

Billy noticed a look of concern sweep across Foster's face. A classic tell.

'I'll look into it,' he said before placing the USB stick on the table in front of Billy. 'Now, down to business.'

Billy had always known that he was good at what he did. From organising the *CSS* in the halcyon days of football hooliganism to selling cars, few could live with him in terms of planning, organising and executing, be it a deal or a ruck.

Yet he also knew that he was at his very best when he was on the ropes and up to about an hour ago, as he'd driven away from *The Top Of The World*, that's exactly where he'd been. Albeit at his own design.

Putting himself in such an obviously vulnerable position over Jamie Brown had been beyond stupid. Not just because it had handed Foster the opportunity to give him a verbal slap down which had left him feeling both embarrassed and vulnerable but because he'd effectively made himself subservient. Something which had all but killed off his plan to seize overall control.

More importantly, by handing over the responsibility for stopping Jamie Brown's article he had left himself not just impotent but reliant on hope. And hope was something Billy didn't do very well.

However, as he'd made his way back to Romford the germ of an idea had formed in his head and now, as Billy waited for his gates to swing open, it was all but fully grown.

It was a risk, a serious risk, but it was one worth taking. Not just for the sake of Hawk's memory and everything that went with it, but because assuming his plan came off, it would protect the one thing Billy cared about above all other, his own self-respect.

'Think you can piss me about do you?' he said out loud as he eased his car onto his drive. 'Well Foster old chap, we'll fucking well see about that.'

PART FIVE

Chapter Thirty One
Monday 9th July 2019

06.30

After a sleepless night that had seemed to involve doing little but nervously overreacting to every single noise in the street outside, Jamie had eventually given up and headed for his sofa and a seemingly endless stream of coffee and Sky News. It was going to be a long day and the thought of it wasn't helped by the fact that the second he walked into work he was going to be bombarded with questions. Since he still couldn't work out if it was his bruised and swollen face or his battered pride that hurt the most, he wasn't looking forward to that at all.

He had even considered calling in sick but only for a fleeting second. With his story now leading in all kinds of different directions, he knew that he had to stay focussed or it would inevitably fall apart. Far better to face the music and keep a firm grip on it than let that happen. Not just for his sake, but for Katie's. She'd worked almost as hard on this as he had.

The key question now was which path to follow. The Graham Hawkins angle had been designed purely to spook Evans and whilst that had obviously worked the only tangible result had been a bloodied nose. 'Journalist gets punch in face' was more likely to galvanise amusement than any other kind of reaction.

The police angle was far more interesting. If he could prove beyond doubt that the police were aiding and abetting vigilantes or even acting as vigilantes themselves, the impact of any subsequent investigation could potentially rival that of the Christopher Lawrence enquiry. That really would be something if he could pull it off, but it was easier said than done. At the moment all he had was what Lisa had told him and what Evans had hinted at, the rest was guesswork. Since Lisa was barely speaking to him there was no chance of her giving him anything concrete and even less of Evans helping him out so he was going to have to find a new source of information if he was ever going to make that work. Maybe he needed to think about taking another crack at the coppers in Coventry.

With a sigh, he glanced at the clock and then headed for the bathroom. All being well, he'd be out of the house before Lisa woke. Another round with her was the last thing he needed.

Claire was still half asleep when the bedroom door swung open and Billy entered carrying two cups of tea.

'You legend,' she sighed without moving. 'Just put it down, I'll drink it later.'

'Who said it's for you?' he replied as he slid back into bed. 'They might both be for me.'

'You wouldn't do that to me,' she sighed as she closed her eyes and snuggled down into her pillow. 'You love me too much.'

Billy glanced down and smiled. She'd mentioned the L word a few times in recent weeks, albeit in jest, but he wondered if this time, in her half-awake subconscious state, there was a more substance to it. Is that what she actually thought? Or was it more what she was hoping for?

He unconsciously reached out and gently touched her shoulder as he wondered if the time had come to give voice to what was the natural and seemingly inevitable next step. In all honesty, he couldn't think of a reason why not. After all, he was happy, she was happy and there was an increasingly normality to their relationship. Maybe it was time.

'What's going on in that head Evans?'

Billy looked down and smiled as she stared up at him with one eye open. 'Nothing,' he said. 'Just waiting for my two cups of tea to cool down.'

Claire wrestled herself into a sitting position, pulled the quilt around her and held out her hand.

'You're plotting something. I can tell.'

'Me? Never,' replied Billy as he passed her a cup. 'You must be mistaking me for your other bloke.'

'Shit, you sussed me. Did you get up last night?'

'Only for a bit. I couldn't sleep and I had some work I wanted to go over.'

'Work. Seriously?' said Claire in a disbelieving tone. 'I'd have said football, cars or porn.'

'I do like a bit of nurse porn,' Billy joked. 'It's the uniform. Speaking of which…'

'Don't even go there,' she said. 'The only thing getting under my scrubs are big pants and a comfortable bra.'

'Just how I like it.'

'Perv. What were you up to?'

'Just a project,' he replied. 'I'll tell you all about it if it comes off.'

Claire threw him a cautious look. 'As long as everything's OK.'

'Couldn't be better,' said Billy. 'Speaking of which, I've got something I need to do this morning but after that, how about I skive off this afternoon and we do something with your day off. We could go up west, celebrate something.'

'Celebrate? Celebrate what?'

Billy smiled. 'How about just being happy?'

'That sounds good to me' replied Claire softly before taking a sip of her tea. 'Are you? Happy I mean?'

Billy leant across and kissed her. 'I'm like a pig in poo,' he said. 'Aren't you?'

A beaming, satisfied smile spread across Claire's face. 'Oink.' she said.

As expected, Jamie had been forced to run the full gauntlet of both questions and piss taking once he'd arrived at work. What he hadn't expected was for Pete to tear into him for not going to hospital and then telling him that if he didn't go to A&E immediately, he'd be fired.

Whilst touched by his editor's efforts at caring, the consequence of Pete's decision was that Jamie had spent almost an hour in the urgent care unit of London Bridge Hospital with only his mobile phone for company. Not that it was doing him any good as the chances of concentrating on anything were remote given the Monday morning chaos of his surroundings.

For the umpteenth time, he threw a look at the receptionist in the hope of getting some attention but drew yet another blank so to try and kill some time he picked up his phone and texted Katie.

'This is fucking ridiculous,' he typed. 'Rescue me FFS!'

The reply was an almost instantaneous and entirely expected 'stop moaning.' With a sigh, Jamie sent her a GIF of a child saying 'I Hate You' and opened the twitter app to read the news.

He had barely made it past the first few headlines when his phone sprang into life. Having forgotten to put it on silent the ringing earned him a disapproving look from the receptionist and so he answered it as quickly as he could. 'Jamie Brown,' he said.

'It's Billy Evans.'

'What do you want?'

'To talk.'

Jamie suddenly felt a wave of irritation sweep over him. Not just because of the situation he found himself in but by the apparent arrogance of the man who had caused it all. 'Well since thanks to you I'm sitting in A&E waiting for an X-Ray,' he snapped, 'how about piss off.'

'I've got a deal for you,' said Billy.

'Mr. Brown?' Jamie looked up to see a male nurse scanning the room looking for him. 'Mr. Brown?' he repeated loudly.

After standing up and gesturing to the nurse, Jamie began gathering his things together and headed for the cubicle. 'I've got to go. What kind of deal are you on about?'

There was a pause before Billy replied. 'One that will make you famous.'

Once he had finished with Jamie Brown, Billy grabbed a coffee, made himself comfortable and prepared to call Foster. He was looking forward to this, although he knew that he was going to have to be at his sharpest.

After running through what he wanted to say, and how he wanted to say it, he dialled the number only to be connected to the messaging service.

'Bollocks,' he grunted to himself as he cancelled the call without leaving anything. 'That's not what I wanted.'

He sat for a moment and wondered what to do next. If he was going to pull this off, Billy knew full well that he had a finite amount of time to seize the initiative and if he couldn't raise Foster soon, the whole thing could go tits up pretty quickly.

'The courier's here,' called Lauren from the outer office.

'One minute,' replied Billy before taking a small pile of thick padded envelopes from his desk drawer and placing them on the desk in front of him.

He stared at them for a moment and wondered if he was doing the right thing. There was no doubt that his plan was a massive gamble but if it came off, he'd be laughing. Then again, if it went horribly wrong at least he'd wipe the smug grin from Foster's face.

'Send him in,' called Billy.

He was about to head for home to collect Claire before heading into London when Billy's phone rang, the legend 'Foster' appearing on the screen.

'I have a missed call from you,' he said once Billy answered. 'Is everything OK?'

'I was just wondering how you're getting on with my problem,' Billy replied. 'Any news?'

'Not yet, it's early days but we're on it.'

Billy took a slow deliberate breath to calm himself. 'Well,' he began, 'just to make sure that you're properly focussed on what we discussed yesterday, I thought I'd give you an incentive.'

'I don't understand,' said Foster cautiously. 'What kind of incentive?'

'I've just sent a file of information to Jamie Brown. Dates, times, photographs and voice recordings.'

'You're not serious.'

'Deadly,' said Billy. 'So, if you don't bury this story, you're fucked. I'm guessing you've got about 24 hours.'

The phone fell silent. It was a while before Foster spoke again.

'That was a foolish thing to do. You should have trusted me.'

'The only bloke I ever trusted is dead. Like I said yesterday, whatever it takes.'

'Well whatever happens, at best you know that you're effectively finished as far as our organisation is concerned.'

'At best?' scoffed Billy. 'So, what's at worst?'

'Treachery isn't taken lightly Mr. Evans. Not by the military, not by anyone. I'm sure even in your world, it has repercussions.'

'True,' said Billy confidently. 'But in my world, we don't do anything unless our backs are covered. And my back is well covered.'

'There'll still be a price to pay,' said Foster with a growing sense of irritation.

'No there won't, not if you want my lads to carry on working with you. But just to be clear, my brief has copies of everything I sent to Brown plus a shit load more and instructions to send it all to every tabloid if anything happens to me.'

'More? What exactly have you sent to Brown?'

Billy laughed. 'You don't seriously think I'd tell him anything that would implicate me, do you?'

The phone went quiet again. Billy listened to the silence for a while and then said 'clock's ticking Mr. Foster,' before killing the call.

'Fuck,' he said out loud as he leant back in his chair. 'That was bloody awesome!'

Chapter Thirty Two
Monday 9th July 2019

15.45

Having hurried back from the hospital, Jamie had arrived at his desk to find the promised A4 sized padded envelope leaning against his computer. The legend 'for the personal attention of J. Brown' written in thick red ink across the heavily sealed flap.

'Shit,' gasped Jamie as he sat down and held it in his hands. He could actually feel his heart racing as his mind ran through all kinds of computations as to what might be inside.

He turned it over and was about to pull at the flap when an alarm bell rang. Over the years he'd heard plenty of stories about the danger of opening unsolicited mail and whilst he'd been expecting this package, was it really beyond the realms of possibility that Evans could send him something untoward? The bruise on his face was testimony to how pissed off he was and from what Jamie had discovered about him over the last week or so, Evans almost certainly had contacts who were more than capable of pulling a stunt of some kind.

He looked across the office to where Katie was sitting and gestured her over.

'Get security to check it out,' she said after he'd brought her up to speed both with its origins and his concerns, 'then for fuck's sake, get it open!'

It was almost an hour before an increasingly frustrated Jamie and Katie were able to examine the contents of the envelope which, despite its size, consisted entirely of a single USB stick.

Having plugged it into his laptop to avoid the possibility of infecting the office mainframe with any kind of virus, they were now sitting in silence as the full implications of what they were looking at began to hit home. For whilst Billy had listed every attack that he had been involved in putting together, including the ones that Jamie had investigated, he had written it in a way which suggested that Foster and his men were responsible for them all.

To back that up, Billy had included various recordings he'd made of conversations between him and Foster and most damningly, a selection of stills from their meeting at *The Top Of The World*. In each one however, his own face had been pixellated out.

'Jesus,' hissed Jamie. Not just in response to what he was reading, but because he noted that Billy had avoided the fairly obvious temptation to implicate Lisa in anything. A detail he decided not to mention to anyone else, including his co-writer.

'Have you noticed something?' he whispered to Katie as he pulled a sheet of paper from his draw. 'Look. Some of the attacks on our list aren't on his.'

'So, there are definitely two groups,' she replied. 'But from the look of this he doesn't seem to know what the other group is up to?'

'Exactly. Either that or he's playing dumb for some reason.'

'We need to show this to Pete,' hissed Katie. 'Right now.'

As one, they looked across the office and seeing Pete at his desk, grabbed the laptop and headed toward him as surreptitiously as they could.

'Pete,' said Jamie is he burst into his office, computer in hand. 'You need to listen to this.'

'In case you hadn't noticed,' their editor replied irritably, 'I'm on the phone.'

Katie reached over and took the phone from his hand. 'He'll call you back,' she said into it before switching it off. 'You need to hear this boss,' she repeated.

Pete leant back in his chair and glared at the two of them. 'This better be good,' he growled.

'It's better than good,' said Jamie as he put the laptop on the desk and pressed play. 'It's dynamite.'

'I'm sorry to disappoint you but I'm not who you think I am.'

'Really, so who are you then? An Ian Foster lookalike?'

'Yes actually, although technically I'm the older one so he's the lookalike. I'm Major Christopher Foster, Royal Military Police. Ian Foster MP is my twin brother.'

'So does brother Ian know that you've got people running around battering members of the public?'

'We'll discuss that once we get to where we're going. In the meantime, why don't we talk about you?'

Jamie leant over and hit stop. 'There's loads more Pete. Film, photo's, names, times, dates, everything.'

Pete Goodwin sat forward and stared, expressionless, at the two people sitting opposite him. 'Where the bloody hell did you get that?'

'Evans sent it to me.'

A smile spread across Pete's face. 'You obviously passed the test,' he said. 'Congratulations.'

Jamie and Katie exchanged glances. 'There is one thing,' said Jamie. 'I gave him my word that I'd keep his name out of it.'

'And d'you want to?'

'Yes,' said Jamie after a pause. 'I think he might have more to give us.'

'OK, he's not important anyway,' said Pete dismissively as he stood up to pace. 'Right, have you got enough here to run with?'

'Yes, I think so. We'll need quotes but…'

'No, not yet. We don't want to spook anyone. Go through everything, check everything and then write it up. You'll need to speak to Ian Foster, but at the last minute.'

'How big d'you want it?' asked Katie.

Pete looked at her aghast. 'A sitting right-wing MP directly linked to a group of ex-servicemen who under the command of his still serving senior officer twin brother are carrying out vigilante attacks across the country. Seriously, what do you fucking think?'

Jamie glanced at Katie and winked. 'We're on it,' he said as he got to his feet.

'You better be, I want to see something by lunchtime tomorrow,' said Pete. 'And one other thing, this stays between us three for now, right? Any of this gets out and you'll both be out on your arses.'

Chapter Thirty Three
Monday 9th July 2019

23.45

Jamie was working in his office at home when he heard the front door slam shut.

Given that Lisa was on duty and mindful of recent events, he saved his work, emailed it to Katie for safety's sake and after closing his laptop, headed nervously downstairs to find Lisa slumped on the sofa. She looked crestfallen.

'What're you doing home?'

'I've been suspended,' she said. Her gaze fixed firmly on the TV screen even though she hadn't turned it on.

'Fuck,' gasped Jamie. 'Why?'

Lisa finally turned her head to stare at him. 'Why d'you think?'

Jamie ran every possibility he could think of through his head and having come up with nothing, simply replied, 'I've no idea.'

With a sigh, Lisa turned back to face the blank screen. 'For a journalist, you're fucking naive sometimes Jamie. D'you seriously not get it?'

'No, I don't. Get what?'

'I told you that there'd be implications for me if you carried on with this bloody story, but you wouldn't listen.'

'Hang on, are you saying that you got suspended because of me?'

Lisa turned to face him again. 'They think I've been feeding you information.' she said. 'No one trusts me, so I'm out.'

'But they can't do that! It's crazy, it's not even true!'

'Well, true or not my career has now officially tanked. Thanks for that.'

Jamie walked across and sat on the coffee table in front of her. 'Lisa, you need to tell me what's going on. I know you know something.'

'Just leave me alone,' she said irritably.

'No, you need to tell me. Are you involved in all this somehow?'

'And what if I was?' she snapped. 'What difference would it make? Would you drop it then?'

Jamie was about to respond but instead, he got to his feet and headed upstairs. Moments later, he returned with a printout of the details relating to the numerous attacks and handed it to her. 'Read this,' he said. 'I'll get us a drink.'

By the time he'd returned from the kitchen with two glasses of wine, Lisa was staring at him, dumbstruck.

'Where did you get this?'

'Evans sent it to me. There are 50 people on that list,' said Jamie. 'That's 50 attacks, 50 people in hospital. Probably more now.'

'This is bullshit.'

Jamie shrugged his shoulders. 'I've checked most of it out, dates, places, the lot. It's kosher.'

Lisa paused for a moment. She looked puzzled, confused even. 'And you think coppers did all these?' she asked incredulously.

Jamie shrugged his shoulders. 'You told me yourself that coppers are involved.'

'I said there are coppers who are sympathetic. That's a big fucking difference.' Lisa took a deep breath, seemingly to calm herself. 'Have you actually checked this Evans out? I have. You name it, he's been involved in it.'

'Yes, of course I have,' said Jamie.

'Yet you're still convinced that he's telling you the truth? Hasn't it occurred to you that these might all be down to him?'

Jamie remained silent. The lack of actual proof in respect of who had actually carried out any of the attacks was a major flaw in the story's chain because in truth, he had absolutely none other than what Evans had told him. However, since he'd also handed him enough hard evidence to go after Major Foster, it didn't really matter. Nor did how he came by any of it. As Pete had made clear, the real story was finding enough evidence to expose the direct link between a right-wing MP and a series of violent vigilante attacks. The rest was largely incidental although the full details would surely follow as it all unfolded.

'D'you know what I think?' continued Lisa. 'I think he's so desperate to stop you running this story about his mate that he'll feed you any old bollocks and you're so desperate for a story that you're falling for it. But all you're really doing is lining yourself up for a massive fall. You know that don't you?'

Jamie simply stared at her as she talked. There was something about her manner that was confusing him. It just didn't feel or sound right. It was questioning when he would have expected it to be more panic stricken.

'What else did he give you?' asked Lisa.

'What?'

'Evans, he must have given you more than this list?'

Again, Jamie hesitated. 'Yes, but Katie has the rest of it,' he lied.

'What was it?'

'He didn't mention you if that's what you're worried about.'

'What was it?' she pressed.

'I can't remember.'

Lisa glared at him. 'In other words, you won't tell me.'

'No,' said Jamie flatly.

'Why not?'

'I think it's best that we keep it to ourselves. For now, anyway.'

'Thanks,' she snorted in response. 'It's nice to know that you don't trust me either.'

There was an awkward silence and then Jamie asked the question that had started to scream at him.

'I've got to ask this Lisa, because I really need to hear you say it. I know you told me that two of these attacks were related to your cases, but were you directly involved in the attacks?'

Lisa scowled at him. 'No. I wasn't. OK?'

'And have you really been suspended?'

'You're fucking kidding me?' she blurted out. The disbelief in her voice almost tangible. 'You think I'm lying to you? Is that it?'

'Well, are you?'

There was a moment's pause and then her face darkened. 'Fuck you Jamie,' she snarled before standing up and heading for the door. The loud slam signalling her departure from the house in the most dramatic and final way possible.

'Well that went well,' Jamie said to himself. 'Great.'

Lisa climbed into her car and sped off. However, as she reached the junction at the end of the road, she pulled over and took out her phone.

'It's me,' she said as soon as it was answered. Her voice a mixture of sadness and embarrassment. 'I gave it a shot, but he won't drop it. He showed me a list Evans had given him but that's all. Listen, did you know that there've been 50 attacks? Yes, I'm telling you, 50! All over the bloody place. No, he said he's checked them out and they're genuine. No, I don't understand either. I tried, but he wouldn't tell me what else he had. Yeah, I'm OK. I'm on my way back to the nick. I'll be about half an hour.'

Lisa put the phone down but rather than drive off she settled back in her seat. She felt absolutely exhausted but more than that, she felt sad. Much as she loved Jamie, the harsh reality was that their relationship had effectively ended days ago. Not because he'd obviously never be able to trust her again, she could have lived with that, but because she'd had to distance herself mentally from what she had suspected was going to start unfolding over the coming weeks. The impact it was going to have on him would be immense, catastrophic even, and the last thing she wanted was to have to be around to witness it.

Ultimately however, it was his own doing. If only he'd listened to her and gone back to the world of celebrity, none of this would have happened.

Yet whilst she felt a degree of sorrow for the way things were going, Lisa had not an ounce of regret. She had all the justification she needed for her role in this saga and even as Jamie had been questioning her, it had been reinforced by the name she had found at number 7 on Evans list. Tommy Lawson. For that was the case that haunted her more than any other. Little Tilly Nelson. Poor little Tilly.

Even now, three years later, Lisa only had to close her eyes to see the films and hear the recordings of Tilly's anguished pleading and the sickening sound of Lawson's voice as he cajoled and encouraged her. All of it underpinned by the guilt and shame of knowing that ultimately it had been her mistake that had allowed him to walk from court.

Yet even as she had stared at his name, Lisa had struggled to suppress a smile at the recollection of the part she had played in arranging the beating that had left him crippled.

It might not be the justice she had sworn to uphold as a police officer, but it was nevertheless, justice and the ghost of Tilly Nelson was all the vindication she needed.

With a sigh, Lisa leant forward, rested her forehead on the steering wheel and burst into tears.

Poor Tilly Nelson.

09.30

After an enjoyable evening spent in the West End of London, Billy and Claire had risen late and tempted as he was to skip work and help her make the most of her second day off, her need to address the growing pile of washing at her house had forced his hand. He was off to work.

However, even as they'd been getting ready to leave, he had felt his nerves start to tingle. Something was wrong.

In truth, it didn't come as too much of a surprise. He'd actually been expecting something to happen ever since he'd spoken to Foster and whilst he was ready for pretty much anything, the fact he had Claire with him gave him additional concern. It was also why he had been hurrying her along on the premise that he had a meeting he had to get too.

It was however, to no avail. For even as Billy passed through his gates, he noticed a car pull out to follow him. The hidden blue lights bursting into life before he had travelled less than 100 yards.

Billy let out a silent curse as a blast of a siren gave additional weight to the demand to turn over. His neighbours would love that, he thought. Just like old times.

'Is that the police?' asked Claire as she looked nervously over her shoulder. 'What do they want?'

'No idea,' replied Billy without taking his eyes off the mirror. 'Wait here.'

Without another word, Billy grabbed his phone and switched on the record function before slipping it into his jacket pocket, climbing out and walking toward the rear of his car. He was however, genuinely taken aback when the door swung open and Lisa Cooper stepped out. She was the very last person he expected to see.

'Sergeant Cooper,' he said as she walked toward him. 'We must stop meeting like this. Your old man'll get jealous.'

Lisa ignored his attempt at humour and nodded toward the Range Rover. 'Who's in the car?'

'Come on,' replied Billy with a wry smile, 'you're better than that. Look, if this is about me smacking your bloke then fair enough, I was out of order. But seriously, hanging about outside my house to hassle me, that's a bit much.'

'I'm pretty sure you know what it's about,' she said, 'so cut the crap.'

Billy was slightly taken aback. When he'd told Foster about her it was in the hope that it would rattle him, and he was fairly confident that it had. Yet Billy had never seriously considered the idea that she might be one of his team, yet here she was pretty much admitting it.

'I'm not sure I do,' he replied cautiously. 'Why don't you enlighten me?'

Lisa took a step forward. 'I need to know what else you've told him,' she demanded.

'What I told who?'

'Don't try to be smart. Jamie, what did you tell Jamie?'

'About what?'

For a second, given the look on her face, Billy thought she was going to explode. 'At least give me a clue!' he continued. Not just to push another button or two but in the hope that he'd get more stuff on tape.

Lisa took a deep and barely controlled breath to calm herself. 'He showed me the bullshit list you sent him,' she said. 'I want to know what else he's got.'

Billy smiled to himself. And there it was. Not only fairly solid confirmation that she was party to what had been going on but pretty damning proof that Foster had a direct link into the Met.

'You can tell Foster that he'd be better off spending his time doing what I asked him to do,' said Billy.

Lisa hesitated for a moment and then asked, 'who's Foster?'

The question gave Billy another jolt, although this time is was more amusement than anything else as he realised that for all her bluster the woman standing in front of him actually knew little or nothing about what was going on. More importantly, her response begged another question and Billy was only too happy to ask it.

'Why don't you ask your old man?'

A hurt look flashed across Lisa's face and picking it up, Billy couldn't help but take another dig.

'Or wouldn't he tell you? Trouble in paradise?'

The two of them stood eyeballing each other and after a few moments, Billy decided that he'd pushed her as far as he could. 'I think we're done here Sergeant,' he said.

'I'll say when we're done,' she barked in response.

'No,' replied Billy in the most condescending voice he could muster, 'we are done. And you can tell whoever told you to sit outside my house that they'd be better off worrying about your fella than me. The clock's ticking.'

'Just so you know,' she said almost apologetically, 'I've been trying to get him to drop this bloody story ever since I found out about it.'

'And how has that worked out for you?' asked Billy sarcastically. 'Tick tock Sarge.'

Without another word Billy turned away and walked back to his car. Within seconds, he was driving away leaving her still standing in the road.

'What was that all about?' asked Claire. 'Are you OK?'

Billy smiled at her. 'Yeah, it was nothing. Just the old bill being a pain in the arse.'

Claire leant forward to look behind in the rearview mirror but seeing nothing, sat back and turned to Billy.

'I always seem to be asking you if everything's OK,' she said. 'Should I be worried Billy?'

'No sweetheart,' he replied, reaching out and squeezing her leg to provide reassurance. 'Everything's going exactly to plan. Trust me.'

Lisa watched the Range Rover speed away and let out a curse. She knew trying it on with Evans was a long shot, but it had been worse than she'd imagined. Now, she just felt like an idiot.

She walked back to her car and climbed in before taking out her phone and dialling. 'It was a bust,' she said as soon as it was answered. 'I bloody knew it would be.'

Leaning back in her seat Lisa listened to the voice on the other end for a moment and then sat forward. 'Who's Foster?'

Barring a quote or two from Ian Foster and the insertion of a few suitably chosen photographs, both Jamie and Katie were confident that their article was as tight as they could possibly have written it given the time they'd had. Now, they were in the period that all journalists dreaded. The no-man's land between having submitted it and it being approved for publication.

'I hate waiting,' sighed Jamie. 'How long does it take to read a bloody article?'

'Jesus,' groaned Katie. 'Will you stop moaning. Are you always this impatient?'

Jamie threw her a look to confirm that he was, and she shook her head in response. 'I can see now why you stayed on the Z-list desk so long,' she laughed.

He was about to reply when he spied Pete on the far side of the office. The editor looked across, caught Jamie's eye and pointed to his door.

'Here we go,' he gulped as he got to his feet. 'Good luck.'

The two of them headed toward Pete's office and were waiting by his door by the time he arrived. In his hands he carried a buff folder that Jamie assumed continued their article and accompanying paperwork.

'Come in and close that,' he said brusquely.

The second the door was closed. He dropped the folder on the desk and motioned the two of them to sit whilst he remained standing.

'This is bloody good,' he said. 'Great work, both of you.'

'Thanks. So, can we speak to Foster?' asked Jamie anxiously.

Pete hesitated and then said abruptly, 'No. Sorry, but we're not running it.'

Jamie and Katie exchanged glances. 'What?' she asked before Jamie could fully grasp what their editor had said.

'We're not running it. Look, I know how much work you've put into it but…'

'This is a joke, right?'

Pete looked at Jamie and shrugged his shoulders. 'It wasn't my decision,' he said.

'Whose was it?' asked Jamie. 'Because this is bollocks.'

Pete sat down at his desk, switched on his laptop and typed something into it. After a few seconds, he turned it round so that Jamie and Katie could see that the screen was filled with the newspaper logo.

'Theirs. The people who pay your wages,' he said in a monotone voice.

'But Pete…' began Jamie only to be stopped in his tracks by his editor holding up his hand.

'How long have you worked the celebrity desk Jamie?'

'About four years,' he replied. 'What's that got to do with this?'

'So how many stories have you buried or stored away for future use? Same with you Katie?'

'But this is different from some z-lister screwing around,' said Jamie almost pleadingly.

'No, it's not. It's just bigger. Look,' Pete continued, 'I know how you're feeling but that's the call. Now get everything wrapped up and on my desk before you go home.'

'Everything?' asked Katie cautiously. 'You want our notes as well?'

'Everything,' repeated Pete firmly. 'I've been told to bury this. Ours is not to reason why.'

He glanced at Katie and nodded at her to leave as Jamie sat, shell shocked by this turn of events.

'If you've got anything to say, let's have it.'

'You mean other than fuck?' said Jamie. 'Because fuck is about all I've got to say.'

'I get that,' said Pete calmly. 'It's a shitty call but it's been made and there's nothing we can do about it. Trust me, I tried.'

Jamie stared across the desk at his editor and nodded. He'd worked for Pete long enough to know that if he said he'd tried, then he would have tried.

With a sigh, he got to his feet. 'What now? Back to celeb's?'

'No,' said Pete. 'I'm gonna put you on features. I reckon you've earned a shot.'

Jamie forced a smile. 'Thanks boss, I appreciate that.'

'Now go get me everything to do with this story and then take Katie and go and get shitfaced. I'll see you both in the morning.'

Pete waited until Jamie had left his office before he picked up his phone and dialled. 'It's done,' he said. 'Yes, I told you, you'll have everything by close of play today.'

He put the phone down and cursed to himself before returning his attention to the myriad of emails clogging up his inbox.

Jamie fell into his seat and let his forehead fall against the desk. He felt empty, he felt cheated and worst of all, he felt betrayed. Not just by the people he worked for, but by Lisa.

Try as he might, he couldn't get his head around the fact that the woman he had been in a relationship with had been living what was in effect a double life. Or more accurately, a treble life. Indeed, he had even begun to wonder if, when she'd told him that she was working nights, she had instead been travelling around the country breaking the bones of some scumbag or other. Not that it mattered any more. There was no way back for them and in truth, he didn't want one. The inevitable separation of assets was going to be a small price to pay.

With a sigh, he sat up and turned on his computer but before he could log on to his account, Katie appeared and sat down beside him. He couldn't help but notice that she looked agitated.

'Our stuff,' she whispered. 'It's already gone.'

Puzzled, Jamie logged on only to find that like Katie, the folder containing all of the work relating to his article had vanished.

'What the fuck?' he said.

Without another word he stood up and headed for their editor's office.

'Our stuff's vanished.'

'Come in, why don't you,' said Pete without looking up from his computer.

'Our stuff,' repeated Jamie. 'It's…'

'Gone. I know. It's standard practice to take documents off the server when a story's shelved.'

'But it's our bloody story,' asserted Jamie in a tone which caused Pete to look up from his screen.

'No,' he replied. 'It's the papers story and it's been archived.'

'That's bullshit.'

'It's policy,' said Pete, returning his attention to his screen. 'I'm still waiting for your notes.'

Jamie stared at him for a moment and then with a sigh of defeat, headed back to where Katie was waiting.

'Here,' he said as he took a folder of notes from his draw and handed it to her. 'You can give him this lot. I'm going to get pissed. Join me if you like.'

Chapter Thirty Five
Tuesday 10th July 2019

15.30

Having done as much as he actually felt like doing, Billy was about to head home when Lauren knocked on his door and entered.

'There's someone here asking to see you.'

'Who?' he asked without looking up.

'It's a soldier,' she hissed.

Billy glanced up and smiled. 'Show him in.'

Lauren ducked out of the doorway and Billy sat back in his chair. Moments later, she returned and showed Foster in. It was the first time Billy had seen him in any kind of uniform and without thinking, Billy got to his feet. An instinctive show of respect.

'Can I get you anything? Tea? Coffee?' she gushed.

'No, thank you,' said Foster. 'I'm fine.'

Billy waited until she closed the door and then the two men shook hands and sat down.

'I've never seen you with your clothes on,' joked Billy sarcastically. 'Fair play, it certainly makes an impressive statement.'

Foster didn't react but instead, reached into his briefcase, took out an envelope and slid it across the desk.

'The text of the article. I thought you'd be interested.'

Billy stared down at the envelope. Tempted as he was to take a look at the contents, that could wait for a while. There was business to be concluded first.

'We had to call in some pretty big favours,' continued Foster irritably. 'But it's done.'

'It's appreciated,' said Billy. 'Seriously. But like I said…'

'Whatever it takes,' interrupted Foster. 'Yes, I remember. I hope you know that you potentially compromised this entire operation, not to mention putting both mine and my brother's careers in jeopardy.'

'I had to force your hand,' said Billy, 'that's how I work. Besides, wasn't the plan always to use Brown to reveal your brother as the top man? Or was that bullshit?'

'It's still our plan but it'll be at a time of our choosing and we'll only know that when we know for sure what's happening with leaving the European Union.'

'When or if?' asked Billy.

Foster smiled 'When,' he replied confidently. 'But there are going to be a few twists and turns before it finally happens.'

'You sound like a man in the know. Should I put a bet on?'

'You can always bet on the British public, Mr. Evans,' said Foster. 'But trust me when I tell you that when the time is right, we'll be in the perfect position to step up to the plate.'

Billy nodded in feigned agreement. He'd heard all this before and whilst he didn't necessarily agree with it, given that the vast majority of people in his world were politically right-wing, it had made sense to get involved from the outset and be a player as opposed to an observer. That's why he had put himself in the frame with Brown, to make himself indispensable.

'Well I'm guessing I'm not exactly flavour of the month,' said Billy, 'So what happens now?'

Foster stared across the table for a few moments. His face expressionless. Billy stared back but he suddenly began to feel uneasy. The man sitting opposite him might be a copper, but he wasn't like the ones he normally dealt with. There was something almost sinister about him and for the first time since he'd met Foster, Billy began to wonder if the stories he'd heard about the military police were actually true. Maybe they really didn't fuck about.

'In light of your actions,' said Foster eventually, 'we have no choice but to suspend all activities for a while. Other papers have run this story and we need it to die down naturally.'

'That's fair enough,' said Billy. 'I'll let my lot know. Is that it?'

Foster returned to his stare and once again, Billy felt uneasy.

'I have to assume,' said Foster after a few moments, 'that your lot, as you call them, won't work for anyone else.'

'They trust me. What can I say?'

With a barely disguised sigh, Foster got to his feet. 'I'll be in touch,' he said before turning and walking out.

Billy watched him go with a mixture of relief and bemusement. Normally he enjoyed verbal sparring with Foster, but he hadn't enjoyed that at all. There was too much unsaid for his liking. More worryingly, he had picked up a hint of something although he couldn't work out if it was a threat or simple distain.

Either way, there was nothing he could do about it and so with a sigh, Billy pulled out his phone and began to compose a message to his lads.

'Who was that?' asked Lauren almost breathlessly.

Billy looked up to see her standing in the doorway, a broad smile on her face. 'Let me guess,' he said, 'a good-looking bastard in a uniform?'

'And some,' Lauren laughed. 'Will he be coming back?'

'I dunno. But if he does and I'm not here, get hold of me immediately. OK?'

Lauren nodded and turned away only to turn back. 'D'you know who he looked like?'

'No,' said Billy, returning his attention to his phone. 'Who?'

'That MP, you know, the Nazi. Well, that's what my fella calls him.'

Billy hit send on his phone and then looked up and shook his head. 'Your fella's a dick,' he said before getting to his feet. 'Now, if it's OK with you, I'm going home.'

Having decided to go to his place and change before he went to Claire's, Billy had just pulled onto his drive when he became aware of a car approaching his rapidly closing gates.

As he watched, the elderly Ford Focus stopped just as they clanged shut but almost instantly, they began to swing open again.

This was trouble, big trouble.

Instinctively, Billy hit the button to open the rear hatch before diving out. By the time the gates had opened enough to allow the car through, he was standing at the rear of his car swinging the baseball bat he kept with him for such an emergency.

'OK, you cunts,' he barked at the four masked men who climbed out. 'I don't care which, but at least one of you bastards is going down with me!'

'Mr. Evans!'

Billy spun around to find Foster walking around the car behind him, still in uniform.

'What the fuck?' he gasped. 'How d'you get in?'

'The same way I knew that you were on your way here and not your girlfriends,' said Foster. 'Billions of pounds of military spending.'

Before Billy could react, he felt himself being grabbed and slammed up against the side of his car whilst expert hands relieved him of his weapon and thrust both arms up his back.

'So, this is it then is it?' growled Billy. His eyes firmly fixed on Foster. 'Payback for almost dropping you in it.'

'We don't do payback,' said Foster impassively, 'but we enforce discipline.'

'You can stick your discipline up your arse,' scoffed Billy as strong hands continued to press him against his car. 'If you seriously think I'll work for you after this you need your fucking bumps feeling.'

Foster allowed a smile to creep across his face. 'You know what I like best about you Mr. Evans? It's not that you're smart, it's that you're greedy. Not for money, for power. You won't give that up, you can't.'

'Wanna bet?'

'Actually, yes. I do. Now, shall we get this over with?'

Billy glared at him. 'Do your fucking worst,' he growled. 'Just don't scratch my motor or I'll get angry.'

Foster nodded knowingly and then turned and walked toward the gates. Billy watched him for as long as he could and then closed his eyes to wait for the inevitable assault. If he was lucky, he'd get at least one solid punch in but either way, it was pretty obvious that he was going to be sore in the morning.

The first blow came not to the kidneys where he expected it, but on the side of his left knee. So well-aimed that Billy was on the floor before he knew it but thanks to an instinct developed over decades at football, he immediately drew himself into a tight ball to protect himself.

There were, however, no further blows. Instead, Billy's entire body went into spasm as he was hit by thousands of volts fired into him courtesy of a taser. He had just about recovered from that when he was hit by a second charge.

He lay for a second with his eyes firmly closed as he felt his body start to relax but Billy knew only too well that if he was going to move, he had to pull himself together and fast. However, even as he tensed his aching muscles to try and get to his feet, he felt his left arm being grabbed and stretched out. Almost immediately, a sharp and expertly applied blow hit his forearm, the resultant thwack being closely followed by a burst of excruciating pain.

'Fuck!' he screamed out loud as he grabbed his wrist. 'You bastard!'

Before he could say anything else, Billy heard the sound of a car starting and turned his head to see his gates swinging open. Within seconds, the four men and the Ford Focus were reversing out and heading off up the road.

He lay back on his concrete drive and tried to fight the pain that was tearing through him. Yet for all that struggle, a part of him knew that he'd got off lightly. Compared to the people they'd been targeting; a broken arm was nothing. At least it would mend reasonably quickly.

With a struggle, Billy worked himself into a seating position and leant against his car, then something lying on the floor caught his eye.

He stared at it for a moment and then realising what it was, said out loud, 'Wankers! They even used my own fucking bat.'

Having left the bar seemingly sober despite his best efforts to get hammered, Jamie had taken a black cab home with the intention of continuing his quest for oblivion on his sofa.

However, as soon as he had walked through his front door he had retreated to the sanctuary of his office where he had grown increasingly angry at the injustice that had been served to him that day.

It wasn't the fact that his first serious investigative piece had been snatched away from publication, it was the indignation at being the victim of political string pulling. It felt very different from the dancing he usually did to the tune played by publicists and agents desperate to keep their clients relevant, this had been done in the name of power and influence. However, Jamie looked at it, it wasn't right.

For the umpteenth time, he picked up the hard copies of the various drafts he'd secreted at home and glanced through them. Surely, he wondered, if Pete wouldn't publish the story on Foster then there had to be some mileage in exposing either Hawk or Evans. After all, he'd garnered a lot of publicity for both the paper and himself with the original vigilante story and this was simply another layer on that. And if Pete wouldn't publish, then why shouldn't he publish something online himself? He had his battered notebook and copies of most of his notes at home so putting a more detailed story together wouldn't be difficult. He could even throw in the stuff about Evans and Hawkins to beef it up even more. After all, irrespective of what his editor had said, this was his story, well, his and Katie's, and surely no one could argue that exposing a corrupt MP and his involvement with a vigilante organisation wasn't in the public interest.

Yet even as he thought about that, Jamie realised that following that path would be a massive risk. He would certainly receive a visit from Evans and who knows how that would end up. Just as importantly, publishing would be a sacking and possibly even criminal offence. Even with his alcohol impaired judgement, he knew that no story was worth that.

With a sigh, he pushed himself back from his desk and got to his feet. His pride and ego had been battered but they would eventually heal themselves. At least he'd been promoted which whilst small comfort, was at least something. What he needed now however, was sleep.

Billy had given up trying to sleep and having left Claire gently snoring, had taken station on his sofa. However, his plan to watch TV to take his mind off the pain had been dashed when he'd knocked his cast against the door frame. As a consequence, he was now cradling his arm whilst praying to any god that would listen that the painkillers he'd taken would kick in sooner rather than later.

Not for the first time that day, his mind returned to the subject of Foster, the cause of his agony. Inevitably there was a part of him already plotting some kind of violent revenge but deep down, Billy had already accepted that he had to let this one go. This wasn't the first time that he'd encountered someone on a different level to him when it came to the use of violence and he only had to think of Samantha to be reminded of the potential consequences of getting into a war with someone like that. 'He who fights and runs away' had never felt more apt.

Yet despite the excruciating pain in his arm, Billy was utterly convinced that he'd done the right thing. Brown had apparently been silenced, Julie was safe from any distress -not that she would ever know what it had cost- and in spite of the fact that his involvement with Foster had clearly come to an abrupt and painful end, he was satisfied that he'd come out on top. He'd miss the buzz of being involved in something, but he'd retained his self-respect and ultimately, that was all that mattered.

The question facing him now was how to replace that buzz, although part of him had started to wonder if he should actually bother. After all, he'd only got involved in this thing with Foster because of Hawk and that particular ghost had certainly been put to rest. It was also safe to say that whilst he would never truly be over the loss of Samantha, the events of the last few months had given him the courage to finally admit that it was OK to move on.

Maybe the lump of plaster he now wore on his arm was the signal that it was finally time to call it quits on the more disreputable side of his life and start a new chapter.

'You OK?'

Billy looked up to see Claire leaning against the door frame, arms folded across her chest.

'This hurts like a bastard.' he groaned.

'It will do you idiot. It's broken.'

'You might want to work on your bedside manner. It's rubbish.'

Claire continued to watch him for a moment and then walked across the room and sat down. 'You were lucky,' she said, 'any worse and that would have needed pinning.'

Billy grunted. He didn't think he'd been lucky at all. It was more likely that whoever had wielded his bat knew exactly how hard a blow to apply to cause just enough damage to make their point.

'Come on then Evans, what really happened? And before you give me any more of that I fell over crap, just think about how many broken arms I've had to deal with over the years.'

Billy looked her in the eyes for a few seconds and nodded. She was right of course, and she deserved better than to be lied to.

'OK,' he sighed, 'but it's complicated.'

'Did it have anything to do with that policewoman who stopped us yesterday?'

'Kind of,' said Billy.

Claire took a deep breath and settled back on the sofa. 'I see. Do I really want to know then?' she asked.

'Probably not,' said Billy calmly, 'but if you ask me, I'll tell you.'

Claire turned her head to look at him. 'That sounds ominous.'

Billy shrugged his shoulders. The movement making him wince and then curse.

'OK,' she said. 'Give me the potted version.'

Billy took a deep breath and went for it. 'The journalist who called Julie was going to write a story about Hawk and me. It was bullshit, but he was going to run it anyway, so I had to stop him. Not for my sake, for hers.'

'And have you?'

'Yes.'

'You didn't do anything...'

'No,' said Billy. 'Nothing like that. I just arranged for his bosses to stop it being published. That's all.'

'So how did your arm get broken?'

Billy hesitated for a moment. 'I pushed my luck a bit too far and some people got upset. This was their way of putting me in my place.'

'What people?'

More hesitation and then Billy took a deep breath and said, 'Old bill.'

Claire turned her head away from him and stared at the TV for a few moments.

'The ones you've been dealing with?' she asked without looking at him.

'Yep,' Billy replied. 'Believe me, it won't happen again.'

'Until the next time you mean.'

Billy reached out and took her hand. 'No sweetheart,' he said. 'I'm done. Honestly.'

She flashed him a look and a half smile. 'Good,' she said.

They sat in silence for a few moments and then Claire lifted Billy's right arm and snuggled down against him.

'I love you Evans,' she said.

Billy gave her a squeeze and smiled to himself. 'I love you too,' he said.

PART SIX

Chapter Thirty Six
Tuesday 6th August 2019

10.15

With his plaster cast freshly consigned to a bin in the orthopaedic department of Queens Hospital, Billy had adjourned to the coffee shop to find that Claire hadn't yet arrived.

After sending a silent curse in her direction closely followed by a text asking where the bloody hell she was and reminding her that she had the car keys, he grabbed a bottle of water and settled back to wait.

Having marked the second anniversary of Hawk's death only a week ago, the hospital and the memories it inevitably dragged up was the very last place he wanted to be. Especially since the evening of Hawk related nostalgia in the company of a group of older *CSS* lads and far too much beer had led to some sobering reflection.

It wasn't that Billy hadn't enjoyed it; it was that he hadn't felt the pull he had expected. *The CSS* were a part of his DNA and he'd never forget or regret his role in their history, but after all the stuff with Foster, he had finally accepted that side of his life as being over.

What he had felt, especially the following morning, was loneliness. The reminiscing over Hawk had finally proven what Billy had long suspected and that was that he still hadn't fully come to terms with the fact that he wasn't around. For all the people he knew, there was no one he could simply sit and talk bollocks with over a beer. He missed that. He missed his mate. He always would.

A ping from his phone dragged Billy away from his melancholy thoughts and having discovered that Claire would be another five minutes, he began trawling through social media to pass the time. Anything to avoid having to look around his surroundings.

'What d'you think of all that then?' asked a voice.

Billy looked up from his phone to discover that the voice belonged to an old man. His worn collar and loosely knotted tie marking him out as being well into his 60's and from the look of him, pretty poor.

'Sorry mate,' said Billy. 'What do I think of what?'

'Him,' he said gesturing toward a television playing silently on the wall across from them. 'That Foster fella.'

A wry smile spread across Billy's face as the sight of Ian Foster MP talking into camera came into focus. Behind him, the Houses of Parliament looked its usual majestic self.

'What's going on?'

'He's kicked off about Boris and what he said yesterday about getting tougher on violent crime. Reckons we need to get the police out on the streets kicking arse.'

'Sounds fair enough to me,' said Billy.

'And me. Dunno why Boris didn't make him Home Secretary. At least he's got some balls.'

After nodding in agreement and smiling at the old man, Billy took out his phone and logged onto the news. It was full of Foster's comments and the reaction from the left which was predictably rabid.

Suddenly, Billy felt a nervous tingle in his stomach as his brain threw a memory into his thinking. Part of the original plan sold to him by Foster had involved his brother kicking up a public storm about the failure of the criminal justice system ahead of resigning from the government. He would then come clean about what had been going on and explain how the attack on his mother had given him the incentive to fight back. Hopefully, hearing him talk about his own experience and seeing the impact his group had been having across the country would galvanise public support for both him and his cause and force the government into more overt action. The ultimate aim being to bring about a return to the traditional British right-wing values of community and respect for the law.

It was of course, all utter bollocks. Billy had seen through that straight away because he'd realised that what it had really been about was power and influence. That had been why he'd jumped on board because if anyone was going to profit from something like this, he was going along for the ride.

Things had gone pretty well for a while but then Jamie Brown had appeared. Whilst Billy thought that he'd managed to contain it initially, Brown had shocked him with the threats about Hawk and from that point on, it was game over as far as he was concerned. Without his input, Foster's plan was going nowhere.

Or was it? For seeing the MP ranting on the news, Billy began to wonder if he had underestimated the Foster brothers. Indeed, the more he thought about it, the more that it made perfect sense to run with it now.

For after three years of seeing the move to leave the European Union stall, the Brexit supporting public had been freshly galvanised first by the EU election results and then the appointment of the overtly right-wing Boris Johnson to the helm. With the left having all but collapsed, the door had been kicked wide open for the centre right to walk in and take control of the political landscape.

Yet if Foster was actually going to run with his plan, Billy knew that he was lacking one significant thing. He didn't have lads doing the footwork any more. Then again, what was to say that Foster hadn't gone looking for troops elsewhere? Billy knew enough ex-forces lads to know that the veteran community potentially provided a rich source of highly disciplined and capable muscle. Indeed, back in the day he'd often thought about how he might have been able to tap into it. With Major Foster an obvious flag bearer for the moral crusade and the veterans increasingly vocal about their perceived injustice at the hands of the government, it would certainly make sense to exploit that pool of talent.

'Shit,' muttered Billy to himself. 'They couldn't have, could they?'

For a moment, he actually felt a pang of regret. The first he'd felt since he'd walked away. If this was indeed going to happen, it would have been an incredible buzz to be one of the main faces when the news broke. Yet almost as quickly, those pangs vanished. However, Billy looked at his life, the bottom line was that he was happy, and life was good. That was enough.

'Hey, you're free! How's it feel?'

'Light,' he said, waving his arm about to Claire's obvious delight. 'And not itchy.'

'Come on then,' she said, holding out her hand. 'Let's blow this joint.'

'Where are we going?' asked Billy as he got to his feet.

Claire looked at him and smiled before leaning in to whisper. 'You've had the bloody cast on your arm for six weeks. Where do you think we're going?'

Billy took a step back. 'Not even dinner first? Bloody hell, so much for romance.'

'There's a McDonalds on the way home,' she said as she led him toward the exit. 'I'll buy you a Happy Meal.'

Like most of the people in his office, Jamie Brown had also been watching Ian Foster on the television but unlike Billy, he wasn't intrigued, he was irritated.

It had taken him a good few weeks to get over the anger surrounding the quashing of his story and here he was being reminded of it all. The resentment, the bitterness and worst of all, the frustration were back and fevering nicely.

It had also dragged up the constantly suppressed issue of Lisa. Within days of their argument she'd moved her stuff out and a few days later, she'd sent him an email demanding that he sell the house and the profits be split down the middle. Then she had seemingly vanished leaving him concerned for her welfare, not that it had done him any good. All attempts to contact her had been in vain.

Now, with the sight of Foster having dragged everything else up, he had also been reminded of her and would now have to go through the process of worrying again. The very last thing he needed or wanted.

However, if Jamie had learned one thing over the last few weeks it was that he had the ability to bury concerns unrelated to his work and so, with a muttered curse, he returned his attention to the task in hand. Within a few minutes, all thoughts of either Lisa or Foster had been placed firmly on the back burner.

With Claire insisting on driving due to her worries about his weakened arm, Billy had settled back in his seat whilst the two of them flirted mercilessly about what was going to be taking place over the next few hours.

As a result, neither of them noticed the black Mercedes following them until they had pulled up outside Billy's house and were waiting for the gates to open.

'Is it them?' asked Claire nervously. Her eyes fixed firmly on her rear-view mirror.

'I don't know,' replied Billy. 'But I'm gonna find out. Go inside and close the gates, OK?'

'But…'

'Just do it, please,' he insisted. 'Don't worry, it'll be fine.'

Before Claire could say another word, Billy pushed open the door and stepped out. Even as he did so, Paul stepped out of the Mercedes and opened the rear door to invite him inside.

Billy walked up to the car and bent down to look inside. 'Major Foster, what a pleasant surprise,' he said sarcastically. 'I'm glad you've popped around; it gives me the chance to tell you to fuck off.'

Foster smiled in response and then held up his hands in mock surrender. 'Fair enough,' he said. 'However, I'd rather that we talk.'

Billy laughed. 'You're kidding right? What possible reason would I have for getting in this motor?'

Foster smiled in response. 'Because you're smart, and I need your help.'

'You do realise that they've only just cut the fucking cast off my arm. You know, the one I got the last time you popped round!'

'Yes, and I'm sorry about that but like I say, I need your help.'

'Tough.'

'Will you at least hear me out? It could be well worth your while.'

At those magic words, Billy hesitated, his interest piqued. 'Shit,' he thought to himself and after a brief glance at his house, climbed into the Mercedes.

Having rushed into the house, Claire was now watching the scene outside unfold from the safety of an upstairs window.

Yet far from being anxious, she was actually intrigued. She would never admit it to anyone else, not even Billy, but she had always found the darker side of his lifestyle particularly captivating.

It wasn't just the secrets of his past or the thought of what he may or may not be getting up to whilst he wasn't with her that she found exciting, it was the schizophrenic nature of his entire character.

On the one hand Billy was this kind, loving and generous man who she adored and on the other, he was apparently a devious, immoral and violent criminal that she knew little or nothing about. How could any woman not find that attractive? She certainly did, or rather, she used to. He had after all, forsaken that side of his life for her sake and whilst she had been incredibly touched by the gesture, it hadn't escaped her notice that he had softened over the last few weeks. She still loved him with a passion, and she was sure that she always would, but Billy was no longer her rough diamond, he had become more a polished pearl.

Now, as she watched Billy climb inside the Mercedes with the dark suited man standing beside it looking for all the world like a Mafia hitman, Claire began to feel that excitement return. Not like before, but stronger. For the first time an episode of her mans' formerly secret life wasn't simply being played out in front of her, she had actually featured in it.

Yet for now, all she could do was wait and see what unfolded and as the tingle in the pit of her stomach grew, Claire began to wonder if this nervous anticipation was anything like the buzz Billy had so often referred to.

If it were, then she finally understood what he meant when he called it addictive. It was after all, both physically and mentally over-powering.

With a sigh, Claire leant against the wall and continued to stare out of the window. Waiting had never been her strongest personality trait, yet as she stared down at the car parked on Billy's drive, it was the only option available.

'Come on then,' said Billy arrogantly, 'convince me.'

'It's the plan,' said Foster. 'The one we outlined. It's on.'

'Yeah, I guessed. I saw your brother on the telly. So, if it's all systems go, what do you need me for?'

Foster gave an almost imperceptible nod and then launched into his pitch.

'I'm sure you don't need me to tell you about the political farce that's currently infecting the country,' he said calmly. 'Well, the fact is that it's all a smokescreen.'

'To con the public again?'

'No,' replied Foster. 'We have an opportunity to destroy the left wing once and for all.' Foster left a pause for effect, but Billy merely stared at him. His face devoid of expression.

'Irrespective of what else happens in the meantime,' continued Foster, 'shortly after this country leaves the EU the various right-wing parties will forge an alliance to gain overall and permanent control of Parliament. From then on, there will be no stopping us.'

'You still think the public will go for something like that after the balls up the Tories are making of Brexit?' scoffed Billy.

Foster smiled. 'I've no doubt about it. The more reputable polls are already showing a very positive response to the Prime Minister and an extremely negative one for Mr. Corbyn.'

'Polls,' scoffed Billy. 'What a bloody scam business that is.'

'Actually, for the most part they're remarkably accurate.'

'I'll have to take your word for it,' scoffed Billy. 'So where do I fit into all this?'

'As you've seen, my brother is currently whipping up a PR storm with his stance on crime. However, within a few days he'll resign from the Tory party citing a personal matter as the reason. The morning after that, a modified version of Brown's article will be published at which point, all hell will break loose. My brother will then kick off a campaign for an even tougher line on crime which will gain huge support from the public. That will eventually lead to the birth of a right-wing alliance. Simple.'

'How?'

'Pardon?'

'How will your brother do anything? He'll be a backbench MP. No one will give a shit.'

Foster smiled knowingly. 'Not for long. But you're going to have to trust me on that.'

'Fair enough,' said Billy. 'But that still doesn't answer my question.'

'When the story breaks,' continued Foster, 'it's inevitable that every newspaper in the land will be searching for dirt on my brother and me. At some point, we will feed them Brown's original story about the attacks and ensure that someone puts two and two together.'

'In other words, you need some up to date news to hand them. Is that it?'

'In a nutshell, yes.'

'Get your own lads to do it. You don't need me.'

Foster took a breath. When he spoke, it was almost apologetically. 'We haven't the numbers. When you pulled out, some of the other activists also took a step back.'

'The serving coppers you mean,' said Billy brusquely.

'Yes. They're er… cautious.'

'In other words, you want me to put my lads back in the frame?'

'No,' insisted Foster. 'I have an assurance that the policy of not investigating attacks will continue.'

Billy hesitated. 'Can I have that in writing?'

'I would if I could,' said Foster with a sly smile. 'But I can give you my word.'

Foster reached into his pocket and pulled out a USB stick. 'On here are 50 targets. The usual feral vermin as you'd expect.' He paused for a second and then added cautiously, 'There are also 50 others.'

'Who are they?' asked Billy having noted a change in the tone of Foster's voice.

'Mostly journalists and left-wing activists.'

'The opposition you mean?'

'Quite. After the news has broken, as long as things go as we are fairly certain they will in terms of public support after Brexit, then it'll be open season. I want to be ready to hit these characters hard.'

Billy settled back in his chair and pondered. There was no doubt that the idea held great appeal but even Billy could see that it was sailing dangerously close to aping the rise of the Brown shirts in the 30's. Did he really want to associate himself with that? There was also Claire to consider. How would she react if he suddenly sprang something like this on her? He certainly wasn't going to risk losing her, whatever the cause. In any event, he would only even consider asking her about it if he had the answer to one very specific question.

'On the off chance I agree,' he said, 'what's in it for me?'

The reply came almost instantaneously. As if Foster had rehearsed the moment numerous times in his head. 'Power Mr. Evans. Power and everything that accompanies it.'

Billy stared across the car and noted the smug expression on Foster's face. He was either raving mad or utterly confident in every word he was saying. Either way, it was clear to Billy that he had nothing to lose and plenty to gain by going along with whatever scheme the Army officer had intimate knowledge of.

'So,' continued Foster as he held out the USB stick, 'will you help change the course of history?'

Billy eyeballed him for a moment and then took the USB stick.

'On one condition.'

'Which is?'

With a smile, Billy slid the stick into his pocket and pulled open the door.

'That my bird lets me.'

Having listened intently to every word Billy had told her since he'd returned from his encounter, Claire had adjourned to the toilet where she now sat deep in thought.

In truth, she was only there because Billy had told her that she had to take time to consider the potential implications of the decision he was asking her to make. In reality she'd made her mind up even as he'd been speaking.

Yet what had hit her the hardest hadn't been the detail it was the fact that Billy had felt the need to ask her. She had never been given that much respect by anyone in her entire life and it was both frightening and electrifying. It was also empowering. And that was seriously exciting.

With a sigh, she glanced at her watch and having decided that she'd taken enough time to satisfy Billy, headed downstairs where he sat waiting patiently on the sofa.

'You OK?' he asked as she sat down beside him.

'If I said no to all this,' she said nervously, 'what would you do?'

'I told you, I need you to be honest. If you're not a hundred percent on board then you must say so.'

'But you won't hate me?'

'Of course not!' replied Billy with a smile.

'Or resent it?'

'Never.'

Claire reached out and took his hand. 'Thank you. You've no idea what that means to me.'

Billy took the USB stick from his pocket and held it up. 'So, shall I bin this then?'

'Are you kidding?' she said with a smile. 'You've got to do it.'

'OK then,' replied Billy with a squeeze of her hand. 'If you're sure.'

'I am, I trust you 100% Billy, I really do.'

'Thanks.'

'I do have one question though.'

Billy looked at her and frowned. 'What's that?'

Claire leant across and kissed Billy passionately on the lips before moving her mouth to his ear. 'Are you going to fuck me or what?' she whispered.

With a function to get to that evening, the last thing Pete Goodwin had needed was to have a last-minute curve ball thrown at him. Yet as he stood in the lift heading back toward his office, he knew full well that the instructions he'd just been

231

given would not only screw up his evening but as a lifelong socialist, they may well haunt him for weeks, if not years.

It had not however, occurred to him to resist. He loved his job and his ambition was such that he had sworn long ago to do whatever it took to climb the ladder to the top. If that meant selling out his political principles, or even his staff, fuck it. He'd have plenty of time for guilt once he'd retired. As the lift doors slid open, Pete's gaze was already firmly fixed in the direction of Jamie's desk. It was, however, empty.

'For fuck's sake,' he muttered as he walked toward it, 'where's he gone now?'

'Katie,' he barked, 'have you seen Jamie?'

'I think he's out,' she replied. 'Can I help?'

Almost instantly, an idea jumped into Pete's head. One which would actually make his task easier.

'Come with me,' he said as he changed direction and headed for his office.

Moments later, she was in the doorway. 'Come in, close the door and sit down.'

'What's up?' she said as she took her seat. 'Is something wrong?'

Pete sat down and eyeballed her. After a second or two, he allowed a smile to creep onto his lips.

'The thing is, I have an opening for a political correspondent in New York. It's a two-year contract, possibly three. D'you fancy it?'

Katie stared back at him, a blank look on her face. 'You're kidding?'

'Why would I do that?'

'Well, er… when?'

'As soon as. I need an answer fast, so go home and think about it.'

'I don't need to think about it,' she said excitedly.

'You sure? Don't you have a bloke to talk to or something?'

'I did have until about thirty seconds ago,' she gushed.

Pete smiled. 'Excellent,' he said. 'It's a great opportunity but you've earned it.'

He paused for a moment to allow her to absorb the news a little more and then said, 'Now, there is one thing I need you to do for me first.'

Chapter Thirty Seven
Wednesday 7th August 2019

08.20

With a still somewhat excited Claire having left for work, Billy had made himself a pot of coffee and taken to his home office to reflect on what had happened over the last 24 hours.

Not only was he about to step back into a world that he'd willingly and happily walked away from only a few weeks ago, but he was dragging his girlfriend with him. Albeit at her insistence. Indeed, Billy had been somewhat taken aback at her enthusiasm for what may lay ahead. It had certainly proved something of a turn on for her which was never to be sniffed at.

The question however, remained. Was he doing the right thing? The more he thought about it, the more obvious the answer. For as Foster had pointed out, the potential in terms of power was immense and power meant not just influence, but money. Just as importantly, if the police really did intend to be half-hearted when it came to investigations, the risk was minimal. How could he turn that down? Why would he even want to?

With the decision taken, Billy fired off a text to Foster closely followed by one to Lauren to tell her he'd be late. He then used his secondary phone to text his lads and tell them to prepare to go back to work. Once that was done, he plugged the USB stick Foster had given him into his laptop and began checking out the 50 names to help him work out who to assign them to. Only once that was complete, and purely out of curiosity, did Billy open the second file and cast his eyes through what was effectively their first proper hit list.

He was quietly satisfied that for the most part, he could have predicted the majority of the people Foster wanted targeting but the sight of Jamie Brown's name attracted a pang of conscience. For all his issues with Brown, he had kept his word and expunged Hawk from his story and even though the revised version had been buried, Billy still considered himself to be in the journalist's debt. But that could wait. He had a business to run and with a satisfied sigh Billy snapped his computer shut and drained his coffee before heading out.

It was good to be back.

Pete finished reading Katie's rewrite of the Foster article and smiled to himself. It was exactly what he wanted. Almost.

However, he had no intention of firing it back to her for a revision. He knew exactly what needed to be done to make it fit for publication and he was more than capable of doing that himself. Indeed, in this instance that was almost certainly for the best given the sensitivity of the changes he was going to make.

'Morning chief. Katie said you were looking for me yesterday.'

Pete looked up to find Jamie standing in his doorway. For a second, he wondered if he should say anything to him but decided against it. Like everyone, he'd find out in the morning.

'Don't worry about it,' he said. 'It was nothing.'

'Cool,' said Jamie. 'Hey, I heard about Katie. Good call, she'll be great.'

'Yeah, she will.' Pete locked eyes with Jamie for a second and then watched him walk back to his desk. Only once he had sat down did he return his attention to the article on his screen.

Scrolling back to the top, he placed his cursor on Jamie's name and without a moment's hesitation, deleted it.

Pete had just finished working on the amendments when he became aware of a furore on the floor outside his office. Within moments, a beaming Jamie appeared.

'Ian Foster's just resigned?' he said excitedly. 'Personal reasons apparently.'

'I heard.'

'What are you going to do? Are you going to run our piece?'

'Tomorrow morning, front page,' he replied calmly.

'Fantastic! What do you want us to do? Should we try and get a quote from his office?'

'I already spoke to them,' replied Pete dryly.

Jamie was taken aback. 'Oh, OK. But how…?' he blurted out before his brain finally caught up with what was happening.

'They called me,' said Pete. 'Don't worry, they didn't say much. I've already done the edits.'

'Can I see it?' asked Jamie after a short but expectant pause.

'No,' said Pete abruptly.

'Why not?' asked a stunned Jamie. 'It's my bloody story!'

'We've already had this conversation. When you're sitting here and your name's on that door, it'll be your story.'

'This is you making some kind of point then?'

'Before you say something you'll regret, I suggest you piss off back to your desk.'

'But…'

'Out,' growled Pete, 'and close the fucking door.'

Jamie glared at his editor for a second or so and then turned and walked out leaving the door wide open. Within a matter of moment's, he'd collected his things and was storming out of the building.

Pete watched him leave and then sat back in his chair. 'Shit,' he mumbled.

News of Foster's resignation had also reached *W.Evans Executive Motors Ltd* in Romford although the reaction there had been very different. Billy was buzzing.

'This shit's actually happening,' he thought as he leant back in his chair. 'Fuck!'

Yet excited as he was, Billy had no idea how best to react. He couldn't exactly tell anyone in the garage and calling Foster to discuss it would be both pointless and slightly juvenile. He couldn't even contact any of his lads because none of them knew anything about what was going on in the background.

In the end, he did the only possible thing he could think of. He sent a text to Claire to tell her to check out the news and then went back to work.

Having spent most of the afternoon in a bar, Jamie was well on the way to being hammered. His mood however, had not improved. This was primarily due to the seemingly constant reruns of the Sky News headlines on the TV behind the bar all of which involved the resignation of a Tory MP and the fact that Boris Johnson now had an effective majority of zero.

Yet even in his drunken stupor, Jamie had begun to wonder if something odd was going on. The only way Foster's resignation made any sense was if someone else had discovered the same information that he and Katie had and had tipped off someone in the Foster camp that they were about to run the story.

However, even that theory made no sense since Pete had told him that he'd already spoken to Foster's people. That meant that he would have had to have known before they announced it. But how?

'Bloody hell,' said Jamie out loud as he pulled his phone from his pocket and dialled. 'I need help.'

'Hi, this is Katie Marshall. Leave a message and I'll get back to you.'

Jamie stared at the phone for a second and then hit the end call button without leaving a message. He hesitated for a moment and then searched through his contacts and hit dial again. To his surprise, it was answered on the second ring.

'Hey,' he slurred. 'It's me.'

Having been a nurse pretty much since leaving school, Claire had seen more than enough of real life whilst on shift to ever worry too much about events outside her personal world. As a consequence, she rarely took any notice of the news and only on world shattering events such as the death of Princess Diana, 9/11 and the London bombings had she ever found herself glued to the television during bulletins.

Yet having seen mention of Foster on the front page of *The Standard*, not only had she read the entire article but she'd listened to the news on the radio whilst driving home and was now sat with a cup of tea in front of the television. She was utterly absorbed by what was happening because whilst the connection might be tenuous, she actually felt a part of what she was watching unfold on screen.

'Have you seen all this?' she asked Billy excitedly as he walked in and kissed her on the head.

'Yeah,' he said as he sat down beside her. 'It's bloody crazy.'

'It's exciting,' she gushed in response.

'This is just the start,' said Billy. 'The shit's really going to hit the fan over the next few days.'

Claire turned to look at him. 'Why?'

Billy returned her stare for a moment and smiled. He'd been involved in a lot of dodgy things over the years, but this was the first time he'd ever willingly shared any of it with a woman. Samantha had never wanted to know a single detail of anything.

Without a word, he headed for his office and returned a few moments later with the copy of the suppressed article Foster had given him.

'Because of this,' he said as he handed Claire the envelope. 'Take a look, I'll make some tea.'

By the time Billy returned, Claire had read through the lengthy article not once, but twice.

'So?' he said as he sat down.

'It's strange seeing it all written down like this,' she said quietly, 'it makes it all seem so real.

'It is real sweetheart. It's very real. But don't go feeling sorry for anyone. I know what these people did remember.'

'I don't,' she replied.

Billy paused for a moment and watched the woman sitting next to him as she went through a thought process of some kind. Even he understood that there was a conflict between her career as a nurse and what he was involved with. 'Are you OK?' he asked after a few moments.

'Yes,' she said. 'Honestly, I'm fine.'

'I told you, if you ever have any questions, just ask them OK? If I can answer, I will.'

'He doesn't mention you in here.'

'No. I did him a favour so he kept me and Hawk out of it.'

A look of surprise shot across her face. 'But you told me Graham wasn't involved!'

'He wasn't. But they were going to say he was. That's what all that stuff with Julie was about.'

Claire fell silent again for a few moments. 'So, was that child killed in the fire anything to do with you?' she asked.

'No. I swear. It was down to Foster. That was actually one of the main reasons why I pulled out.'

Claire sat for a moment in silence. 'OK,' she said. 'There's nothing else like that?'

'Not that I know of,' said Billy, 'and that's the truth.'

With a satisfied nod, Claire picked up her cup and took a mouthful of tea.

'So, what's the plan for tonight mister?'

Courtesy of a helpful Uber driver, Jamie had just made it into his house and was about to collapse onto his sofa when his doorbell rang.

'Oh, for fuck's sake,' he groaned. 'What now?'

He staggered back up the hall and pulled the door open only to be shocked almost sober by the sight of the person standing on his doorstep.

'Hey,' he blurted out. 'Why didn't you use your key?'

'I didn't think it was right,' replied Lisa. 'Although if I'd known you were wrecked, I wouldn't have bothered coming around anyway.'

'Sorry, I've had a shit afternoon at work.'

'Welcome to my world, Jamie.'

Without another word, he turned and walked back up the hall. Lisa watched him for a second and then followed, closing the door behind her.

'What d'you want?' she asked.

'I dunno, I just missed you,' he said as he slumped on the sofa. 'I tried to get hold of you a few times. Where were you?'

'Hiding out mostly,' Lisa replied. 'I had some leave owing so went and stayed with an old colleague. How've you been?'

Jamie shrugged his shoulders but said nothing.

'I'm actually glad you called. I wanted to say sorry,' she said. 'I was pretty crappy to you at the end.'

'Yeah, you were. Fancy a drink? For old times' sake.'

'I think you've had enough for both of us.'

'Bollocks,' said Jamie as he started to get to his feet. 'I haven't even had enough for me yet.'

Lisa shook her head. 'Sit down you idiot, I'll do it,'

Jamie watched her grab two glasses and a bottle of Vodka from the drinks cabinet and forced a smile as she sat down on the other end of the sofa. 'Old times,' she said as she handed him a glass and filled it, 'and happier days.'

Jamie nodded and downed his drink. She refilled it immediately.

'I've resigned from the force,' she blurted out.

'Bullshit,' he scoffed in response.

Lisa downed her shot and then shrugged her shoulders. 'It's true. Too many ghosts. Easier to jump than be pushed.'

Jamie stared at her aghast. 'Seriously? Christ, Lisa, I'm sorry.'

'It's OK, at least I kept my pension. Plus, I get to sleep at night.'

The two of them sat in silence for a few moments then downed their drinks. Lisa refilled them and settled back into the soft cushions.

'What's happening with you? What happened to the big story?'

'They buried it, the bastards. But I think they might actually be running it tomorrow.'

'Tomorrow? Why?'

'Foster. He quit so it's suddenly news again.'

Lisa stared at him, bemused. 'Foster? You mean the MP? That's who you kept talking about?'

'No,' said Jamie who was feeling drunker by the second. 'His brother.'

'What? His brother? I don't understand.'

Jamie emptied his glass and leant back in his chair. 'His twin brother, the one in the army.'

Lisa watched Jamie lapse into unconsciousness and let out a silent curse to the effects of alcohol.

She genuinely had no idea what Jamie had been talking about but then she realised that it wasn't her problem any more. Instead, Lisa was just glad to be back in her own home.

After a glance at Jamie, she plumped up the cushions to make herself as comfortable as she could, emptied her glass and within a matter of moments, was fast asleep.

Thankfully, as with all her nights of late, Tilly Nelson once again left her in peace.

Chapter Thirty Eight
Thursday 8th August 2019

06.45

Once again Lisa was dragged from her sleep by the persistent ringing of Jamie's phone.

However, with little or no interest in knowing who was calling at such an obviously ungodly hour, she waited until it stopped and then began to drift back to sleep. She had almost made it when it started ringing again.

'For fuck's sake,' she muttered as she forced open her eyes only to see Jamie still enjoying his alcohol induced coma on the other end of the sofa. Whilst tempted to kick him awake she knew that it was hardly worth the effort. Particularly with her head banging like a steel drum at the Notting Hill Carnival.

Instead, she dragged herself upright and rescued his phone from the floor.

'Katie, it's Lisa,' she said. 'Sorry, he's…, whoa, slow down! What are you talking about?'

Billy was also woken early by his phone only in his case, it was the ping of a Google News notification.

He was still reading what the internet had delivered him when he felt a hand creeping up the inside of his leg.

'You can knock that on the head mush,' he said without looking away from his phone, 'I'm reading something.'

'You're reading? Seriously?'

Billy glanced down to see Claire looking up at him, a sly smile on her face.

'Don't even think about it,' he said.

Without another word she slid under the duvet. Billy waited for a moment and then said, 'You do know it's ten to eight.'

There was a moment's pause and then Claire burst from the bed. 'Shit! Why didn't you wake me?' she said, only to stop dead when she saw the clock. The numbers 7 and 10 shining brightly on its face.

'I told you,' said Billy cheekily. 'I'm reading. But since you're up, go stick the kettle on.'

'Twat,' she hissed as she slid back into bed and sat beside him. 'So, come on then, what's so important? And if you mention West Ham, you're a dead man.'

Billy turned to her and smiled before handing her the phone. 'Better.'

'You arsehole. You've totally shafted me.'

Pete settled back in his chair and clasped his hands together as he stared at a clearly furious Jamie who had seemingly appeared from nowhere.

'Come in, why don't you?' he said sarcastically.

'What the fuck's this?' Jamie said, throwing a copy of the paper on the desk. The headline 'Exclusive: Tory MP Foster linked to vigilante attack' uppermost.

'I know what it is, I put it there.'

'Why?' continued Jamie angrily. 'That's what I don't get.'

'Why what? Why did I rewrite it or why did I take your name off it? Because you do know that the second answers the first.'

'You're fucking kidding?' gasped Jamie incredulously. 'You've rewritten it to make him look like the bloody victim! The only thing missing's a picture of his mum's headstone!'

Never one to shy away from confrontation, Pete would normally have been happy to play word games with Jamie for a while but something about his tone was already starting to piss him off and whilst he could understand his employee's angst, he wasn't going to take any shit.

'I don't fucking kid, Jamie, so here's the deal. I rewrote the article because this paper is chasing the right-wing market. Your version of the article may well have destroyed Foster and that would have impacted on the paper.'

'You're saying it was a commercial decision to not even reference any of the attacks we wrote about two weeks ago or

241

mention that little matter of his twin brother being behind them all?' scoffed Jamie. 'That's bullshit!'

'Yes, it is. But that's how it works. If you don't like it, I'll happily put you back on the celebrity desk.'

Jamie sat and seethed. Pete watched him and softened slightly.

'Sit down for Christ's sake. I knew you'd react like this, that's why I took your name off it. You'd never have squared it with your conscience.'

'It's not about the bloody credit, it's about the truth.'

'It is the truth,' said Pete. 'Just not all of it. Look, you've seen what's going on. Boris is desperate to get votes back from the Brexit Party, so he's pushing everything from no deal to more coppers on the streets. You really think the Tory supporting owners of this paper are going to be the one who fuck it all up?'

'It's bullshit.'

'True, but at least you get the satisfaction of knowing that your articles drove him to come clean.'

'Yeah, but he's still off the hook.'

'He's also out of government. For now, anyway.'

Jamie sat back. He was spent. More than that, he was pissed off. Pete looked at him and half smiled.

'Political journalism is a shitty game, Jamie, but it's a lot easier to play it if you learn the rules. Now, I've got work to do and you'd better have.'

With a sigh, Jamie dragged himself to his feet and headed back to his desk.

Pete watched him for a moment and then dragged his attention back to his screen. Jamie might not know how to play the game, but he certainly did, and he had a very good idea what was going to unfold over the coming weeks. If he was right, his employee's current mood was going to be nothing compared to the resentment that would soon consume him.

'Bloody journalists,' he muttered.

Unlike Jamie Brown, Billy Evans was having an awesome day. With the media full of Ian Foster's resignation, he had spent much of it listening to events about which he not only had intimate knowledge but a vested interest.

Most interesting of all was seeing how different the MP was from his brother. He was more assured and certainly more charismatic but behind it all he was clearly highly motivated. Yes, he'd walked away from the government, but it was pretty obvious that he wasn't going far. There had already been rumours that he'd turned down an invitation to stand for the Brexit Party at any future general election whilst the local Tory Party office had put out a statement saying that it would not accept his resignation. He was very much their man.

Already becoming something of a hero with the general public judging by the almost universally positive reaction on the morning radio talk shows, Ian Foster's status had seemingly leapt to new heights when he'd appeared on the lunchtime TV news in the wake of the prime minister announcing that as well as the police, he was going to be throwing money at the prisons.

Rather than talk about his personal situation and the death of his mother, Foster had gone on the offensive and stated live on air that the government needed to stop being reactive to crime and start being pro-active. Hit the criminals hard, fast and if they need punishing, then actually punish them had been his message.

It had in many ways been a masterclass in how to come out of a bad situation looking like the good guy and by the time Billy called it quits and headed for home, it seemed like Ian Foster was the only subject anyone was talking about.

Having had a coffee with Katie to clear the air and wish her well on her assignment in the States, Jamie had also headed home.

He was slightly surprised to find Lisa still there but whilst naturally cautious, there was also a sense of relief that he wouldn't have to spend the evening alone. Not least because he wasn't sure that his liver would take another hammering.

'You wanna talk about your day?' she asked him as they sat eating dinner. 'I'm guessing it was a toughie.'

'That's an understatement. I'm so sick of seeing Foster and the bloody hypocrisy he's spouting.'

'Yeah well, what did you expect. He's a Tory. Well, he was anyway.'

Jamie let out an audible sigh. 'I feel like I'm consorting with the enemy,' he said.

'Yeah, me too,' she replied before picking up a white paper towel and waving it above her head.

'Funny,' said Jamie.

'I thought so,' she replied with a smile. 'By the way, I met your Billy Evans a couple of times. He's a cocky bastard ain't he.'

'And some.'

'Did you know he got attacked? Had his arm broken.'

'No, when?' asked Jamie, slightly taken aback.

'About six or seven weeks ago. Everything went quiet after that.'

'What d'you mean?'

'It all stopped. People began to get nervous.'

'What people?'

'Everyone I guess, certainly my lot. I think it was your articles that spooked people.'

'Well at least I achieved something.'

'Yeah, well. Anyway, that's when I decided to get out for good.'

Jamie began to feel his journalistic instincts start to tingle but well aware that the wound which had scarred their relationship was far from healed, he had no choice but to tread warily.

'So how many policemen were actually involved?'

'I don't know,' she said apologetically, 'honestly, I don't. It was all kept very cloak and dagger for obvious reasons. There were three of us at my nick, but I heard that there were coppers all over the country.'

Jamie took a deep breath and asked the question that had been nagging him ever since they'd started talking, 'Did you actually go on any?' he asked.

Lisa threw him a look but far from being embarrassed as he'd expected, her face was cloaked in what he could only take as pride.

'Only two,' she said. 'One in Barnet, one in Northampton. And before you say anything, I'm not sorry. They both deserved it.'

Jamie looked at her, unsure if he should feel horrified or angry. His professional curiosity was throwing questions at him but mindful of who he was talking to, he took care to adopt a conversational tone.

'OK,' he said slowly, 'where did Evans come into it?'

'I'd never heard of him until you mentioned him. Same as Foster.'

'How did you get involved?'

Lisa baulked at the question. 'You're interviewing me again,' she said.

'Sorry, I didn't mean to. This whole bloody story had got under my skin. Well, you know what that's like.'

'Fair enough I suppose.' Lisa fell silent, she did indeed know. She might not be a copper any more, but there were certain cases which would linger with her forever. 'There was this one particular case,' she began, 'a girl. She was only a tot, gorgeous little thing. Her name was Tilly Nelson.'

It had taken Lisa nearly a half an hour to tell Jamie about the Tilly Nelson case and another hour for the tears to run dry. Even Jamie had shed a few as for the first time he'd heard his former partner unload chapter and verse about the realities of her work and the full impact it had made on her both as a policeman and a female.

Now, he was sitting watching her from across the room as she read through his notes and the story that Pete had canned.

'Jesus Christ Jamie,' she said as she finally finished. 'I didn't know about any of this. What are you going to do?'

'Nothing. There's nothing I can do. The paper won't publish it...'

'There are other newspapers.'

'Yeah, and if I talk to them, I'm screwed.'

'Me too I suppose.'

Jamie looked at her and smiled. 'Yeah, I suppose you would be,' he said. 'Maybe I should use it to extract my revenge after you dumping me.'

'Do your worst,' she laughed. 'But seriously, what are you going to do?'

With a resigned sigh, Jamie said the only thing that he could possibly say under the circumstances.

'I genuinely don't know.'

The two of them sat in silence for a few moments and then Lisa said cautiously, 'd'you fancy going out for a drink?'

Chapter Thirty Nine
Friday 9th August 2019

10.30

Like the rest of the country, both Billy and Jamie had woken to find blanket media coverage of Ian Forster's resignation.

Some of it inevitably focussed on the political implications, not just for the man, but for both the Tory party and the government. Other outlets had focussed on the personal side with his twin brother, Major Christopher Foster of the Royal Military Police, receiving more than passing scrutiny in some quarters. However, with the public increasingly coming out in support of Ian Foster and his hardline stance on crime, not even the most vehement anti-Tory journalists had dared tear into a decorated war veteran. The result being that like his brother, Major Foster was also beginning to be regarded as something of a hero.

The one constant in pretty much every publication was an examination of the incident that had kick started the whole saga. However, with neither of the Foster brothers willing to speak about it and their mother long dead, it was all largely speculative. What had been confirmed however, was that there would be no police action taken against either brother. With the victim of the revenge attack refusing to speak to anyone about it, they had nothing to base any charges on even if they had wanted to.

This had effectively cleared the way for Ian Foster to return to the Tory fold with more than one commentator claiming that moves were already afoot to lever him into a cabinet post as a way of exploiting his newfound popularity. However, the MP had thus far declined to comment which if anything, had added fuel to the rumours.

For Billy, it wasn't simply exciting, it was inspiring. He'd never once doubted that he was doing the right thing because everything he did was underpinned by thoughts of Hawk and the satisfaction having the shit beaten out of Ashley Bennett had given him. Yet now that same sense of gratification was being endorsed by people across the country who were jumping behind the Foster's to show support. It wasn't just Billy caught up in it either. By lunchtime at least two thirds of his lads had messaged him to express exactly the same sentiment. Everyone was buzzing and with enthusiasm for the task in hand at its highest, Billy did what he'd been waiting to do ever since his last meeting with Foster.

He picked up his phone and set his lads back to work.

For Jamie however, the day could not have been more different. For having left Lisa asleep in the spare room, he'd headed for work and endured the entire journey being reminded of Ian Foster MP. Each mention feeling akin to a kick in the nuts.

His mood deteriorated further when even as he'd walked into the office, news had broken that his paper had secured exclusive rights to the only interview the Foster brothers were going to give to any media outlet. Given the week he'd been having, Jamie had half expected Pete to ask him to do it.

Instead, he'd had been left alone. Festering in the knowledge that whilst the world and his dog seemed to be lauding them, Jamie had accrued more than enough evidence to cause major problems for the two men who were due to arrive in the building at 2.00.

Part of him had actually wanted to hang around to introduce himself. If only in the hope that he would see something in either of the brothers to show him that maybe Pete had indeed done the right thing.

Yet a bigger part, the better part, had realised the folly of that idea and that the more likely outcome would be that he would make a twat of himself and get fired. Far better to get out of the building and lick his wounds in Starbucks than risk that.

His plan had almost worked. However, as he'd stepped out of the lift in the lobby, he'd come face to face with Major Christopher Foster who had arrived earlier than expected. His immaculate uniform totally at odds with the surroundings and ensuring that any hopes he might have had of making a subtle entrance were null and void.

Yet whilst the sight of Major Foster had shocked him, what had stunned Jamie was that the man he'd been desperate to expose, had not only recognised him but had immediately left his seat and headed toward him.

'Mr. Brown,' he'd said as he approached and thrust out his arm, 'I don't believe we've actually met.'

Jamie had reluctantly taken the officers hand, the strength of the grip almost making him wince as he'd replied, 'I know we haven't. My editor wouldn't let me.'

'Well now we have,' Foster had beamed before finally releasing Jamie's hand and adding, 'could I have a word, in private?'

Despite the fact that Jamie was effectively on home turf, it was clearly more of an instruction than a request and whilst tempted to refuse on the pretext that he had somewhere else to be, the journalist in him was still curious to hear what Foster had to say.

'Sure,' he'd replied before leading them both over to a quiet corner of the lobby and sitting down. 'So how can I help you?'

What had happened next had chilled Jamie to his very core. For after taking a casual look around to check that no one was within ear shot, Foster had leant forward and said softly, 'We're watching you Mr. Brown so I'd advise against trying to cross us. If you do, I give you my word that it won't end well for you.' With that, he'd stood up and headed back toward the reception desk even as someone had arrived from upstairs to collect him.

A shocked Jamie had continued to stare at the officer until he was out of sight and only then had he fallen back into his seat. The movement accompanied by a relieved and vocal 'fuck'.

Yet as he'd replayed the encounter in his head, Jamie had realised that once he'd been collected, Foster hadn't even stolen another glance in his direction which somehow served to make the whole experience even more sinister.

He'd then sat for a moment, reflecting on what had happened before heading for the exit. However, instead of a local coffee shop Jamie had gone home where he now sat on his sofa nursing a beer and describing his encounter to Lisa.

'Honestly,' he said, 'seeing him in his uniform the only thing I could think of was the fucking Gestapo. Scared the shit out of me.'

Sitting opposite him, Lisa said nothing although in truth she knew exactly what he meant. Ever since 52% of the population had voted to leave the European Union, comparisons with 1930's Germany had been thrown around to the point where the accusation of fascism had lost any real meaning. Yet even as that social media fuelled verbal battle had raged, she and her colleagues had secretly been indulging in practices which no matter how you looked at it, bore frightening similarities to those carried out by the brown shirts of the Nazi party.

For Lisa however, those comparisons were meaningless. Her feelings had nothing to do with politics they were entirely based on the concept of justice and as such, she had never once doubted that she was doing the right thing. That was until the situation with Jamie had exploded. For the second she'd been told to keep a close eye on him, doubts had begun to surface and as it had all begun to unfold, Lisa had inevitably begun to consider things in a different light. It had been an increasingly uncomfortable process, and in the end, had been partially responsible for driving her from the job she'd once loved.

'What are you going to do?' she asked.

'I don't have a bloody clue,' sighed Jamie. 'What would you do?'

'I don't have a bloody clue,' she repeated with wry smile. 'Honestly, I don't. But isn't the real question more along the lines of what can you actually do?'

Jamie sat in silence for a moment. 'Well, either I do nothing and watch the fucking Nazi party take over, or I somehow get what I have out there and spend the rest of my life looking over my shoulder. Some choice.'

'The Nazi party? D'you seriously think that's what this is all about?'

'Well maybe not the Nazi's, more like Nazi-lite. But honestly, when a bloke in uniform tells you that you're being watched, it's hard not to make the comparison.'

The two of them sat in silence for a while and then Lisa spoke up.

'I think you know what you've got to do,' she said. 'You'd never be able to live with yourself if you didn't at least try.'

With a sigh, Jamie nodded. She was right of course. Indeed, even whilst they'd been sat there, he'd been thinking of who he could send his file too to obtain maximum exposure.

'I'll get fired, maybe worse, and it'll be dangerous,' he said. 'They'll come after me.'

'Us,' corrected Lisa with a half-smile. 'Come after us. You know we could always just say balls to it all and leave.'

'What, the country?' asked Jamie.

'Why not? We've got no real ties here. My sister's always asking us to go out to Canada and you've got family in New Zealand. Either way it'd be a fresh start.'

'As a couple you mean?'

Lisa looked at him and shrugged her shoulders. 'Would that be so bad?' she asked nervously.

Jamie looked at her for a moment and then smiled. 'No,' he said. 'It wouldn't be bad at all.'

Having spent the entire afternoon at an auction, Billy had popped home to spend an hour or so with Claire before she started a week of nights.

Like him, she'd also been keeping abreast of the news and was equally caught up in the excitement of it all. So much so that for a brief moment Billy had actually wondered if it might be prudent to remind her that nothing they were involved with was for public consumption. However, he had quickly realised that she was smart enough to know that and issuing a warning might well prove counterproductive. The last thing he wanted to do was patronise her and potentially piss her off.

Once he'd seen her off to work, he'd then checked in with his lads before settling down for the evening. With the football season beginning the following day and West Ham kicking off at 12.30, it would mean an early start and a long day but for the first time in a good few years, Billy was actually looking forward to it.

Pete Goodwin was just sitting down for dinner with his family when his phone rang.

In accordance with the rule of his house which forbade telephones at the dinner table, he let it ring but took a mental note to check for any message after they'd eaten. However, having been caught up in conversation with his wife and two daughters, it was almost an hour before he found the time to listen to it.

'Fuck it,' he hissed angrily, hitting the return call button even before the recording had come to an end. However, before it connected, he cancelled it and cradled the phone in his hands. Much as he hated the idea that had just come to him, the news he'd just received could actually be made to work to his advantage and save him an awful lot of hassle in the future.

He continued to ponder for a few moments and then with his mind made up, flicked through his contacts until he found the name he was looking for.

'It's Pete Goodwin,' he said once the call was answered. 'I just thought you'd want to know that Jamie Brown just quit.'

Billy had been about to go to bed when the call from Foster had come.

At first, the news that Jamie Brown had resigned from his newspaper had raised a wry smile but then Foster had continued. Without the constraints of the newspaper, Brown was a loose cannon and as such, he needed to be dealt with.

Billy had immediately passed that particular responsibility straight back to the military man. After all, Foster and his brother had much more to lose than he did and if his men could break into his place with all the security Billy had, then they'd surely have no problem gaining access to a mid-terraced house in North London.

Yet as the conversation had continued, Billy had begun to feel slightly uneasy at the direction it was taking. Foster wasn't talking about the kind of justice he had signed up to deliver, he was hinting at something worse. Whilst he had no real compassion for Jamie Brown, Billy still regarded himself as being indebted to the journalist for keeping his word over Hawk even though in the end, it hadn't come to anything anyway.

With that thought uppermost in his mind, he had told Foster to leave Brown to him. He'd deal with the reporter, but he'd do it in a way that would settle his debt.

It was the very least he could do.

Chapter Forty
Saturday 10th August 2019

08.30

Having taken the decision to resign, Jamie and Lisa had talked long into the night about what they should do next.

After much soul searching, they had elected to seize the opportunity to start afresh in Canada.

With Lisa's sister and her family having ample room for them, it made the most sense. It also meant that they'd be able to make the initial move sooner rather than later and start to lay the foundations of their new life.

As a journalist with a wealth of international celebrity contacts, Jamie was fairly certain that he'd have no problem finding work whilst a brief look at the relative websites showed that Lisa would eventually have a good shot at joining the Canadian police, if she ever wanted to go down that route.

An additional consequence of that decision was that it afforded Jamie some genuine justification for not publishing his story about the Foster's. Thus far all he'd had was the fear of potential repercussions and whilst that had been a genuine concern, it hadn't been sitting well with him. Jamie was many things, but a coward wasn't one of them. At least now he could offset that with the thought that by sitting on the story it would almost certainly make Lisa's potential application to the police a little more straightforward, not to mention the matter of citizenship. After all, it didn't take a rocket scientist to work out that being linked to a story which impacted directly on the political landscape of one of their greatest allies might not curry favour with the Canadian authorities.

If all went to plan, he could always publish once they were settled although that assumed that the story didn't simply fizzle out of its own accord over the coming months. If that proved to be the case, then any concerns for their safety would be groundless anyway but for the moment it was very much a case of better safe than sorry.

Having decided all that and then discussed the practicalities of selling their house, it had been the early hours before Jamie and Lisa had finally found the strength to confront the issue of their actual relationship and the impact of recent events. However, after some soul searching, both had agreed that whatever had happened over the last few weeks should be consigned to history as nothing more than a blip, albeit a large one. Only once they were both fully content had they retired to bed with the clock nudging 03.30.

Neither of them was therefore thrilled to be woken up by someone banging on the front door at a little after 9.00.

At first, they'd tried to ignore it, but it had been so persistent that Jamie had eventually given up and gone downstairs to see who was giving him so much angst. To say he was shocked to find Billy Evans standing on his front step was an understatement.

'What the bloody hell do you want?' he blurted out nervously.

'A chat,' said Billy even as he barged past him and headed inside.

'What the fuck?' shouted Jamie as he hurried after him. 'Get out or I'm calling the police.'

Billy stood in the middle of the kitchen with his arms folded. 'No, you won't,' he said confidently only to smile broadly when Lisa hurried in and stood beside Jamie. 'Well, well. It looks like they're already here. Morning sarge.'

'You've got precisely ten seconds to get out,' growled Lisa.

'You're not even going to offer me a cuppa?'

'Nine, eight, seven...'

Billy held up his hands in mock surrender. 'OK,' he said. 'Look, I've come to repay my debt.'

'Six, five...' continued Lisa forcefully.

Jamie put his hand on her shoulder to stop her. 'What debt?' he asked curiously.

Billy threw a curious look at Lisa. 'OK, before I say anything, I've got to ask. Does he know what I know about you?'

'Yes,' said Jamie. 'I know everything.'

'So, are you regular old bill or still double agenting?' Billy asked Lisa. 'Cos it would be handy to know.'

'Not that it's any of your bloody concern,' Lisa barked in response, 'but I've quit the force.'

'Actually,' replied Billy smugly, 'it's very much my concern. I don't want you grassing me to Foster.'

'Grassing? For what?' asked Jamie.

Billy turned his gaze to the man standing in front of him and uncrossed his arms. 'For what I'm about to do.'

Billy Evans didn't like being in debt. In fact, it was a source of personal pride that he generally conducted his life with no arrears, be they financial or personal. Be it money or favours, he was owed, not owing. That's how it worked.

It was therefore with some satisfaction that Billy headed back toward Romford with the knowledge that his debt to Jamie Brown had been fully repaid.

Obviously, there was a risk that warning the journalist of Foster's intention to silence him would come back to bite him on the arse but that was a risk Billy had been happy to take although in truth, it was fairly remote. He couldn't imagine that Jamie Brown was going to be telling many people that he'd been placed on a hit list and had been forced to flee the country of his birth for his own protection.

It had however, been interesting to discover that Lisa Cooper had retired from the police. Billy didn't imagine for a moment that Foster wasn't already aware of that development and for a brief moment he had considered the possibility that she was still working both sides of the fence. That would certainly have explained why he hadn't told him about it. Yet there had been something about her manner that had quickly convinced Billy that she was on the level. The harshness that had been so evident on the two occasions he'd encountered her had gone replaced by what he could only assume was a degree of uncertainty, if not fear.

Anyway, whatever the truth of Foster's knowledge of Lisa Cooper's career, Billy had done what he'd had to do and if there were going to be consequences, he'd deal with them as and when. Before that there was the small matter of the opening day of the season and an afternoon with the lads.

For the first time in a long time, Billy suddenly realised that he was actually looking forward to it.

PART SEVEN

The Epilogue
Thursday 24th March 2022

16.00

With a sense of satisfaction, Jamie Brown settled back in his chair and took a drink from the bottle of water on his desk. His manuscript was shaping up very nicely.

Whatever his thoughts on their politics, there was little doubt that the Foster brothers had proven to be an extremely lucrative income stream since they'd first come crashing into his life almost three years ago. The global fascination with both them and their central role in the evolution of post-Brexit Britain showed no sign of waning and as one of their leading and most informed critics he was in pretty much constant demand by the world's media.

That would hopefully be boosted further by the release of his forthcoming book on their controversial rise to power. All he had to do was finish it and hand it over to his increasingly eager, if not desperate publisher. That would hopefully be before his parents arrived in two weeks' time although if it wasn't, he didn't want to think about how Lisa would react. It was unlikely to be pretty.

It would have been finished already had he been able to go back to the UK to conduct his research but the fact he hadn't was entirely his own fault. It had after all, been his decision to announce his arrival as a political commentator with one of Canada's more prestigious left-wing newspapers by publishing a column in the days after the general election in which he'd accused Ian Foster and his twin brother Stephen of being directly linked to a series of vigilante attacks across England.

Whilst the article had been a global smash it had not been so well received in the country he still called home. There, it had been derided as little more than the rantings of a bitter and twisted hack taking potshots from the other side of the Atlantic. That however, had been nothing compared to the more personal and hate filled attacks Jamie had endured on social media. So vitriolic had it become that he'd been forced to close his accounts for a while but not before he'd been left in no doubt that were he to ever to show his face at home again it would prove to be a huge and potentially dangerous mistake. Not that he missed it much. Jamie had a better idea than most ex-pats of what had been happening to the place he and Lisa had left behind, and it held little appeal for either of them.

The changes had begun fairly soon after he had fled in the wake of Billy Evans visit. With Foster continuing to ride the wave of popularity that had begun after his resignation from the Tory party, he had shocked the establishment even further by standing down and putting himself up for re-election as an independent. His rationale being that a victory would secure a mandate from his constituency to kick start a national right-wing alliance to drive through Brexit and rebuild a nation trapped in a political quagmire thanks to the fanaticism of the socialist left.

Despite all the major parties fielding heavyweight candidates against him, his plan had been a resounding success. Ian Foster had obliterated the opposition with one of the largest by-election majorities in recent history and with that endorsement secured, had immediately gone on the offensive.

However, whilst his stance had captured the attention of the public, it had all seemingly come to nothing when the government had been forced to delay Brexit and then call a general election.

Suddenly, with the country seemingly more divided than ever, talk had turned to tactical voting and a possible hung parliament with many on the left suggesting that Brexit might be stalled for years.

In the event, thanks in no small part to the Brexit party capitulating and the left tearing themselves apart, both Labour and the Lid-Dems had been all but wiped out by a huge Conservative majority.

Yet in the months after the election, it had begun to become apparent how much of a role the newly reelected Ian Foster had played in the victory. Stories of underhand tactics and even threats became commonplace and in the end, Jamie had persuaded his newspaper to take the lead in the attack on the still independent MP by publishing his article in Canada.

However, whilst the negative impact on his own personal life had been immense, the opposite had been true of Ian Foster whose popularity amongst the right-wing voting public had soared. There had even been calls in the tabloids for him to be shoehorned into the cabinet despite not holding the Tory whip.

Foster had modestly dismissed that idea and had insisted that he was happy on the back benches. That had changed in the summer of 2020 when, with the public increasingly frustrated by a stalling Brexit and the Labour Party starting to make ground under their new leader, the home secretary had suddenly and unexpectedly resigned.

In what many had claimed was the final part of a calculated plan, Ian Foster had immediately rejoined the Conservatives and been installed into the post with a pledge to carry through his dream of making his country great again. It was an appointment that had been greeted with almost universal approval. Not just from the party faithful and the voting public, but from the remnants of the Brexit Party who fully endorsed what was immediately labelled by the media as a right-wing alliance. The impact on Labour had been devastating as the rejuvenated swing toward the right had effectively wiped them from the news agenda.

For Jamie, watching from the other side of the world, the whole sorry saga had been observed with a sense of dismay and foreboding. He had experienced a glimpse of what the Foster brothers were capable of but with one of them having been handed real power, he couldn't even begin to imagine what they might do. It hadn't taken long to find out.

Almost immediately after taking his post, Foster had got to his feet in the House of Commons and announced that one of the Brexit Parties key pre-election promises had been enacted by the government and with immediate effect the overseas aid budget was being slashed by almost two thirds. Fifty percent of the almost ten billion pounds saved annually was being handed to him and every penny of that money would be pumped into the police, the prison service and the border force agencies. He was, he said to roars of support from the packed benches behind him, taking the country to war against crime.

This however, had just been the start. Within weeks Foster had again got to his feet in the House and announced that he was scrapping the policy of policing by consent. 'The good, honest law-abiding people of this country didn't need a police service, they wanted a police force. That's what I am going to give them and I'm going to lead it from the front!' he'd raged.

He had begun to deliver within days. First by replacing every senior officer he considered less than hard-line and then by scrapping quota led recruitment policies for all three services. His assertion being that the country deserved the best public servants possible and he didn't care what race, religion or sexual orientation they were.

The impact had been startling. Not simply in terms of morale amongst the rank and file officers but across the country as a whole. Public confidence in both the police and the judiciary began to return within weeks as criminals quickly began to discover that this new regime was very different from the one they'd been used to. Even minor crimes were being treated with the severity the public were increasingly demanding.

Yet Foster hadn't only gone on the offensive against criminals, he'd started two additional battle fronts. The first had been against anyone under the watch of the security services who fairly quickly found themselves snatched from their homes and placed in internment camps guarded by Army personnel.

The second and more controversial had been against illegal immigrants. To the dismay of the left but the delight of the public, new and almost draconian powers had been handed to Immigration Enforcement Officers allowing them to arrest and deport people within a matter of days, often without any right of appeal whatsoever. In addition, anyone caught trafficking or even employing illegal immigrants faced swift and severe consequences ranging from seizure of assets to imprisonment.

To strengthen his crusade further, the new Home Secretary had also demanded that the military be handed a major role in border security and with the defence secretary in full agreement had installed his newly promoted brother into a revamped Office of Homeland Security to oversee the entire operation.

Within days of taking his new post, the now Lieutenant Colonel Christopher Foster had not only deployed armed units of the Military Police into every major entry point but had tasked the Royal Navy with patrolling the English channel. Their strict orders being to return to the mainland anyone caught trying to cross illegally and offload them on the beaches if the French authorities wouldn't take them. This had caused all sorts of problems with the International community but Foster had dismissed them out of hand. 'These people are a problem for Europe, not us!' he'd raged in the House.

To a growing majority of the British public Ian Foster could do no wrong. For the first time in living memory there was a genuine belief that they had someone in power who was actually delivering on his word and who didn't take crap from anyone.

Yet for those who'd wanted to listen, stories had also began to circulate about a darker side to this new regime many of which were frighteningly familiar to Jamie. Where the street justice he'd discovered being delivered by the likes of Billy Evans had been administered in the shadows, these new tales talked of people being dragged from their beds and spirited away by the police before ending up in hospital with injuries of the type Jamie was all too familiar with.

There had also been strong rumours of anti-government activists being rounded up and placed in the same internment camps as suspected terrorists and in recent weeks Jamie had even begun to hear whispers of people simply disappearing altogether. More worryingly from a personal perspective had been a suggestion that he'd been placed on a list of undesirables and potentially faced arrest if he ever returned. Rumour or not, he had absolutely no intention of ever testing it out.

Thoughts of home suddenly reminded Jamie of something and he returned to his computer to scan through his manuscript. 'I bloody knew it,' he muttered as he corrected the name Teddy Miller to Teddy Miles.

It was a small but important detail but having only discovered the previous night that the old man had died in 2020, he at least owed him the courtesy of getting his name right. Especially since he had played a pivotal role in Jamie's initial interest in the story.

The memory of Teddy Miles suddenly brought to mind another name that had passed through Jamie's thought process many times over the last two years, certainly far more often than the old mans. Indeed, it had been whilst conducting one of his frequent searches for news of Billy Evans that Jamie had stumbled upon a memorial for Teddy.

As usual, his search had been fruitless and other than the fact that *W.Evans Executive Motors Ltd* was still apparently trading, he had never been able to find anything about Billy that was post-2019. It appeared that Evans had vanished without a trace, yet something about the idea didn't sit comfortably with Jamie. Even with his limited experience of the man, it just seemed to be out of character.

There was of course, always the possibility that with his former clandestine activities now apparently standard police practice, Evans had effectively been made redundant and had just walked away. Having glimpsed a more human side to him at their last meeting, there was actually a large part of Jamie that hoped that were indeed the case.

Yet increasingly, as rumours of disappearances had begun to surface, Jamie had begun to wonder if Billy had become a victim of his own design. He had after all fed him all kinds of information much of which had formed the basis of his numerous articles and certainly featured in his forthcoming book. That can't have gone down well with the Foster brothers so maybe he'd paid the ultimate price. That would certainly explain why even emails sent to the garage had gone unanswered.

The thought suddenly struck Jamie that given his role in the whole sorry saga, if Billy Evans had indeed vanished off the face of the earth, he would have to include details of it in his book, if only for the show value. It would mean a bit more work on his part, but it would certainly be worth it.

With that in mind, Jamie sent an email to his secretary asking her to find the name of an Essex based private detective and with a glance at his watch, returned his attention to his manuscript.

He'd do another hour and then head for home. Traffic permitting, he'd be home in time to put his baby daughter in the bath.

A little over an hour later, Jamie headed for the underground car park and made his way through the parked vehicles to his SUV. Having secured a promise from Lisa to keep the baby out of the water in exchange for a large Pepperoni Pizza and a portion of chicken wings, he was looking forward to spending an evening at home with his young family.

Barely ten minutes later, the SUV eased its way out into the late afternoon Vancouver traffic but by then Jamie Brown was already dead. Strangled by a heavy duty cable tie pulled so tightly around his throat that it had not only starved him of oxygen and rendered him incapable of speech but had been impossible to even loosen let alone remove before unconsciousness and then death took him.

For Warrant Officer Alex Lewis of the Special Boat Service, it was almost mission accomplished. All he had left to do was park the SUV in a secluded spot close to Brown's home in Richmond, walk a few miles to his own car and then head for the airport to await his early flight. It would be days before the body would be found and by then he'd be back home in London. Having previously scouted the area to make sure that there was no CCTV coverage that might potentially identify him, he was fairly confident that he'd be effectively untraceable. Just as importantly, if he knew his colleagues at the Special Operations Executive, by the time any investigation began they would already have intimate knowledge of the contents of the laptop that his target had been carrying with him and which would soon be on its way back to London.

It was routine stuff for someone as experienced as Alex although he had taken some pride in his choice of weapon. The cable tie was inspired, Not only was it quiet and very effective but being easily concealed he'd been able to bring it with him from the UK which effectively cut off that avenue of investigation. All he had left to do was snip it off the body and put it in his luggage with the latex gloves he was still wearing. Not just to negate any risk of it being found by the Canadian police and giving up its grisly secrets but for it to become the latest item of memorabilia in the small glass cabinet in his quarters.

He'd accrued a nice little collection of mementoes since he'd been seconded to Homeland Security and placed with the SOE and this would fit in quite nicely. Not that any of them reminded him of the actual victims, Alex had no feelings for them at all. His job wasn't to reason why, it was to carry out his mission as tasked by someone higher up the chain. If there were regrets or sleepless nights to be had, they were theirs and theirs alone. As far as he was concerned, they were welcome to them.

In common with all overseas operations, Alex only sent his mission complete message once he'd cleared customs at Heathrow. As a consequence, it was almost 11.00 before it was received by his handler at SOE headquarters and another hour and 20 minutes before it had been confirmed and then relayed to the originator of the mission. There, it was read immediately although it generated a very different reaction to that of the highly professional handler. This time the message generated a wry smile because this mission had not merely been extremely important, it had been personal.

With a contented sigh, Billy looked up from his phone and uttered a silent prayer of thanks. To say that he was relieved to be able to draw a line under this particular matter was an understatement.

In the wake of Jamie Brown fleeing the country, Foster had been convinced that Billy had tipped him off and for a while, things had been decidedly frosty between the two. So much so that for a time, Billy had not only felt that he was being eased out of the firm but that he might actually be looking at another broken arm. Maybe worse.

Thankfully, primarily by employing the age old tactic of feigning indignance at being accused of grassing coupled with the fact that under his leadership his lads had been busily and ruthlessly working through their list of targets, Billy had eventually convinced Foster to ease off and look elsewhere for someone to blame.

However, whilst Jamie Brown had stuck to his word and never revealed the truth despite frequently mentioning his enforced abdication over the following two years, Billy had never been comfortable with the idea of that shadow hanging over him. When he'd discovered that Brown was writing a book about the Foster brothers, he certainly wasn't going to risk the truth coming out and had decided then and there that the time had finally come to do something about it.

Luckily, having been installed as a senior advisor to Homeland Security, Billy had ample opportunity to drop a few hints about rumours of fresh information and potential damage to the home secretary. From that point on, having already been categorised as an enemy of the state following the publication of his article in the Canadian press, the journalist's fate was sealed.

That had been a week ago but in truth, from the second Billy has signed the order authorising the mission, it was effectively game over. Removing potential problems was after all, what the SOE had been established for and what they had proven to be remarkably efficient at.

But confirmation was confirmation and the text message he'd just received didn't simply tell Billy that Jamie Brown was dead, it told him that both his secret and his highly lucrative and influential status within the corridors of power, were finally safe.

He looked up to see Claire approaching with a tray of tea and cake. Her face covered in what had seemingly become a permanent grin.

'Busted!' she said. 'So much for you taking a bloody day off to come shopping with me.'

Billy placed his phone down on the table and stood up to take the tray from her.

'Sorry,' he said. 'It was just work stuff.'

'So, what was so important?'

Billy allowed a wry smile to crease his lips. 'Nothing,' he said. 'Nothing worth bothering about anyway.'